STEALING
the
LEAD

IAN MITCHELL-GILL

 FriesenPress

One Printers Way
Altona, MB R0G 0B0
Canada

www.friesenpress.com

Cover Models: Morgan L. and Connor D.

Photos by: AM Photography

Special thanks to Justin Bruckmann for the location and inspiration.

ISBN
978-1-03-914504-7 (Hardcover)
978-1-03-914503-0 (Paperback)
978-1-03-914505-4 (eBook)

1. YOUNG ADULT FICTION, GIRLS & WOMEN

Distributed to the trade by The Ingram Book Company

This book is dedicated to the artists on the stage and on the mats.

CHAPTER 1

There are no guarantees in life. Everything can change because of one unexpected event, and nothing will ever be the same.

"This is not happening. This is *NOT* happening!" wailed a tall brunette across the desk at the woman seated before her. It was a small office, neat, and the large windows brightened the room considerably. Small bookshelves surrounded the plain desk. It was the perfect atmosphere for Southwood High School's guidance counselor to ply her trade. The young woman brought her hands up to either side of her face and clenched her fists. Her eyes welled with tears, and she snatched a tissue from the strategically positioned box.

Ms. Blake, the guidance counselor, nodded her understanding and pushed the tissue box a little closer. "Just take a moment, let it sink in. Take your time with this, Morgan." She was an older woman, wearing a blue skirt and blazer. Her hair was short, and gold earrings flashed against her dark skin. Her brown eyes were framed by fashionable glasses.

"*No!* No, this is the worst. It's my senior year. I've been working for this competition since I walked into this place!" The teen put her elbows on the desk and put her face in her palms. "I'm the defending champion and nobody has *ever* won two years in a row. That would get me in any dance school in the country. This was my whole future and the dance team is counting on me too." She sniffed back some tears, sat up straight, and ran her palms over her hair and down her neat ponytail. "Tell me again, and please tell me how this happened. Maybe there's time to fix it."

Ms. Blake sighed. "Okay, Bernie Pollard won't be attending this school any longer, and he asked me to let you know."

"Why? Is it those jocks on the football team again? That's no reason to leave school."

"Morgan, that's not it."

"Then *what?*"

The counselor took a tissue for herself in one hand, and her glasses in the other. She wiped the lenses as she spoke. "Bernie's father landed a great job offer on the east coast, and they had to pack and move fast. He barely had enough time to come and get his transcripts before he was on a plane. When I saw him in the office, he asked me to explain it to you."

The striking teen's eyes flashed. "But I'm his partner! He couldn't tell me this himself?"

Ms. Blake tilted her head to one side and smiled. "Bernie had this crazy idea that you'd take it hard and might be a little emotional. Don't know where he got a ridiculous idea like that."

The teen frowned at the sarcasm. "We were gearing up for nationals. Our dance team did better than we ever had last year, and we were looking to do even better."

"Can't you find another partner?"

"Are you serious? Do you know how hard it was to find Bernie?" It was true. For Morgan Laflamme, the young man had been a rare find. He was the right height, he was reliable, and he was easy to boss around.

Ms. Blake was not only the guidance counselor, she also took an active interest in the dance team and supervised their practices and competitions. She knew about the pile of bodies that weren't up to the challenge of being the dance captain's partner.

"What about Hector?"

"Hector!?" Morgan recoiled in horror.

"He's very good," Ms. Blake reassured her.

"Oh, sure, he's great. Trouble is that he's a *SHRIMP!*"

The guidance counselor held up her hand to stop Morgan, wincing at her choice of words. "Okay, let's try hard to ignore that awful term for smaller people and move on. Do you think it matters that much?"

In answer, Morgan rose to her full height. "Take a good look. I'm five ten in flats and taller in heels. If I dance with Hector, I'm going to look like Godzilla, and he's going to look like a five-year-old dancing with his big sister."

Ms. Blake looked the dancer up and down. She had a point. Wearing her black leggings made her sleek form look longer. Her arms were folded on her white sweater, and she was leaning on one hip.

The older woman motioned for the younger to sit. Morgan rolled her eyes and sat back in the chair.

"Morgan," said Ms. Blake, "I know this is disappointing, but you're missing the big picture. You've done some amazing things in your time with us. You get great marks, you're respected in the school community, and you took this dance team from barely existing into a cohesive team that wins. You're on the hip-hop team, so you can still get at least one more win at the nationals. Maybe you can find another partner, or be happy with your role on the team as it is."

Morgan considered that and shook her head, looking down at the ground. "But this was my year. When the audience heard, 'Please welcome last year's champion, Morgan Laflamme!' I picked out a song, a style, and I've already choreographed half the number. Sure, I want good things for the team, but I want my name to be remembered when I apply to dance schools."

Ms. Blake gave her a small, patient smile. "If memory serves, Bernie wasn't terribly enthusiastic when you first approached him. You won him over, maybe you can do it again?"

"I know everyone in the school at this point and I can't think of a single guy who would, or could, make it work."

"I don't know what to tell you, Morgan. Keep your eyes open, consider the guys on the team again, and give the student body a fresh look. Try to find someone with potential." Ms. Blake tilted her head. "You've done it before."

"Yeah, yeah. Is there anything else?"

"No, Morgan. That was the only thing I needed to discuss with you."

The young woman stood up, brushed her long, dark ponytail over her shoulder, and moved to the door. She let out a big sigh when her hand clasped the doorknob. Turning a softer face to her guidance counselor, she said, "Thanks for letting me know. I'll see you after school tomorrow at practice."

"I'll see you then. It'll all work out somehow, Morgan, wait and see."

Morgan managed a small smile as she left the office and walked quickly to get out of the school as soon as possible. There were few students in the hallways, as most had gone home or to extracurricular activities.

She went through the doors at the back of the school and made her way to the parking lot. Her mind churned as she tried to recall students tall enough to be her partner, but she was coming up empty. She marched to her turquoise mini convertible, tossed her bag into the backseat, and sat behind the wheel. She stared at the keys in her hand. *Oh, this is going to work out alright, Ms. Blake*, she thought to herself. *But I'm not going to "wait and see."*

CHAPTER 2

When Morgan arrived home, she slammed the door of her compact convertible harder than she needed to and stormed up the front stairs of her large, spacious house. Shifting her bag back and out of the way, she punched in the security code, walked in the front door, and stopped dead in her tracks. Her eyes widened as she took in the sight in front of her.

Her little sister, Taylor, was dressed in a white martial arts uniform and holding an aggressive stance. One foot was forward and hands were balled into fists in front of her face. Her green eyes glared malevolently, and she started to smirk. "*HIYAAAAH!*" she screamed at the top of her lungs. Morgan stood there, staring at her. Taylor stood up straight and grinned. "Gotcha," she said as she pointed at her big sister.

"What are you doing, weirdo?"

Taylor's face fell. "I'm going to my first karate class tonight, remember?"

Morgan didn't. "Oh, I get it. No need to attack family members in the foyer, though," she said as she walked by.

The youngest sister shrugged and cartwheeled away. "I'm going to be *dangerous!*" she cackled as she rotated down the long hallway.

"God help us," Morgan muttered as she headed towards the kitchen. She could hear her mother chopping vegetables before she saw her. Where Morgan was tall and had dark hair, her mother was average size, with light brown hair and hazel eyes. She wore a comfortable pair of jeans and a grey sweater.

Rachel Laflamme was a woman of many talents. Besides being an accomplished accountant, she was also a leader in the community and an exceptional cook. She had often joked that her meals had been the source of her oldest daughter's unusual height. She saw Morgan as she looked up. "Oh, hi love. How was your day?"

Morgan brought her hand to rub her eyes and her shoulders fell. "Oh, I just had my entire world fall apart. That's all!"

"That's nice," her mother said without looking at her. "Can you get me the carrots out of the fridge? I'm in a bit of a hurry."

Morgan scowled at her, but went to the fridge. "Did you even hear a word I said?"

Rachel stopped working the knife on the cutting board and gave her a kind smile. "Yes honey, I did. I also know that things tend to hit you hard at first, but you always see a way out after you've had a little time to process." She went back to cutting and her smile grew. "You get that from your father."

"What does she get from me?" her father asked as he strolled into the kitchen. He was a tall man, with dark hair and eyes, wearing a suit and carrying a tie. Grey was starting to speckle his hair, and it only made the successful lawyer seem more distinguished.

"Her temper, Patrick," Rachel said with a chuckle as her husband gave her a kiss on the cheek.

Her husband smiled and nodded. "Ah, the famous 'Laflamme fire.' What's wrong, Morgan?"

"My dance partner has left the state."

Her mother looked up from her work quickly and gave her daughter a wink. "Nothing you did, I hope."

Morgan let out an exasperated sigh. "Very funny. Of course not. His father got a new job on the east coast. They had to leave pretty quickly."

"Must have been a good opportunity," her father mused.

That was too much for Morgan. "Ugh! Don't you care about how this affects me? I'm state champion, and it was my year to defend. My *LAST* year to defend it. This meant so much to me and now … now it's been taken away."

Her parents gave each other a glance. Her father raised his collar and wrapped the tie around his neck. He was working the knot as he spoke to his daughter. "Morgan, that is unfortunate. I understand it's a setback. But, please … let's keep some things in mind. You are a talented and accomplished dancer, and this is only the beginning of your journey."

"I know, Dad, but I really wanted this," she said softly.

"I understand, dear. I know what you're like when you set your sights on a goal. It's not over yet." He finished tying the knot on his tie and looked down. It was uneven and poorly done. He looked at his daughter, pointed to the tie, and started again. "You see that? I had everything I needed, and I've done it a thousand times. It didn't work out the way I wanted, so I'm going to try again." This time, the knot was completed quickly and perfectly. "You have to press on. Keep trying."

Morgan considered this and came to a different realization. "Wait, why are you getting dressed up? You're not going to work, are you?"

"No, dear. Your father and I have an important dinner to attend. We're leaving after I get you and your sister something to eat. You're taking her to her first karate class, remember?"

Both of Morgan's hands came up in protest. "No way. I'm dealing with a crisis right now!"

Her father took a deep breath and let it out. "Well, my darling daughter, we bought you an expensive convertible with a custom color and all the features. We told you that we'd only do it if you would step up when we needed you to help run errands."

"Yeah, but I thought that would be going to the store, or picking something up for you."

"And you are," her mother added. "You're dropping off Taylor at her class, and picking her up for us."

"Do I have to?"

"Yes, honey," said her father. "With a great convertible comes a little responsibility."

CHAPTER 3

"I can't think of anybody. Certainly not any seniors," Morgan said into her phone. She was sitting in her car in the parking lot outside a gym called MMA World, waiting for Taylor to finish karate. She had no intention of setting foot inside, and it was a nice night anyway. No chance of rain, and a warm breeze moved her ponytail.

"What about Chad? I think he's always had a bit of a crush on you … and he's pretty tall," Olivia's voice came into her ear. Her best friend for years, Morgan could always talk about anything with the blonde beauty. Aside from having great fashion sense, Olivia was also a total extrovert and the life of any party. You would always get honesty from that girl, even when you didn't want it.

"No, basketball players are certainly tall enough, and they have timing, but they don't use their feet like a dancer does."

"What about a football player? Pretty sure Steve Harris would jump at the chance to get close to you." Olivia finished with a giggle.

"Oh, *gross!*" Morgan couldn't help but laugh too. "You think I'd want to invite the biggest bully in the school onto our team? He's pushed the dancers around for years."

"You might have to start considering dudes that are younger than you are. I mean, is it really that hard to find a tall guy who wants to dance?"

Morgan frowned and brought her hand to her forehead. "It's more than that. They don't just have to *want* to dance … they must have some natural ability. They need timing, an awareness of what their partner is doing, good footwork. They need a strong work ethic. You know that, Olivia. You're one of the best hip-hop dancers I've ever seen."

"Thanks, babe. I'm not gonna lie, I'm glad that I'm not you right now. You can always put together a trio, or … maybe a solo? I mean, what else can you do?"

"I don't know. I really don't." Morgan looked up as she saw the door to the gym opening. "Gotta go, Liv. The kids are starting to come out. See you tomorrow."

"Okay, g'night Morgan."

Taylor came bouncing through the parking lot, still wearing her loose martial arts garments and glistening with sweat. She plopped into the convertible and burst out, "That was awesome! We worked out, did throws, kicked and punched bags … oh, and I hit that one kid in the face. But it was an accident. He's fine."

Morgan gave her a stern look. "You're sweaty. You couldn't have a shower before you got in my car?"

Taylor shrugged. "I didn't bring anything to shower, and I don't think that they have showers in there anyway."

"People work out, get stinky, and leave like that? That is disgusting."

Her younger sister started waving frantically at a large figure walking across the parking lot. He was wearing loose black track pants, old sneakers, and a big, grey, shapeless hoodie that covered his face. Realizing that she hadn't been seen, Taylor leaned over her sister and honked the horn.

"Hey!" Morgan protested.

"It's one of the instructors. He's nice. He helped me," she explained as she resumed waving.

The big figure smiled faintly and waved back before turning to get into a beat-up old Volvo. The car had grey primer paint everywhere and a mismatched black front quarter panel. The windows were dirty, and there were no hubcaps on any of the wheels.

"Well, his car sucks," Morgan noted.

Taylor stuck her tongue out at her. "He's nice. I like him. Can we go home now?"

"Yeah, I could use a good night's sleep. Maybe everything will look better in the morning."

"Sorry it sucks to be you. I'm having a blast."

Morgan glared though the windshield as she fired up the flashy little car and zipped out of the parking lot.

CHAPTER 4

The front stairs belonged to the dancers. They owned that space; it was theirs. As long as anyone could remember at Southwood High, different groups met before the school day in specific areas. The football players congregated near the parking lot, making fun of anybody who walked by. The misfits were under a large oak closer to the sidewalk. The stoners laughed raucously in the smoker's area, and it wasn't always cigarettes they were firing up.

There was still a half hour before the first bell rang, so all the groups had only begun to form. The dancers were represented by "the triumvirate." It was formed by the three young women who led the dance team in all ways. They were dressed to kill; their makeup was immaculate, their hair perfect, and each carried a purse that was worth a month's salary for most people.

Morgan was dressed in her usual black leggings, with a colorful t-shirt beneath her denim jacket. Her dark hair was swept back in her trademark ponytail, which hung to the middle of her back. Over her shoulder hung an elegant, black Prada purse. She was saving her allowance for something more impressive. A pink backpack leaned against the wall.

Olivia Stark stood on the first stair, making herself a little taller, and making it easier to talk to her best friend. She wore a white hair band to keep her long, blonde hair out of her face. Her skin was perfect, and her cornflower blue eyes were piercing. A denim skirt showed off her toned legs, and an oversize grey sweatshirt arranged itself on her shoulders. She too wore a purse that few could afford.

The last member of the triumvirate, and perhaps the most striking, was Tonisha Smith. Her eyes and white teeth flashed, contrasting against her incredibly dark skin. Her hair was arranged in long, perfect braids. She was slightly shorter than Olivia, but her personality made her seem bigger. Her body was toned like an Olympic gymnast, and she wore a tight-fitting pink skirt and matching jacket that showed her physique off. She too wore an expensive purse. In fact, her Gucci Dionysus was the priciest item owned by her group of friends. She liked that.

"I don't know why you don't come on over to hip-hop full time. You're already a part of the co-ed. Why not join the female group?" Tonisha said.

Morgan smiled at her friend. "I like hip-hop, I do. But, honestly … ballroom is my first love. You're the best on the team for hip-hop, Tonisha."

"Don't let Hector or Lucas hear you say that," Olivia added.

Tonisha pointed a finger at Morgan. "Say, why can't I be your partner? Pretty sure I can lift you."

All three laughed at that. "Sorry, shorty. Unless you can dance in stilts, it's not going to fly," Morgan said with a smirk.

Tonisha's white teeth flashed in a grin. "Not my fault you're a 'Glamazon.' What did your parents feed you, anyway?"

Suddenly they heard a commotion, and the three of them turned their heads. The football players had a smaller boy surrounded. It was easy to identify the parties involved, as the players on the football team were large and all wore school jackets.

"Steve Harris, captain of the football team and full-time creep," said Olivia.

"I know, right? Doesn't he have anything better to do?" Tonisha said, with a shake of her head.

Morgan glanced away from the group that had gathered to watch and pointed towards the parking lot. "Who's this now?"

A familiar-looking old Volvo was sliding silently through the parking lot and came to a stop in one of the parking spots designated for visitors. Morgan recognized the car from the MMA gym where Taylor had gone for her first day of training.

This did not go unnoticed by the football team, and since they weren't sure if it was a person of authority, they took their attention from their prey. The younger and smaller boy didn't stick around. He dashed away, blending into the crowd.

The same large figure that Morgan had seen her sister wave to was exiting the car and reaching in to pull out a backpack. She noticed that he was wearing the same comfortable, but shapeless, clothes he'd worn when she saw him last. The *exact* same black jogging pants and grey hoodie. Only the shoes were slightly less worn. She couldn't make out the face under the large hood.

"Oh hey, I think we have a new student," Olivia whispered to her friends.

"He's got a driver's license, so he's probably a senior," said Tonisha.

Morgan frowned. "Who transfers halfway through the school year?"

Olivia shrugged. "Could be lots of reasons. I'm going to see if I can find out a little more."

The football team and other students watched the young man move past them quietly. He didn't give them so much as a glance and marched right up the stairs. A few students were buzzing about him, and Morgan herself was becoming curious.

When he made it to the top of the stairs, Olivia planted herself right in front of the door and held out her hand. "Hi! My name is Olivia. Are you new here? Let me be the first to welcome you to Southwood—"

"Stop," the tall stranger interrupted. He held up a grimy hand to halt her. "I don't have time to talk. They're expecting me in the office and I can't be late." He reached out a hand speckled with dirt and a healthy amount of grime under the fingernails. Olivia's nose wrinkled as her own hand was enveloped in the large and filthy one of the young man in front of her. He gave her hand a gentle shake, walked around her to grab the door, and looked back down at the blonde, who was left standing there speechless. "Thanks for the welcome," he said, and went in the school.

Morgan and Tonisha burst into laughter at their friend's complete and utter failure to gain information, and for that matter, attention. Olivia herself rolled her eyes and turned back to her friends. The rest of the school turned back to their own friends, and the buzz of conversation grew again.

"Never thought you'd meet someone immune to your charm, huh, Olivia?" Tonisha teased.

Olivia laughed. "Did you see how dirty he was? Those finger-nails … *Yuck!*"

"That wasn't dirt under those nails. That was grease and grime," Morgan said, grimacing.

"That was a big, dirty white boy," Tonisha agreed. "Did you get a look at his face?"

"Couldn't make out much. Just … scars."

"Scars?" Morgan asked.

"Yeah, a pretty deep one above his left eye and a smaller one on his lip."

Tonisha chuckled. "So he's a beat-up, big, dirty white boy." All three of the friends laughed at her correction.

Olivia got a faraway look. "Nice eyes, though."

Morgan blinked and cocked her head to one side. "Really?"

"Yeah," Olivia confirmed. "Very blue."

CHAPTER 5

"Kyle Branch, that's your name?" Ms. Blake asked the teenager sitting across the desk in her office. He had taken down the hood at her request, revealing a strong face, black short-cropped hair, and a tanned complexion. The stubble on his chin was dark and evenly spread on his square jaw. The scars on his face told her that this was a young man who had absorbed some punishment in his time. But what held her attention were his clear, luminous blue eyes.

He nodded to answer her question.

"Okay, and I see you've filled out the paperwork so we can request your file from your old school." She turned some pages in front of her. "Michigan? Well, hopefully California will be a nice change for you. What brings you to Irvine, if you don't mind me asking?"

He gave a slow shrug of his shoulders. "Family. I have an uncle who lives here."

"Anybody else?"

"No."

Ms. Blake nodded. "I see. What are your goals for the rest of the year?"

Kyle pursed his lips and considered that. "I want to finish the year, get the best marks I can, and stay out of trouble."

"That's it?" Ms. Blake sat back in her chair and narrowed her eyes at the young man. "Is trouble a problem for you?"

"I don't understand your question."

She put her elbows on the armrest and held her pen between her hands. "I guess what I'm asking is, do you often get in 'trouble?'"

He rubbed a big hand on his chin. "Ah, I get it. Listen, it was a tough high school I attended. Sometimes people would try to push you around, but I'm not an easy mark. I was left alone, for the most part. Like I said, I'm here to get good marks."

She smiled at that. "Thinking about college?"

He returned her smile. "Depending on it. I'm trying hard to save the money, but without the marks, well, it's kind of pointless."

She nodded and moved some more papers. "You seem like a fit young man. Do you have any interests, hobbies, or sports you like to play?"

He shook his head. "I have lots of interests outside of school, and that keeps me pretty busy."

"That's going to make it harder to make friends. Joining a team or club would help with that."

"I'm not here to make friends. I'm here to learn and get good marks."

She tapped her pen on the papers in front of her. "I admire focus, I do. I have to tell you, Kyle, that sounds like a lonely way to live."

"I'm pretty comfortable with my own company."

Ms. Blake took a long look at the young man in front of her. She'd had countless students sit in front of her to discuss everything from academic goals to their home situations. She'd learned to trust the instincts that she'd honed over the years. Her intuition was telling her that there was more to this boy. One thing that she didn't feel was any deception. He looked you in the eyes and answered your questions. He was, as they say, a "straight talker." She appreciated that.

She stood up from her chair and gathered the papers. He stood up too, towering above her. "Well, Kyle," she said, "that sounds pretty good. Let's get you a locker, and I'll help you pick out your courses. When that's done, we'll print out a schedule for you. How does that sound?"

"That sounds pretty good."

She turned and motioned for him to follow. "Come with me, and … welcome to Southwood High."

CHAPTER 6

"I've got a name," Olivia said with a sly smile. She was in the cafeteria, already seated with her lunch. Morgan and Tonisha had arrived. They always ate lunch together, and always in the same spot.

"What?" Tonisha asked, one eyebrow raised.

"The new guy. Who else?"

Morgan shrugged and took a bite of her wrap.

"You're not a little curious?" Olivia asked.

"A little," Tonisha admitted. Morgan shook her head and kept munching.

Their conversation was interrupted by a familiar face. Lucas Quintana bounced into the cafeteria and plunked himself down in the chair beside Olivia. He was small, his black hair was spiked up, and he wore a little mascara. With his black silk shirt, he looked refined. "Hey, what are we talking about?"

"The new guy," Olivia said, poking him in the shoulder.

"Oh! Have you seen him? He's kinda scary-looking," he said with a shudder.

"Not your type?" Tonisha asked with a smirk. Lucas was one of the few openly gay students in the high school, and a member of the dance team.

He gave her a withering look. "You know I like 'em pretty. That big galoot needs a serious fashion makeover."

"I know, right?" Morgan said with a chuckle. "It looks like he's in prison, or about to be."

All three laughed at her barb.

Tonisha stopped and patted Lucas's hand. "Speak of the devil, and he appears."

All four of them turned to follow their friend's gaze. They weren't the only ones. Most of the conversations in the cafeteria had ended, or lowered, as heads turned to watch the big teen paying for a drink at the cash register. He was wearing his usual loose-fitting clothes, and counting coins that he was digging out of his pocket. When the count was right, he handed the change to the cashier with a small smile and carried his tray into the big room.

He looked around, saw an empty seat, and strolled over. He sat down heavily and set his lunch down, in a large plastic bag that he had placed in the middle of the tray. He fished out a sandwich made with a hamburger bun and took an enormous bite. He started opening the milk carton that he had purchased. He never looked up at the students staring, just kept his eyes on his food. At that rate, the sandwich wouldn't last long. The buzz of conversation returned to normal.

"I give you, 'Kyle Branch,'" Olivia said, flourishing her hand.

"Kyle? That's his name?" Lucas asked with a frown.

Olivia nodded. "You were expecting something different?"

"Well, I thought it'd be rougher-sounding. He's kind of butch."

"He has a job at an MMA gym," Morgan announced, and took another bite of her wrap. All three of her friends turned to her with wide eyes.

"How do you know that?" Tonisha asked.

Morgan shrugged. "My little sister takes lessons there. I saw him walking out."

Olivia looked scandalized. "I'm the one who digs up the dirt."

"That boy eats like a pig," Tonisha observed, as Kyle shoveled another huge bite of the sandwich into his face and poured some milk into his mouth to soften it.

"HEY!" Lucas protested, and jumped to his feet. A French fry that had been liberally dipped in ketchup had landed on his immaculate shirt. He glared at a nearby table, where the football players were sniggering.

Tonisha's eyes burned. "Those guys are the worst. Why can't they leave people alone?"

Lucas sat back down. "Don't bite, girl. That's what they want." But his eyes betrayed his thoughts, and it was clear he was more bothered than he let on.

"I can't wait until we graduate and we don't have to share a school with them anymore," Olivia whispered.

"COME ON!" Lucas shouted, as another dripping fry landed on his shirt. Again, the football team was laughing, and two of them high-fived. It was the usual suspect.

Morgan stood to her impressive height and scowled at them. "I see you, Steve Harris!"

The team laughed louder, and Steve waved at her with a sneer. They suddenly stopped their commotion and stared at something behind her.

The new guy had finished his lunch, and was strolling down the middle of the cafeteria towards the situation. His hood was up, hiding his face, and he carried his food tray. Every student watched as he moved through the room. Every footstep he took could be heard in the silence.

He got to the table where the dancers sat, hesitated, moved some things around on his tray, and grabbed a handful of something. He took another couple of steps until he was standing right beside the dancers. Lucas's eyes were wide, and the three young women stared with their mouths open.

He slowly placed a handful of napkins and wet-wipes in front of Lucas with one grimy hand. With the same hand, he gave the dancer a pat on the shoulder and walked away. Nobody said a word or made a sound as he continued walking to the end of the cafeteria, threw out his garbage, and plunked his tray on the pile. He turned and left the cafeteria, the students continuing to stare behind him.

Nobody knew who was first, but someone started applauding. It wasn't long until many other pairs of hands joined in to show their approval. Lucas stood up so the entire room could see him and started using the napkins to clean up his shirt.

Amid the cheering, the football team were muttering amongst themselves as the student body expressed their opinion. It was the talk of the school, and it wasn't long until everyone at Southwood High had heard the tale.

The only person who was completely oblivious, and had no idea how much it mattered, was Kyle Branch.

CHAPTER 7

After school, Morgan and Tonisha entered the utility room on the first floor: a big, whitewashed room with green tiles on the floor. A pile of old desks was pushed to one corner. The school had put mirrors on one wall to help the dancers see what they were doing. The captains of the team were surprised to find they were not the first to arrive at dance practice. Hector Santana, Olivia Stark, and Lucas Quintana were huddled together, talking something over.

There were a few surprising things about that situation. Morgan and Tonisha were almost always the first to arrive at practice. They were the most organized and focused students, so it wasn't hard for them to make the transition from locker to dance practice when the school day was over. The other dancers would arrive after the team captains had already put down their bags and fired up the sound system.

It was also odd that Lucas was there so early. He was certainly a good student, well-organized, but he preferred to be fashionably late. Morgan often teased him that he liked to be "fashionably" anything.

"Hector!" Morgan declared when she was closer to the conversation. "Where have you been?"

Hector was wearing his usual t-shirt and jeans. He preferred his head shaved and wore a large cross around his neck. "Funeral, had to be there," he explained, with the hint of a Spanish accent.

"Oh, Hector. I'm so sorry."

He waved a hand at her. "Don't be. It was a distant cousin that I barely knew. But, you know, family is family."

"I hear that," Tonisha agreed.

"We were filling him in on the excitement yesterday," said Olivia.

"I don't know if I would call it 'excitement,'" Morgan countered.

Hector shrugged. "Who is this guy?"

"New guy, big white boy," Tonisha answered. "You'll know him when you see him. Tall, scars on his face, and he dresses like a bum."

"More like a convict, if you ask me," said Morgan.

"Dirty," Olivia said with wide eyes. "Dirty hands."

Hector laughed. "You make this hombre sound like Frankenstein's monster."

"He has nice eyes," Olivia said with a smile. "Very blue."

They stopped their conversation to look at more members of the dance crew as they arrived at the utility room. A couple of sophomores were talking about the same subject. Two others were looking down at their phones.

"I kind of wonder why he did it," Tonisha said quietly.

Lucas smiled. "I actually asked him."

All the dancers' eyes goggled. "You did!? You actually *spoke* to him?" Olivia screeched. "What was that like?"

"Terrifying," Lucas said with a giggle.

Morgan leaned toward him. "How did it happen? Tell us."

Lucas held up his hands to quiet her. "Okay, okay, Glamazon. I saw him getting a drink of water from the fountain on the second floor, sixth period. I guess we have a spare at the same time. I figured that was the time to ask."

"Hurry up, Blake's gonna be here soon," Hector pressed.

"Alright, alright. So I walk up to the big fella, and he starts moving like he's going to walk right by me without noticing me. I swear, the guy didn't seem to recognize me."

"I guess he's dumb," Morgan concluded.

Lucas shook his head. "No, no, I don't think so. Anyway, I looked up at him …"

"Were you scared?" Olivia asked.

"You have no idea," Lucas laughed. "I give him a wave, and I say, 'Hey, big guy, thanks for what you did in the cafeteria.' Well, he looked kind of confused."

"Really?" Tonisha asked.

"Yeah," said Lucas. "He said, 'Sorry, friend, I don't know what you mean.'"

"You're kidding?" said Morgan. "Oh, man, he *is* stupid."

"No, that's not it," Lucas said. "So I remind him of what happened and then he gets it.

'Oh, yeah … you were the guy?' he asks."

"He didn't recognize you?" Hector asked.

"No, he didn't. I asked him why he did it."

"And?" Olivia said, exasperated.

"He said, 'I saw a guy with ketchup on his shirt. I had some napkins and stuff I was going to throw out. Figured the guy could use it. That's all.'"

The dancers looked at each other, as if to confirm they'd heard Lucas right. "That's a weird answer," Morgan said with a grimace.

"Yeah, I thought so too. I thanked him for what he did. He said, 'No big deal, dude.' Then he kept walking down the hall." Lucas wore a small smile on his face. "It wasn't a big deal for him, just something he did. I don't think he gave it much thought. It meant a lot to me, though," he finished quietly.

"Did you tell him that?" Olivia asked.

Lucas shook his head. "He was already too far away. He's a big guy, and when he starts walking he moves fast."

The door to the utility room swung open, and all the dancers in the room looked over to see the guidance counselor, Ms. Blake, walk in with her arms full of folders. "Morgan, Tonisha, let's get this rehearsal moving. I have a stack of paperwork to deal with, so I'm going to sit in the corner while you whip 'em into shape."

The room laughed at that. It had the virtue of being the truth. In answer, Tonisha clapped her hands. "Line up! Morgan's going to fire up the music, and you had BETTER be in position!"

Everyone in the room started running in different directions as Ms. Blake made her way to one of the old desks in the corner.

Hector, Tonisha, and Lucas found their positions quickly at the front of the crew. "You're right," Hector mumbled. "That was a bit of excitement in the cafeteria."

Olivia smiled ear to ear. "Yeah, well, it's not over yet, because I hear Steve Harris is *pissed*."

CHAPTER 8

"There he is," Lucas said quietly to the rest of the dancers eating lunch in the cafeteria the next day. He was turned in his seat, looking behind him, and Hector was doing the same. Olivia, Morgan, and Tonisha craned their necks to see what Lucas was pointing out.

Sure enough, there was the young man, wearing his loose clothing and carrying a tray with a plastic bag in the middle. He was counting his change again, but there was less of it. The drink he was purchasing was smaller than the one from the day before. He paid for his beverage and sauntered over to an empty seat, close to where he'd sat the day before.

Morgan frowned. "Uh, exactly why are we watching this guy?"

"Yeah, the big boy is buying lunch. Who cares?" Tonisha agreed.

Hector turned to face them with a small smile. "You're about to get a lesson in how things work around here … if you're a guy."

"Here we go," Lucas hissed. Three football players walked up to the long table where Kyle sat. Steve Harris, team captain, led the group. He was wearing his team jacket, though it was a little warm for it. They all were. His light brown hair was coiffed to perfection, and there was a smug look on his face. He was flanked by Richie Green, a speedy, pale-skinned defensive back, and Tony "Two-Ton" Stevens. The big African-American loomed behind his captain, glaring malevolently.

"I think you've made a mistake, buddy," Steve announced with a smirk.

Kyle was chewing on a bite of his sandwich. He didn't look up as he mumbled through his food. "Oh yeah? What's that?"

Steve leaned forward and put his hands on the table, looking down at his prey. "Well, we all have our favorite place when we eat lunch, and you're where the football players sit."

"Well, that's not true," Kyle said after swallowing his food. "You guys ate lunch yesterday, and you weren't sitting here."

The malicious smile on Steve's face grew. "Ah, well, we decide every day where we sit and sometimes it changes. See, we run this school, so we sit where we want to sit." The football players behind him chuckled at his explanation.

Kyle smiled too, and nodded. "Okay, I get it now." He slammed his hands on the table and stood up fast, firing his chair straight back into the table behind him. The football players stopped smiling and took a step back. The entire cafeteria stopped their conversations and held their collective breath.

Kyle's face was made of stone, and his blue gaze burned into the wide eyes of Steve Harris. He was a lot bigger than they'd figured when he was sitting, and now that he was standing, he was even taller than Tony. Kyle was so quiet and relaxed that it was easy to overlook his size. Now he was alert, focused, standing tall, and more than a little incensed. They had awakened the giant, and they knew it.

A teacher in the cafeteria approached the situation. "Uh, hey, guys, is everything okay?" It was the biology teacher, Mr. Ryckman. He was a large man himself, with a full beard, and his hair was curly and wild on top. He wore a neatly pressed dress shirt and a conservative tie. He was smiling pleasantly, but his eyes told a different story as they darted between the two adversaries standing in front of him.

Kyle gave a small laugh and turned to collect the chair he had shoved behind him. "Aw, it's alright, sir. Just somebody trying to be something they're not." He sat down and took another bite of his lunch.

Mr. Ryckman turned his attention to the football players. "Steve, Richie, Tony … you guys need something?" Ryckman knew who the instigators were.

"No, we're good," Steve said, with a dirty look at Kyle.

"Glad to hear it," Mr. Ryckman said. "Perhaps you'd better find a seat and have some lunch." His eyes grew hard. "I think I see some seats over there, where you always sit."

A few students who were listening in chuckled. Ryckman knew what they all knew. It was Steve Harris who caused this trouble. It always was.

The football players slunk back to their teammates, trying hard to look smug and victorious. It was all about appearances. Some of the players were smiling, like something had been accomplished, but the three young men who had approached Kyle knew different.

"You're Kyle Branch, right?" Mr. Ryckman asked.

"That's right," Kyle mumbled, mouth full.

"I think you're in my biology class tomorrow. Welcome to Southwood High," the teacher said with a smile.

Kyle gave him a grin. "Thanks. I like your welcome better than the football team's version."

Ryckman chuckled and looked like he wanted to say something more. Instead, he walked away, smiling.

"Ugh! I HATE that macho crap," Morgan said.

"Really! It's so stupid," Olivia agreed.

Lucas rolled his eyes. "Oh yeah, it would have been so much better if they had given each other dirty looks and sent some nasty texts."

The dancers laughed. "Let me enlighten you, chicas," Hector offered.

"Oh, please do," Olivia said.

Hector smiled and slowly shook his head. "Guys like Steve feel like they gotta be the biggest dog in the room. When Kyle helped out Lucas here, it showed him up."

"Well, that's pathetic," Tonisha muttered.

"I agree," Hector said. "But that's the way it is."

Morgan held up a hand. "So, excuse me, but what is this nonsense we saw today?"

Hector pointed a finger at her. "That was the football team trying to get some respect back."

"Did they?" Olivia asked.

"Oh no!" Lucas said with a chuckle.

"Definitely not," Hector said with a grin.

"I'm lost," Morgan said. "So did Kyle do the right thing?"

Lucas and Hector looked at each other. "He did the only thing he could," Lucas explained.

"Yeah," Hector added. "If he didn't stand up for himself, they would have been on him for the rest of the year."

"So the drama is over then?" Olivia said with a smile. "Well, I guess that's a good thing."

Hector and Lucas looked at each other again. They sat back in their chairs, and Lucas let out a sigh. "I wish that were true. But that's not how it works."

CHAPTER 9

M r. Ryckman was right. First period, the day after the showdown in the cafeteria, Kyle entered his biology class, waited until every student had already picked a seat, and then sauntered in to find an unclaimed seat. It happened to be right beside Lucas Quintana. While few students were openly homophobic, fewer still would sit with him.

A few students giggled when the grubby teenager plunked himself on a stool beside the more polished dancer. Lucas himself seemed a little nervous, but nodded to his new biology partner, and Kyle returned the gesture.

Morgan and Olivia sat beside each other in the same class. Olivia was fascinated with Kyle and watched his every move. Morgan was indifferent, but saw the humor in the strange pairing. "Talk about the odd couple," Olivia whispered.

"Yeah, the fashion plate and the caveman," Morgan agreed.

Mr. Ryckman focused the class, outlining the task and the materials they would need to complete the experiment. Bunsen burners, beakers, lighters, and a long talk about being safe with the gas. Some were paying attention, others had checked out. Lucas was surprised to see that his partner was furiously writing every instruction down with a pencil.

After the instructions had been given, the students were encouraged to begin. The whole class started moving. Some students were fetching the burners, while others grabbed the other supplies. The noise level dipped a bit when all the students had their materials and concentrated on the task at hand. Olivia bumped Morgan and pointed a finger behind her to direct her attention.

When Morgan turned her head, she found that Lucas and Kyle were well on their way to completing the experiment. The burner was set up, a nice level flame, and their water was approaching the boiling point. Lucas was performing the experiment and talking to Kyle. The big teenager was writing the notes to complete the assignment as the smaller partner directed him. Not what she would expect.

This did not go unnoticed by their instructor. Ryckman took some time to see what Kyle was writing and how the experiment was going. He said something specifically to Kyle, and he stopped writing. The big student said something softly to his teacher, and Mr. Ryckman considered his words. Lucas excused himself as he reached past his partner to fetch his bag. Then he quickly fished out a couple of pens and gave them to Kyle.

The teenager gave Lucas a clap on the shoulder that wobbled the dancer, and started to write on the paper in front of him. Olivia looked at Morgan and shrugged. Morgan returned the gesture. They were sure to get the scoop from Lucas. He'd be dying to talk about this.

"So what was that like?" Olivia asked as the three dancers marched down the hall.

"What? What was what like?" Lucas said with a smirk.

"Come on," Morgan admonished. "You know what we're asking."

Lucas smiled. "Actually, it was cool. He was easy to work with, and more than happy to do his share. Maybe a little more."

Olivia made a face. "More? What does that mean?"

Lucas narrowed his eyes. "Well, he was willing to do all the writing, and when Ryckman told him that the work was good, but shouldn't be in pencil, he seemed kind of sad."

"Is that why you gave him the pens?" Morgan guessed.

"Yeah, he didn't have one. I felt kind of bad for him."

Olivia gave him a playful pat on the shoulder. "Aw, that was nice of you."

"That's not all," Lucas said with a laugh. "He rewrote the whole assignment in pen. I think Ryckman liked that."

"So he's a good guy?" Olivia pressed.

"Yeah," Lucas confirmed. "Quiet, doesn't say much."

Morgan raised an eyebrow. "You think maybe he's ... well ... like you?"

Lucas grinned at her. "Nope! That one is hopelessly heterosexual."

The three friends chuckled at that. They parted ways and started heading to their next class. "See you at my locker later, Morgie?" Olivia called down the hall to her friend.

"It's *Morgan*, and yeah," the tall brunette called back.

Olivia and Morgan were walking down the hall on the second floor, talking about how the hip-hop crew was coming together. It was well after the bell, and most of the students had gone home. The halls were empty. The blonde suddenly did a double take as they passed the computer lab, and stopped. She grabbed Morgan's arm and pulled her a step backward. "Check it out."

Sure enough, there was Southwood's newest student on one of the computers, working hard. Morgan gave her friend a look. "Come on, Olivia! You gotta stop stalking this guy. He's a nobody."

"I know, I know. I'm curious. You KNOW how I have to know what's going on."

Morgan shook her head and started walking away from the situation. "The guy doesn't own a pen, of course he needs to use a school computer."

Olivia looked back over her shoulder at the lab, where Kyle was working. As she walked on, she considered her friend's callous comment. It made sense. She stole a last look and then ran to catch up with Morgan.

CHAPTER 10

"*What?!* Come on! I took her last time." Morgan's arms were crossed on her chest, and she was glaring at her mother. Taylor was behind her, wearing her martial arts gear. She was ignoring the conversation and, instead, practicing her stance, letting out the occasional kick and punch.

"Morgan, your father has a late meeting tonight, and I've got some work to catch up on in the study."

"Would it be the end of the world if she was to miss a lesson?"

"No way!" Taylor protested. "It's Judo night tonight. I'm not missing that."

Mrs. Laflamme raised an eyebrow. "Really, Morgan? You'd be okay with missing a dance rehearsal?"

Morgan considered that, rolled her eyes, and looked down at the floor, defeated.

"Besides," her mother continued, "it's only for an hour."

"Fine," Morgan muttered, and stomped off to make sure her phone was charged.

"YAY!" Taylor cheered. Then her face dropped, and she leapt into her stance. "I mean, KIYAAH!"

"How much longer are you going to do this, anyway?" Morgan asked her sister, as the convertible whizzed down their street.

"I don't know, until it's not fun anymore," Taylor answered.

"Dressing in that white outfit and beating up on each other is fun?"

Taylor looked at her sister and grinned. "Yeah, it is. But it's more than that. It's about learning something new and getting it right."

Morgan stole a quick glance at her sister. "Getting what right?"

"The move, the technique, whatever we're working on. There's actually a lot to it."

"And tonight is Judo night?"

Taylor's eyes widened. "Yeah, I've never tried it before. I'm a little nervous, but I mostly want to know what it's like."

Morgan wrinkled her nose. "Well, whatever. You'll have to tell me about it, because I'm not setting foot in that place."

"Yeah, so I'm sitting in the parking lot. I guess this comes with the convertible." Morgan was sitting in her little car, talking on her phone with Olivia. Class had begun, so nobody was coming or going. The parking lot was deserted. Only a bird chirping in the dusk interrupted the quiet.

"Hey, look on the bright side," her friend's voice crackled in her ear. "It won't be long until Taylor learns to drive. Then she can take herself to whatever madness she's gotten herself into."

Morgan gave a small smile at that thought. "You think my parents will buy her a car nicer than mine?"

There was a pause as Olivia thought about that. "Would Taylor want a car like yours? She'll probably ask for a monster truck." They both laughed.

Morgan looked up as she saw a car pull into the lot. The primer-coated Volvo slowly rolled to a stop in a parking space beside her. Only one person in the city drove a car like that. Sure enough, Kyle Branch hopped out and sauntered into the gym.

"Hey, the guy you're so curious about just got here," she informed her friend.

"*Really*?" Olivia squawked. "Oh yeah, he helps out there, right?"

Morgan inspected the nails on one of her hands. "I guess so. That's what Taylor says, anyway."

"So you've never seen him when he's in there?"

"I'm not going in there. It'll smell."

There was a pause before Olivia exploded, "Oh no! You *HAVE* to. Aren't you the least bit curious?"

"No."

"Well, I'm not there. Can't you go in for a little while? Then you can report what you saw to me."

"The smell, remember?"

"Breathe through your mouth," Olivia laughed.

"I'm not doing it."

"I'd do it for you!" Olivia whined.

Morgan brought a hand to her temple and let out a big sigh. "You would because you're the nosiest person in California."

"True, true," Olivia answered. "But I'd also do it for my best pal."

Morgan put the phone down on her leg, as if to remove the entire conversation. She groaned and brought the phone back to her ear. "Fine! But you're going to owe me for this one."

"You're the best!" her friend cheered into the phone. "Call me when it's over. Tell me everything!"

Morgan climbed out of the car, stretched, and started walking to the front door. She started breathing through her mouth before she got there.

CHAPTER 11

To her surprise, the gym was a clean place, albeit a little warmer than she would have liked; someone had put some work in on sweeping and mopping up. A kind-looking older gentleman sat behind a large desk, surrounded by the shoes that the students had left before entering. He smiled at her. "Hi there, I'm Paul and this is my place. Would you like to try some classes?"

Morgan held up a hand to stop him. "No, thanks. I'm here to see how my sister is doing."

Paul nodded and tilted his head. "Out of curiosity, which one of my students is your sister?"

"Taylor."

He thumped a hand down on his desk with a laugh. "I should've guessed by your height. They grow 'em tall in your family."

Morgan smiled. "How is she doing?"

"That firecracker is doing well. We have to calm her down sometimes before she kills somebody!"

She brought a hand to her mouth as she laughed. "Yeah, that's her."

"Well, please leave your shoes with the rest, and you'll find a bench for spectators inside the room."

She nodded her thanks, slipped off her shoes, and started into the gym. She first noticed stalls like you'd see in a bathroom, but there were no toilets inside. Obviously, they were for changing. She passed those and hung a right to step into the main area. There were red mats on every part of the ground, and kids in martial arts gear of every color were scattered all over. She saw the bench and took a seat not too far from the other parents watching their kids. Though she called up a news site on her phone, her attention was focused on the class. Olivia was right, this was kind of interesting.

It didn't take long for her to spot Kyle. He was easily the biggest person in the room, and his white martial arts uniform was the most worn. She had to wonder if anything he owned was in good condition. The belt around his waist was in good shape and looked new. It was black. That was a surprise that was sure to entertain Olivia.

She scanned the room to find her sister. Again, it wasn't hard to find her gleaming white outfit; she was one of the tallest kids. She had a slightly taller boy in her grasp. She had one of his sleeves in a tight grip, and her other arm was snaked around his waist. She took a step into him, turned away, and pulled him over her back. She threw him to the mat, screaming, "DIE!"

A few of the other students stopped what they were doing and stared in horror. Taylor held both of her hands above her head in victory. Kyle sauntered over, a faint smile on his lips. He checked on the student still lying on the mat to make sure he was okay. He bent at the waist to lower himself to talk to Taylor. It was a quiet conversation, and the young girl was nodding her head occasionally. Eventually, Kyle straightened up, and Taylor gave her partner a hug, and then threw him again … but with much more control.

Morgan was watching all this, but trying hard to hide it. She was hoping that Kyle would notice she was ignoring him. It was doubtful he didn't recognize a classmate with her unique height and appearance. But he made no effort to acknowledge her presence. To her irritation, Kyle *was* ignoring her. She preferred to be the one doing the ignoring.

Kyle walked to the center of the mats and clapped his hands together a few times to get the students' attention. They stopped what they were doing and circled around him. "You're doing a good job," he encouraged, "but you're trying to do everything with your arms." He beckoned for another adult wearing a brown belt to come over. "You're learning a basic hip toss, or 'Ogoshi.'" He grabbed the other instructor, stepped in, and elevated him easily. The man went up over Kyle's hip and landed gently on the mats, but thumped his hand for control as he hit.

Morgan was done pretending to look at her phone. She was riveted to the action on the mats.

Kyle stood the other instructor up again. "You want to see that slower?" he asked his young charges.

Every head nodded with a smile.

"Okay, first off, this throw is mostly done with the feet. We'll cover the arms first, but I want you to pay attention to the footwork when we get there."

Mostly done with the feet. Morgan considered that statement. She leaned forward and put her hand on her chin, her brown eyes wide and unblinking.

Kyle grabbed the other instructor's sleeve. "Sure, you have to control the arm and move in relation to your partner's frame ..."

Move in relation to the frame of your partner ... something Morgan herself had heard many, many times as she learned how to dance with a partner.

"You need to put your arm under their arm," Kyle continued. "But here comes the part with the feet. You remember me telling you about the feet, right?"

All the youngsters nodded their heads, and Morgan nodded hers slightly too.

"Okay, here it is." The big teenager stepped one foot between his partner's stance, and the other quickly joined it. He turned his body as he stepped, and his hip rotated into the man who was assisting with the demonstration. "You see how I have to step quickly and keep my feet together? Well, it's not enough that I move my feet right. They must be placed correctly in relation to my opponent's feet."

Feet must be moved correctly, but in relation to your partner. That was something Morgan had said to Bernie, her old partner.

Kyle held up a finger. "Now here's the magic. After your feet are placed correctly in relation to your partner, your hip must move below theirs, and you pull their frame forward and load them up." He did as he said, and the man helping him smiled, as his feet were no longer touching the ground and he was balanced precariously on Kyle's hip. "Now I rotate, *gently*," he said, with a stern look at Taylor, who grinned sheepishly and turned a little red.

Kyle then turned the man slowly and held his arm as he went to the mat. "See? I can easily get him up with proper footwork and hip placement, and I can control his descent by holding onto his arm. Now watch it a little quicker."

He nodded to the other instructor to ensure he was ready, and the nod was returned. Kyle moved so quickly that the man was elevated and headed toward the ground in an instant. Again, he controlled the descent, and the man didn't hit the mats with the force that could have rattled his teeth.

Morgan was impressed with his efficiency and speed, but the things he said and demonstrated echoed in her mind. *Proper footwork ... in relation to your partner ... hips in position ... pull frame forward.* These were all common instructions in the world of ballroom dance. Things she had said many different times in different ways to the people she was teaching.

"So there you have it," Kyle said cheerfully. "Treat it more like a dance and less like a throw, and it might come easier. Give it a try."

Morgan watched in awe as the youngsters partnered up, immediately doing better. They clearly were focusing on their feet and their hips, and were reaping the benefits.

"Like a dance?" one mother said to another beside her.

"Most violent dance I've ever seen," They both gave a small laugh.

Violent, okay, Morgan thought to herself. *But the footwork, proximity, movement ... it's a dance for sure!* She couldn't help but smile. Morgan Laflamme had found the answer to all her problems. She'd found her partner. He just didn't know it ... yet.

CHAPTER 12

"Are you CRAZY? You are. You've gone crazy!" Olivia screeched at Morgan. They were sitting in the cafeteria, discussing what Morgan had seen the night before. Olivia was staring at her wide-eyed; she hadn't touched her salad yet.

"I know! I know what this must sound like," Morgan said, with a shake of her head. She put her wrap down and clasped her hands on the table as she gathered her thoughts. "You should have seen it. Everything he was teaching was so similar to what I do—to what I had to learn, and what a new partner is going to have to learn."

Olivia gave her a hard look. "I guess your next routine is going to involve dressing in white pajamas and throwing each other on the floor over and over again? Does that sound right?"

Morgan burst out laughing at the image and put her hand to her forehead. Olivia laughed too. People stared at the two teens as they enjoyed their laughing fit.

"I'm telling you," Morgan said after catching her breath, "everything, and I mean EVERYTHING, before he tossed that guy was dance. It reminded me of a move Bernie and I performed our first year together."

"One move? You're basing all of this on one move that you saw?"

"*No, no, no,*" Morgan replied, holding up a hand to stop her friend. "It's a few things." She started counting her reasons on her fingers. "One, he can move his feet very well. Two, he has an awareness of what his partner—"

"Opponent," Olivia interrupted.

"Whatever," Morgan continued. "He has an awareness of where the other person is. That's important in ballroom. Actually, it's key."

"Okay, what else?"

Morgan went back to counting on her fingers. "Three, that guy has a black belt. Do you even know what that means?"

"Do *you?*" Olivia countered.

The brunette took a deep breath, running her hands over her head and down her long ponytail as she collected herself. "Well, it means Steve Harris has definitely bitten off more than he can chew."

The blonde laughed and pointed a finger at her to signal her agreement, as she shoveled some salad in her mouth.

"I also know that it's rare, and it takes a lot of time and focus to get one. You've got to be dedicated, tough, and good with your body to wear one. I mean, do you know anybody else with a black belt in a martial art?"

Olivia thought about that and shook her head to concede her point.

"Four, and this is crucial, it's the thing *NOBODY* can teach and nobody can learn."

"He's big?"

"He *is* big," Morgan said with a chuckle. "I'm a tall woman, and I need a tall man to make it work. How tall do you think he is?"

"Oh, he's at least 6'3". Remember him looking down his nose at Steve?"

Morgan smiled and counted the last finger on her hand. "And here's number five. It's the thing that's probably the most important."

"I can't wait," Olivia said, and took a drink of her diet soda.

Morgan's eyes lit up. "I'm Morgan Laflamme, and when I set a goal, it gets done. I have decided, *absolutely decided*, that I'm going to defend my first-place finish last year, and I need him to do it."

"No matter what?" Olivia asked quietly.

"No matter what."

Almost in answer to their discussion, the subject of their conversation walked into the cafeteria and sat in the first empty chair he could find. He wasn't wearing the same clothes, but they were as large, old, and shapeless: green track pants and a faded black sweatshirt with the hood up, hiding his face.

Olivia stared hard at him as he stuffed his face with a sandwich. "I've got to tell you this as a friend, Morgan. I think you've lost your mind."

"I know what it sounds like, but I know talent when I see it. Besides, with my instruction, he'll be a champion in no time."

Olivia continued to stare at the young man. "Here's something you're not considering. Has it ever crossed your mind that he's an MMA fighter and has zero interest in ballroom dancing? I mean, he's not exactly doing much. I hear he does a good job in class, he's quiet, and he seems a decent guy—but *NOT* a dancer."

Morgan waved a hand in dismissal. "I'm not worried about that part. I'm sure I can convince him." She looked over her shoulder at Kyle as he stood up and started moving to dispose of his tray and garbage. She turned back to Olivia. "Trust me, he'll be all for it. I'm going to be the best thing that's ever happened to this guy."

CHAPTER 13

The day moved slowly for Morgan. When she sat in history class, she was thinking about how to introduce herself and her brilliant idea to the martial artist. When she daydreamed in Spanish class, she was thinking about how to explain it, how to make sure he could understand how great they would be. If she explained it right, she had no doubt that he'd jump at the chance. I mean, who wouldn't? A chance to learn and work with a national champion and win hardware at the biggest competition in the country? It was a once-in-a-lifetime opportunity.

While she wasn't worried about convincing him, she was nervous about approaching him. This was a big guy, who faced down the meanest bullies in the school and didn't blink. A teenager who earned a black belt in at least one martial art, who kept to himself and didn't seem to want any social interaction. She remembered how Olivia had crashed and burned in her attempt to talk to him.

By the end of the school day, she'd decided that Olivia would have to be there. Maybe seeing her face would put him at ease. She knew all too well that two pretty girls can convince a teenage boy to do anything. Her friend's blonde beauty and her own dark, striking appearance always afforded them special treatment. Besides, Olivia would do anything for her. There was no doubt.

"No way. Absolutely not. Uh-uh!" Olivia's eyes were wide and her hands were up. They were taking a break at dance rehearsal, and Tonisha was on the other side of the room talking with a few of the sophomores. Morgan had casually mentioned that she would like Olivia's company when she enlightened Mister Kyle Branch about his great opportunity.

"Yes, you will," Morgan said, without looking at her.

"No, I WON'T!"

Morgan turned her eyes on her best friend. "You would actually let me approach that big scary guy alone?"

"Maybe," the blonde answered without looking at her.

"You don't want to be there to hear what goes down? You aren't interested in what he says? You aren't curious?" Morgan pressed.

"A little."

"So it's settled then? After rehearsal, we'll see if he's around?" Morgan said with a smile.

"Yeah. But sometimes it's not easy being your friend," Olivia said with a pout.

Morgan grabbed Olivia in a big hug. "But it's never dull."

Tonisha clapped her hands in the center of the room to signal that the break was over. "Okay, on your feet. We've got more to do!"

As they took their positions, Olivia looked over to her friend. "This might be the first time I'm actually NOT looking forward to the end of rehearsal."

Morgan smiled at her.

"Oh my God, oh my God, oh my GOD! Are we actually doing this?" Olivia whispered to Morgan as they crept down the hall towards the computer lab. The halls were deserted, and they hadn't seen another student since rehearsal ended. They were shoulder to shoulder, moving at a snail's pace.

"Calm down. He might not even be there," Morgan whispered back.

The door to the computer lab opened wide, and Kyle strode into the hall, marching away from them. His hood was up, and he carried his bag in one hand and books in the other.

"He's leaving. You're going to have to call him," Olivia hissed.

Morgan raised a hand and half-heartedly called, "Uh, excuse me!"

Kyle kept moving down the hall until he was almost at the corner.

"*HEY, BRANCH!*" Olivia bellowed down the hall.

That stopped him dead, and he slowly turned towards them. Morgan's eyes bugged out, and she gave a hard look at Olivia, who shrugged.

"You wanted his attention," said Olivia. "You're up."

They hustled up to him, and Morgan put on a winning smile and held out her hand. "Hi, I'm Morgan Laflamme."

Kyle took off the hood, and his blue eyes burned into hers. He dropped his bag and reached out to shake her hand. Morgan winced a little at the power in his grip, and she noticed the dirt under his fingernails.

"Maybe you've heard of me?" she asked, with an eyebrow raised.

The young man shook his head with no expression.

"Ah, well, maybe you've heard of our dance team at Southwood?"

Again, he shook his head. The silence lingered. Olivia bumped her with an elbow to spur her on.

"Right, well, we have a dance team. I'm a captain, and Olivia here is on the team too." Morgan gestured with her thumb at the blonde beside her as her friend offered a weak little wave.

"So I was at that place you teach, MMA World, did … did you see me there?"

A shake of the head, and still his expression hadn't changed.

"Oh, well, I was there," she said, rolling her eyes. "Yeah, I just said that. Taylor, she's my sister, do you know her?"

"Yes," he said in his quiet, low voice. "I know Taylor. Cool kid."

"Oh, good!" Morgan said a little too loudly. "Well, I saw you teaching that hip throw thingy, and I noticed you move your feet well. You had a good feel for where the other person is, and we need that on the dance team. In fact, you could—"

"No," Kyle interrupted.

"What?"

"No, I won't join your dance team, or any other team or club at this school."

There was a momentary silence as they absorbed his meaning.

Morgan blinked and tried again. "I don't think you understand. You see, this is actually a great opportunity."

Kyle held up his hand to stop her again. "No, I think it's you who doesn't understand. I work two jobs, and I'm trying to get good enough grades to go to college. I don't need any distractions and I'm busy enough. The last thing I want to do is dance," he finished, with a shake of his head.

"But you would be dancing with me."

"Okay, listen. Marion, is it?"

"It's *Morgan*," she answered with a glare.

"Okay, Morgan. I'm sure you're a very good dancer—"

"National champion," she interrupted.

"Yeah, that's good," he agreed. "You're a pretty girl, and I'm sure you're used to getting your way, but it's not going to happen."

Morgan and Olivia stared at him, their mouths open.

"Thanks for the offer," he concluded. He collected his bag from the floor, turned on his heel, and continued his way down the hall.

The two young women were frozen, unable to speak, as they watched him walk down the hall and disappear into the stairwell.

"Wow, that went even worse than I thought it would," Olivia muttered.

"B-but ... but ..." Morgan stammered, staring after him, tears welling in her eyes.

Olivia touched her arm to get her attention. She shrugged. "Well, at least he thinks you're pretty."

CHAPTER 14

Morgan ate her cereal grudgingly, staring straight ahead. Her eyes were puffy from crying, and her voice was hoarse from a few primal screams she had let out in her car. Her feelings swung from crushing disappointment to rage.

How could he not see it as clearly as she could? How could fate be so cruel as to take away one dance partner and tease her with another? She hated Bernie for leaving, and was furious at Kyle for brushing her off like that. Never, NEVER had anyone been so indifferent to her point of view. *The big dummy doesn't know what he's missing,* she thought as she shoveled in some more cereal.

She grimaced and pushed the bowl away from her. She'd been too slow, and the milk had made the cereal too soggy to enjoy. Another chance missed. "Story of my life," she muttered to herself.

Taylor sat across from her, staring, as she too worked on her breakfast. Their parents were talking softly in the vast kitchen, aware that their eldest was out of sorts. They also knew that she'd talk about it when she was ready.

Unfortunately, little sisters don't have the wisdom that comes with time and experience. "You okay, Morgan? You look awful," Taylor asked through a mouthful of cereal.

Morgan looked at her for an eternity, then slammed down her spoon and sprinted back to her room.

"Nice," Taylor's mother said pointedly at her youngest, and followed Morgan down the hall.

Taylor threw her hands up and looked at her father. "What? We were all thinking it."

Her father shook his head. "We were also waiting for the right time to talk about it."

She thought about that. "Oh. Well, you can talk about it now. No more waiting. No need to thank me."

Morgan ran right to her dresser and looked in the mirror. She barely recognized herself. Her ponytail was not neat, and her skin was blotchy, but her eyes alarmed her the most. They had dark circles under them, and they were so ... so ... *red*. They looked like a couple of dark marbles floating in bourbon.

She hurled herself onto her bed and shouted into her pillows. She stopped when she heard a gentle knock. "Go away, Taylor!"

"It's your mother. May I come in?"

Morgan had to think about that. Part of her wanted to be alone, forever. Her mother was also the easiest to talk to, and if there was one person who could see what mattered, it was her. "Yeah, okay. Come in."

Her mother came in, sat on the bed beside her, and started rubbing her back. "Want to talk about it?"

Morgan let out a shuddering sigh. "There's not a lot to talk about. I lost my dance partner, thought I'd found another one, and I completely struck out." She sat up on the bed and looked at her mother. "I thought things were finally going my way. I thought I had the answer and I could dance for the national championship." She gave the pillow a swat in frustration. "I was wrong, and now I'm right back where I started, but I got to make a fool of myself too."

Her mother considered her words. "Wrong? You are many things, baby girl, but 'wrong' is rarely one of them. Did you ever consider that you were right about your choice in partner?"

Morgan sniffed and wiped a tear away. "What do you mean?"

Her mother patted her leg. "You're a dancer. Nobody knows dance like you, and if you thought you'd found someone to fit the bill, you were probably right. But we both know a true dancer will always *want* to dance. They have to, and they can't help it."

"He could have done it, Mom. He's too dumb to understand."

"Oh, I wouldn't say that. He's just not a dancer," her mother said with a chuckle.

Morgan pointed to her eyes. "I *can't* go to school like this. Can I stay home?"

"A little makeup, hairstyle, and some of my magic eyedrops and you'll be fine."

"I don't know if I can face my friends after this kind of failure. I feel like an idiot."

"You shouldn't," her mother said with a shake of her head. "You had a problem and you tried to solve it. It didn't work. That's all."

Morgan laughed. "That's one way to look at it."

"It's the only way to look at it," her mother said, and she gave her oldest daughter a kiss on the forehead. "Go to school. It could turn out to be a great day. You never know."

CHAPTER 15

Morgan walked down the hall to her homeroom, hoping to avoid Olivia. "Hey, Morgie! You okay?" she heard called down the hall. She'd hoped for too much.

She turned to face her friend. "It's MORGAN. And yeah, I'm fine. Why?"

Olivia was wearing a pink dress, and her hair was braided. Her brows furrowed above her cornflower blue eyes. She leaned in and took a good look. "Hey, your eyes are a little red."

Morgan waved a hand at her face. "Allergies. No big deal."

"Good. You coming to rehearsal tonight?"

"Yeah, not looking forward to it, but I'll be there."

"Better be," Olivia said with a grin, pointing at her friend.

They started walking down the hall together, waving occasionally at friends or acquaintances as they passed. "I have a conversation with Ms. Blake after rehearsal that I'm not going to enjoy," said Morgan.

"Giving up on the ballroom?" Olivia asked.

"What else can I do?"

Tonisha brought rehearsal to a stop with some encouragement. "Okay, okay! It's coming, boys and girls. We've made some big jumps, but we've got more to do. Stick around and stretch a bit if you like, but this rehearsal is done."

All the sweaty dancers in the room groaned in relief. Ms. Blake raised her voice from the back of the room. "One more thing. Come see me to get the paperwork for nationals. I need you to fill out these forms carefully."

Some of the dancers grabbed their things, while others took the opportunity to stretch. A small lineup formed in front of Ms. Blake. She took the time to go over the forms with each of the dancers, and they thanked her as they left. Morgan took her time and made sure to be the last in line. What she had to say was not for an audience. As it was, she was the last person left in the room.

When her turn came, Ms. Blake gave her a smile and started searching through the paperwork. "Ah, Morgan. I take it you're waiting for the ballroom form?"

"I'm afraid not, Ms. Blake," she murmured.

Ms. Blake stopped and looked up at the tall teenager. "No? Ah … you were unable to find a partner, I take it?"

Morgan fought back tears and took a deep breath. "I thought I had it solved, but I was wrong."

"That must have been hard to say."

The brunette rolled her eyes and wiped away a renegade tear. "You'll never know."

"Don't worry, you still have the hip-hop group. Have you considered leading another team? Maybe the pom-pom class?"

She stiffened. "Cheerleading? So the tall girl can be in the back row? Sorry, I'll pass."

"Just a thought," Ms. Blake said, holding up her hands. "Don't be surprised if I ask you about other possibilities. You can always say no."

Morgan nodded and turned for the door. When she put her hand on the doorknob, Ms. Blake called out to her. "I know it hurts, Morgan. But you'll always have that national championship you won last year. Few people ever attain that."

She managed a weak smile, croaked a "Thank you," and left. Morgan hugged herself as she walked to the second floor, opening her locker without thinking about the combination. She was almost in a trance. Explaining it all to Ms. Blake made it seem real. Her dream was over, and what she'd accomplished last year would have to do. It wasn't enough.

She walked down the hall and came to the large window that looked over the parking lot. How could this have happened to her? What did she do wrong in a past life … or this one? She shook her head, trying to stop thinking about it. She didn't want to cry again.

Suddenly, Morgan noticed a figure walking alone through the parking lot. The walk, the size: it could only be Kyle Branch. He was walking toward the old Volvo. Her face grew hard.

"Why didn't you give it a chance, Kyle?" she whispered to herself. Again, she shook her head, trying to forget the disastrous conversation. He was who he was. Nothing to be done about that.

She looked to her right as she saw three figures walking fast towards the same destination. Steve Harris, Richie Green, and Two-Ton Tony were on a collision course with the new guy. "Uh oh," she said out loud. It was like watching a car crash. She didn't want to see it, but she couldn't bring herself to look away.

They got to Kyle as he was about to put his key in the door of the old car. She couldn't hear, but they obviously were calling to him. He pulled down his hood to reveal his face, and he turned so that he was square with the three youths.

Steve was doing all the talking. No surprise there. She could tell that Kyle wasn't saying much, but he said something. Suddenly, Steve pulled out something from his pocket and held it up. Even at a distance, she could tell it was a knife.

"Oh God," she gasped, as she brought a hand to her mouth. "No, don't do it, Steve. Please don't do it."

Kyle held up both hands, almost in surrender. He was saying something to Steve's smug face. The football captain looked back at his friends with a sneer. That was a mistake. Faster than Morgan could see, Kyle's right hand flashed out, and he smashed Steve on the jaw. Morgan could hear the impact through the window.

"Whoa!" she exclaimed as Steve's eyes rolled up into his head and he dropped. The other two football players' eyes goggled, then grew mean. Richie jumped forward and tried to get Kyle in a headlock. The big fighter brought his hips in and elevated Richie six feet in the air. He paused for a second, then slammed his assailant to the pavement. Richie was squirming on the ground and holding his shoulder.

Morgan couldn't believe what she was seeing. She wasn't the only one. Two-Ton Tony had watched two of his friends incapacitated by this big newcomer, and he had a tough decision to make. He made it.

The big football player crouched into a fighting stance and inched forward. Kyle gave him a slight smile and said something. Then he mirrored his assailant and eased into a fighting stance too. But where Tony plodded closer, Kyle glided in and out. He was incredibly light on his feet, and soon he was circling the rather helpless-looking Tony.

Kyle took a quick step forward, turned on his hip, and thundered a low kick above the knee of Tony's lead leg. Morgan could hear the thwack from the school. "Owww! That's gotta hurt," she said with a wince.

Tony backed up, holding his knee, grimacing in pain. He got back in his stance and moved more tentatively toward Kyle. The big teenager didn't hesitate as he stepped forward again and landed the same kick to the exact same place. Morgan could hear the impact, clearer than before.

That was it for Tony. He screamed and crumpled to the asphalt, holding his knee. Kyle looked down at him, shook his head, and started looking on the ground for his keys. He found them, opened his door, and started driving away. He didn't get far, as a police car came screaming into the lot and stopped right in front of the old Volvo. The officer exited the cruiser, gun in hand, and trained it on the driver.

"Oh, no, no, no!" Morgan said to herself. "It wasn't his fault ..."

Kyle exited the Volvo without protest and did as he was told. He was ordered to put his hands on the hood, so he did. The officer came closer and cuffed the big teenager. Kyle stared straight ahead. Another police car arrived as Kyle was being helped into the back of the first one, an ambulance just behind.

Morgan looked at the car that held Kyle. She couldn't see him, but she could imagine him sitting in the back. She figured he probably wasn't saying a thing. It was at that moment that Morgan Laflamme realized that she was probably the only person who'd seen the whole thing, and knew the truth.

CHAPTER 16

By first bell, everybody knew. Anybody who was anybody was talking about it. Like all juicy stories, it evolved as it was told. When it started, Steve Harris and his friends were approaching Kyle to see if he was interested in joining the football team. Supposedly, Kyle freaked out, pulled a knife, and attacked. Luckily, Steve disarmed him, or it could have been much worse. Steve was happy to show everybody the small cut on his hand.

By lunchtime, people were saying that Kyle had pulled a gun. That was quickly corrected, and the story went back to where it started, where Steve Harris wanted it to be.

And there in the middle of it all sat Morgan Laflamme. The *only* person who had seen what happened. She marveled at the way this lie was making its way around the world in no time at all.

Morgan sat there at lunch, listening as the tale was repeated, discussed, and debated. She didn't reveal her secret when the dancers ran up to her and told her. She pretended to be surprised.

Her friends debated the facts. Lucas defended Kyle and pointed out Steve's well-known track record when it came to bullying, intimidation, and violence of any kind. Olivia, strangely quiet during most of the discussion, agreed. Hector and Tonisha found it easier to believe that Kyle carried a knife. He was the new guy, after all. He also looked like a pretty rough customer.

The only thing they all agreed on was that Steve's story was a little off. Inviting Kyle to join the football team? While feasible, it sounded … wrong. When had that ever happened before?

Through it all, Morgan listened and offered no opinion. It was unusual for her, or any high school student, to say so little about such a big happening. So much so that Olivia tapped her hand. "What do you think of all this, Morg?"

And there it was. The perfect opportunity to drop a bombshell. The perfect time to drop the truth like six tons of bricks. But it wasn't the right time for her. There was another conversation she needed to have first.

Morgan gave her friend a hard look. "Call me Morgan, PLEASE! And as for that fight everyone's talking about? Well, we may never know what really happened."

Olivia looked down at the floor as she considered that. "Yeah, I guess … I guess that's true."

"Too bad nobody saw it," Hector offered.

"Yeah, it is," Lucas agreed. "Because without a witness, Kyle Branch is always going to be the bad guy."

CHAPTER 17

For the first time in her life, Morgan was early to school. Ever since the altercation, she'd avoided the other dancers. She started hanging around the first floor of the school. She was biding her time. She was waiting.

It was the second day after the incident when it finally happened. She was sitting on the floor cross-legged, pretending to read a book, when she heard two sets of footfalls coming down the hall. The dress shoes that rapped the floor belonged to their principal, Mr. Hayes. A small man with a calm demeanor, he wore his usual brown three-piece suit and perfectly round glasses. He was frowning as he looked down at the tiles on the floor, the light gleaming off his bald pate.

Kyle Branch and his sneakers were responsible for the other footsteps. He walked beside Hayes, towering over the older man, his mouth fixed in a grim line. His eyes were a little wider than usual, and he stared straight ahead. This was not a happy man.

The two walked by Morgan. Kyle didn't glance her way, but Mr. Hayes nodded a hello, and she raised a hand to return the greeting. They went further down the hall and stopped at a locker. Kyle grabbed the lock and opened it. Mr. Hayes was talking quietly, so that what he had to say stayed between him and Kyle. The principal gave the big teenager a pat on the shoulder, and Kyle nodded and said, "Thanks." Mr. Hayes headed back the way he came, still looking deflated.

Morgan stared at her book intently, but she was waiting for the principal to be out of sight. When he rounded the corner, she turned her gaze to Kyle. He had a plastic bag in one hand, and was stuffing his few belongings from the locker into the bag with his other hand. It looked like his time at Southwood High was over.

She took a deep breath. It was now or never. She stood up and started walking toward him. She held her books against her chest, almost defensively, as she walked closer to him. With every step, he grew larger and she felt smaller.

Kyle slammed the locker shut and started marching down the hall to leave the school for one last time. He was heading in her direction, but he didn't give her a glance as he marched.

He had just passed her when she finally found the courage to speak up. "Uh—*Kyle!*"

He stopped dead in his tracks, turned, and gave her a hard look. "Not today, princess. I've got no time for you or your ideas." He turned and started striding away.

"I know what happened, Kyle. I was there. I saw it!" she called after him.

He froze and looked over his shoulder at her. His blue eyes were wide. "What did you say?"

"You heard me," she said. "I saw that fight in the parking lot. I know what happened, and I know that you're completely innocent. How about that?"

He turned and walked right up to her, until he was standing close. Too close. "How? I didn't see you."

She swallowed. "I'd finished rehearsal, and I took a moment for myself. I was looking out the big window that looks over the parking lot. I'm telling you, I saw the whole thing."

He regarded her skeptically. "What do you think you saw?"

"I saw Steve Harris pull a knife and get knocked out for his trouble. I watched Richie try to grab you, and you lifted him up and bounced him off the cement." She tilted her head. "You turned Tony's leg into hamburger with not one, but two low kicks. You are one dangerous guy."

Kyle blinked and absorbed what she said. He shook his head and raised his arms up helplessly at his sides. "So are you going to tell anybody? They think I was the one who started it and pulled the knife!"

She nodded. "Yes, that's what everyone is saying. Especially Steve Harris."

"So is there a reason you're not telling the principal what you saw?"

She smiled maliciously. "I was waiting to talk to you. There's a little business matter I wanted to discuss with you."

He held up both hands to stop her. "Oh no! This isn't about that dance thing again, is it?"

She smiled wider.

"Come on, I told you I don't have time for that."

The smile left her face. "Huh! Well, that's too bad." She turned and started walking away. "Well, it was unpleasant meeting you, Kyle. Good luck in your new school!" she called over her shoulder, waving without looking back.

"Whoa, you don't understand! The cops are pressing charges. It's their word against mine, and the law is always going to side with three locals over me."

Morgan stopped and turned to face him. She gave an exaggerated shrug and started walking away again.

"WAIT!" he barked down the hall. He took a deep breath to compose himself. "Okay, okay. What do you want?"

She smiled again and marched right up to him, looking in his eyes. *Olivia was right, they are pretty blue*, she thought. "I'm so glad you asked. Here are the terms," she said, a gleam in her eye.

"Terms? What do you mean terms?"

"First off, you're my new partner for the ballroom competition at Nationals."

He took a step back. "No! No way."

"Second, you will attend two rehearsals a week with me. They're only an hour long—"

"No!" he interrupted. "Didn't you hear what I said?"

"Third, you will attend a longer two-hour rehearsal every weekend," she said, ignoring him. "Not sure yet where we're going to do that."

"It's not going to happen anywhere," he protested. "Because it's not going to happen!"

Her brown eyes grew hard and she glared into his angry face. "That's too bad. I guess I didn't see anything at all."

His eyes goggled and his jaw dropped as he came to a full realization of what was going down. He closed his eyes and let out a big sigh. Then he leaned up against the lockers and looked at the sky. "You're blackmailing me. I don't believe it!"

"No," she said, and pointed a finger at him. "I'm negotiating aggressively. And to prove it, I'll even sweeten the deal."

He raised one eyebrow at her. "Oh, I can't wait to hear this."

She grinned. "I'm actually going to pay you for your time and effort. I've been saving my allowance for a new purse, so I'll give you the money instead."

He shook his head slowly. "You think a little chump change—"

"Five thousand dollars," she interrupted.

He did a double take. "I knew you were crazy, but what kind of a nutcase pays five grand for a bag? You could buy a car for that."

"I *have* a car. What I don't have is a dance partner."

The big teenager took a long look at her and then covered his face with his hands. "You won't tell the principal because it's the right thing to do?"

"I could," she admitted. "But we'd both be missing out if I did that."

He dropped his hands from his face and gave her an incredulous look.

"Think about it," she said, pointing at her temple. "You're going to be able to stay in school, avoid jail, make serious money, and you might even enjoy it."

He folded his arms on his chest. "You're serious about this. You won't say a word unless I agree to this insanity?"

She pointed a finger at him and nodded with a grin.

"But I work two jobs ... I can't lose either because I'm dancing with some—"

"We can work around your work schedule. You won't miss a single minute of work. I promise!"

He sat there, dumbfounded. "What choice do I have?"

She grinned ear to ear and held out a hand. "So we have a deal?"

Kyle's fists balled at his sides and he turned red. He took a cleansing breath and let it out slowly. "Okay, okay. You have a deal," he said between clenched teeth. He held out his big mitt, and Morgan grabbed it with both of hers and shook it enthusiastically.

"You're not going to regret this!"

"I already do," he muttered to himself.

She started jogging away from him, heading toward the office. "Wait!" he called out to her. "Look, uh ... what's your name again?"

She scowled at him. "I told you, it's Morgan."

"Right, right. What happens now, Morgan?"

She pointed a finger at him. "I'm going to talk to the authorities. I was going to anyway. Leave all that to me. You come to the utility room when hip-hop finishes up after school tomorrow. You're getting your first lesson." Morgan turned and ran out of sight.

"And where's the utility room?" he asked, but she was long gone.

CHAPTER 18

"That's ... that's quite a story, Morgan." Mr. Hayes was sitting behind his desk. Morgan was sitting in the comfortable chair facing him, and the chair beside her was occupied by one of Irvine's finest. Officer Gatlin was middle-aged and a little soft around the middle, but his eyes were sharp, and the pencil he used to write every word she said was sharper.

"It's true," she said. "Every word of it." She turned to face Gatlin. "Isn't that right, Officer?"

He was still writing in his pad, but he raised his eyebrows in surprise. "It does fill in a few blanks for us."

"I'll bet Kyle told you the exact same thing," she said with a smile. "I'll also bet you didn't find any of his fingerprints on the knife. In fact, I know you didn't."

"Officially, I can't comment on an ongoing investigation." He stood up and let out a big breath, favoring her with a tight-lipped smile. "Unofficially, you've pretty much confirmed everything we suspected. What we had didn't make any sense. Thank you for coming forward, Miss Laflamme." He turned to Mr. Hayes. "I'll be in touch. Now, if you'll excuse me, I have some paperwork to complete, and new charges to file."

"Thank you, Officer Gatlin," Hayes said, as the lawman left the room. He tapped a pen on his hand and looked up at Morgan. "I'm grateful to you too, but I do wish you'd come to me earlier. Why didn't you? If you don't mind me asking."

"I didn't want to get involved. I thought someone else would have seen something, or the police would have figured it out."

Hayes nodded his satisfaction. "That's reasonable. We aren't sure who called the police, but they were called the minute that knife came out." He let out a big sigh and rubbed his tired eyes. "This isn't going to make my job any easier."

"But you know the truth now. You don't have to expel Kyle."

The principal held out a hand to her, and she took it. "Thanks again for coming to me. It couldn't have been easy, but it was the right thing to do."

"You're welcome. Bye," she said, as she too left the room.

Hayes smiled and shook his head. "Good for you, Kyle," he chuckled to himself. He looked at the papers on his desk. There was only one form he had to complete before he left for the day, and he was looking forward to it. Kyle Branch was reinstated as a student.

CHAPTER 19

"**Y**ou *actually knew?!* This whole time you *knew?* Why didn't you say something? At least tell your best friend," Olivia reprimanded Morgan, as they sat in the cafeteria the next day.

"I didn't want to get involved. I figured someone else must have seen it and would speak up," Morgan explained. She looked into the distance. "I wonder who called the cops that day? I didn't."

Hector, Tonisha, and Lucas almost ran to their table, carrying their trays in front of them. They sat down together and all started talking at the same time. Hector motioned with his hands to indicate his mind was blown, while Tonisha was saying something about telling her the story—Lucas was doing a happy dance in his seat.

The entire school was starting to hear the truth. Morgan had called Olivia after her meeting in the principal's office. Olivia, as predicted, made phone calls of her own and used social media to spread the word. Everyone in the school knew that Kyle Branch was an innocent man.

If the students were quick to discuss the fight in the parking lot with one side of the story, they were more excited to discuss the latest turn of events. They didn't know much about the new student, but they knew the three football players all too well. Three bullies calling out the new guy, pulling a knife, and taking a beating. Worse, they lied about who started it and who brought the weapon in the first place. Everyone was talking about it, savoring it in the retelling, and celebrating their outrage. Some defended the football players, but they were few compared to those who despised their actions. They were righteous in their indignation, and they relished the justice.

"So what was that like to watch?" Lucas asked. "Was it scary?"

Morgan thought about that and nodded. "When I saw the knife, I was pretty worried. After he knocked out Steve, everything else happened too fast to think about it."

"That could have been bad ... *so* bad," Olivia mumbled.

Hector held up a hand. "Is it fair to say Kyle can fight?"

"Like a demon! I've never seen anything like it."

Tonisha laughed. "There are some pretty rough hoods out there. Our boy probably has seen more of that stuff than we could imagine. Irvine is pretty tame."

"It's weird," Lucas said, looking at the table. "If it wasn't for his size, and the scars, I would never have guessed he's a tough guy."

Olivia gave him a sideways look. "Are you serious? When I look at that ogre, that's all I see."

"Yeah, I know what you mean," Lucas agreed. "But I was talking about his personality. As a biology partner, he was easy to work with, not pushy at all."

Morgan smiled. This was good news for her, but it wasn't common knowledge that she had a new dance partner. She was going to hold those cards close to the vest.

"Hey, there he is," Hector hissed, and gestured with his head toward the other end of the cafeteria.

Sure enough, Kyle was in line, waiting for his chance to purchase something on his tray. Lucas grinned. "Gotta go!" he said, and walked away from their table and towards the cash register.

"What is *he* doing?" Olivia asked. Hector and Tonisha shrugged.

"No idea," Morgan answered with a shake of her head. In fact, she did have an idea, but she wanted to see it go down.

The dancers watched as Lucas approached Kyle and started talking. He was using his hands a lot and smiling. Kyle seemed a little taken aback and said nothing. At first, he was shaking his head and holding up a hand to try and stop Lucas, but he wasn't having it.

Lucas grabbed the small carton of milk from Kyle's tray and jogged back into the food service area.

Hector and Tonisha looked at each other. "I think Kyle's going to murder him," Hector said with a furrowed brow.

"What is that dude *thinking?*" Tonisha asked.

Morgan smiled and pointed. "No, that's not it. Look!"

Lucas had returned to Kyle and plopped a larger carton of milk on his tray. They could see Kyle mouth his thanks, and Lucas continued to be animated as they approached the cashier. The little dancer reached in his pocket and paid for the drink. After they walked from the cashier, Lucas gave him a pat on the shoulder and waved goodbye.

Kyle walked over to the area he usually frequented. Half the students immediately picked up their things and scurried away. It was interesting to note that a few said "Hello," or waved a greeting, before they stood up to flee.

The dancers could hear the football players buzzing nearby, and none of it sounded kind. But without Steve Harris in the middle of it all, they weren't as bold. And there was another sound that Morgan and her friends could discern: the occasional call of "Way to go, Kyle!" or "Nice going, big guy!" could be heard from different corners of the cafeteria. Each time, the football players would turn to try and figure out who was supporting their nemesis. It was a failure, because every time they tried to get a bead on one comment, another voice would call, "Yeah, Kyle!" or something similar.

Lucas returned to the table, sat down, and leaned in to talk with his friends. "What did you do, Lukie?" Tonisha asked with a grin.

"Oh, that was so cool," Lucas said with a giggle. "I welcomed him back, told him I would give him my notes from the biology class he missed, and offered to pay for his drink."

"He didn't want that, did he?" Morgan guessed.

"No, he didn't," said Lucas. "But I can be pretty persuasive."

"Looks like Kyle has some fans in the school now," Olivia mused.

Morgan thought about that. "Not everybody. What's the story with the three guys Kyle beat up?"

Hector raised a hand. "Well, the word going around is that they're suspended."

"*What!?*" Morgan exclaimed with a scowl. "After I told them what happened? They should be expelled, like they were going to do with Kyle."

Tonisha nodded. "I hear that, girl. The word is that Steve plead guilty, and claimed he never planned on using the knife. Since Kyle wasn't hurt, they gave him probation and community service. The others got off with a warning. They took the injuries into account. That's why they're getting off a little easier."

"Yeah," said Hector. "Steve has a bad concussion, Richie earned a broken collarbone, and Tony is looking at surgery for his knee. Besides, we all know Steve is well-connected. You had to know they'd let him graduate."

"So they're going to be coming back," Morgan stated.

Lucas frowned. "That ... that could make things a little tense around here."

An awkward silence hung over the conversation. They all turned to look at Kyle as he quietly and innocently ate his lunch.

CHAPTER 20

"*Again!* Let's do it again," Tonisha called with a clap of her hands. The hip hop squad were glistening with sweat and breathing hard. They could barely manage half-hearted groans as they moved back to their first position. "Last time, people. Last time!"

The captain of the hip hop team started the music and ran back to her position. Ms. Blake was in the corner, watching while working on some papers. Her gaze shifted from the team back to the page in front of her.

The team was on. Morgan, Hector, and Lucas were in the back line, holding a difficult pose, while Tonisha, Olivia, and some first-year students moved in synchronicity in the front row. They also froze at the same moment, letting the three dancers in the back strut to the front and perform their own set of moves. Morgan stood tall in the center of the three, while Lucas and Hector flanked her as they completed their share of the choreography. The three dancers stopped dead, holding a pose, and the other dancers took the spotlight. They had completed one figure together when the door to the utility room opened and someone stepped in.

Kyle Branch stood there, larger than life, and looked straight back at them. He wore the same baggy green track pants and shapeless black hoodie. The entire dance crew came to a stop and regarded the young man who had disrupted their rehearsal. One of the sophomores walked over to the small player and turned off the music.

Ms. Blake shifted her focus from her paperwork to the young man, who stood impassively and faced them all. She stood up slowly and shifted her glasses. "Kyle? Are you okay, honey?"

His face turned to her, and he nodded with a hint of a smile.

"Did you come to see me?" Ms. Blake asked as she left her desk and started walking towards him.

Kyle shook his head and pointed an accusing finger at Morgan. "No, I'm early," he explained.

All the dancers turned to look at Morgan, and she couldn't hold back her smile.

"Uh, that's it for today," Tonisha called to the dancers. "Good job," she said, as her gaze went from Kyle to Morgan and back again.

Morgan walked up to Ms. Blake as the rest of the dancers started gathering their things and heading for the door. They were talking to each other in hushed tones, and stealing glances at the fighter, Morgan, and Ms. Blake. Olivia gave her best friend a wave as she left. "I'm calling you later," she whispered.

Kyle took a step into the room to allow the dancers to leave and stood there with both hands in his pockets. Morgan came up to him, her arms folded on her chest. She looked at him for a moment, and he stared back, saying nothing. When she came to stand beside him, she grabbed one of his arms with both hands, steering him closer to the guidance counselor.

"Ms. Blake," she said with pride, "I'm going to need that paperwork after all." She patted Kyle's arm and grinned. "I'd like to present my new dance partner for nationals."

A silence lingered as Ms. Blake took off her glasses, looking from Morgan to Kyle and back again. "Really?"

"That's right," Morgan confirmed. "He's my partner, and we have some work to do."

The older woman still looked dubious, but managed to spur herself into action. "Right, right! Okay, great." She went back to the desk, where her bag and papers were. "I'll find the forms. I can only give you a half hour today. I guess you two can start practicing."

Morgan turned to Kyle quickly, and her long ponytail whipped behind her. She grinned up at him. "We have a long way to go, but we're going to do it … *and we're going to win.*"

CHAPTER 21

"Ready for your first lesson?" Morgan asked.

Kyle shrugged and looked at the floor. "That's why I'm here."

"What style are you going to teach?" Ms. Blake asked from the other side of the room.

Morgan walked over to the small speaker and hooked up her phone. "I've thought about that a lot. I decided that a Rumba would be easier to learn, and could steal the show."

"A Rumba?" Ms. Blake murmured. "Very traditional, classic style. You can deliver it with a lot of heat and passion. I like it."

"A room-bah?" Kyle asked with a frown.

"Rumba," Morgan corrected. "It's said a little faster, and there's no 'room' in the pronunciation."

"Whatever," Kyle muttered, shifting his weight from foot to foot and looking at the ground.

Morgan looked at him and raised an eyebrow. "You're not going to wear that hoodie, are you? You'll roast in that thing."

Kyle shrugged and walked over to a few empty desks in the corner. He pulled his sweatshirt over his head and dumped it on the closest desktop. He pulled down the blue t-shirt, which was wrinkled and had a few holes, turned to face his partner and strode back to the middle of the room.

"There, that's better," Morgan said, blinking. *It certainly is!* she thought to herself. Kyle's arms were well-developed, and his forearms were corded with muscle. A large, thick scar ran down the outside of his right forearm. His chest was thick, and his waist was narrow. She had expected him to be more padded around the middle, as the sweatshirts he wore concealed his true build.

She walked up to him and brought her hands together. "Okay, let's start at the beginning. Do you know how to do a basic box step?"

Kyle looked up as he thought about that. He nodded and dropped into a low stance, bringing both hands up in fists to protect his face. He tilted his chin down and moved away from her, then toward again.

Her eyes widened and she burst out laughing, "No, no … it's not a *boxing* step, but something called a 'box step,'" she explained through her laughter.

Ms. Blake frowned. "You've never done any ballroom dancing before, Kyle?"

He shook his head. "First time."

Morgan put a delicate hand on his arm to reassure him. It felt like warm steel, thick and unyielding. "That's okay, I'll show you how." She stood beside him and looked down at both their feet. She pointed to her left foot and started. "You step forward with your left foot, then bring your right foot up to touch it, and then step to your right."

Kyle gave it a try and looked at her when he finished.

"Not bad," she said with an appreciative nod. "This time, glide your right foot just over the ground. It may be a step, but you want to make it smooth."

"Glide?" Kyle clarified.

"Yeah, try it."

He took a breath and executed it to perfection.

"*Yes!* Yes, that's right," she cheered. "Now your right foot steps back, and then the left glides to touch it, and you should be right back where you started."

"What?"

"Here! I'll show you what I'm talking about." She showed him the entire step from beginning to end. "You see?" she asked, looking up into his face.

"Yeah, got it," he mumbled, and showed her that he did indeed have it down.

"Great," she said, with a clap of her hands. "Okay, let's do it together, to reinforce what you've learned."

She counted to four as they both executed the step in unison. They moved faster and smoother as they repeated it over and over.

"You're a great teacher, Morgan," Ms. Blake observed.

"Thanks." Morgan smiled. "But I've seen Kyle move his feet before. I knew he'd be good."

"When did you see that?" Ms. Blake asked.

Morgan looked at her as she continued to step. "He teaches my little sister martial arts." She stopped dancing, and Kyle followed suit. "Okay, now it's time to try it as a couple."

"Do you want music?" Ms. Blake called, as Morgan moved to stand in front of Kyle.

"Not yet. I don't want to distract from the other elements." She looked at Kyle. "Okay, big fella, reach out your left hand and turn the palm up like you're holding an apple."

He did as he was asked.

"Good, okay, now put your right hand right here, on my hip."

He reached out tentatively, and she grabbed his wrist and placed his large hand where she wanted it. "Yes, now I put my right hand in your left ..." She placed her hand, and recoiled when she felt a good deal of moisture. His palms were covered in sweat. "Oh, *gross!*" she muttered and walked away.

Kyle wiped his palms self-consciously on his track pants.

She went to the sink and grabbed a couple of paper towels in one hand. Then she turned on her heel, marched back up to him, plunked the paper towels in his left hand, and put her right hand on top of the pile.

"Sorry, I'm a little nervous," he explained, looking at his shoes.

"It's okay," she said. Inside, she was kind of amused, and a little touched that this dangerous fighter was intimidated. She couldn't help but feel a little sorry for him.

"Now," she began, "you do the same thing, but keep your arms firm. That's called your frame, and it's not supposed to sag."

He nodded his understanding, and she felt his arms tense to hold her in position.

"Good! That's right. Now I'm going to pull you toward me, and I want your left foot to move first, okay?"

He nodded. "Okay."

"Normally, it's your job to lead the dance, but I'm going to have to lead until you learn the steps." She took a deep breath. "Okay, like we did together. I'll be moving my feet out of the way so you have to do it right. Here we go," she said, tugging him towards her.

He moved his left foot on cue, and the right went to its proper destination too.

"Yes!" she cheered, and pushed him to make him back away.

Again, the right foot moved back as it should, and she was relieved when his left glided into the right to bring them back into their original position.

"Well, Mister Branch," she said with a grin, "you just completed a perfect box step." She gave him a playful punch on the shoulder. "We're on our way."

"And that's where we stop," Ms. Blake interrupted. "That's all the time I can give you today. This was a bit of a surprise. I can hang around longer after the next rehearsal."

Morgan nodded her understanding. "Good start." She looked at Kyle. "We're going to have to meet on our own to practice." She went to grab her phone. "I'm going to need your number, so I can text you and we can figure out another time to rehearse."

He shrugged. "Don't have one."

Morgan looked at him with wide eyes. "You don't have a phone?"

He shrugged again.

"Okay, well, what's your number at home? Your land line."

"Don't have one of those, either."

This time, Ms. Blake and Morgan were both staring at him. The dancer brought her hand to her chin. "Well, how do I get hold of you?"

"There are only four places I can be. School, the gym, work, and home."

"Fine," Morgan said, with a shake of her head. "What's your address?"

"Uh, yeah, about that." He ran a hand through his hair while he looked at the ground. "It's not my home. It's a place I live."

Morgan and Ms. Blake looked at each other. Morgan started tapping on her phone. "Well, I guess you'd better give me that." She stopped and pointed a finger at him. "Oh, you're eating lunch with us tomorrow."

"What?"

Morgan smiled as she pulled up her contacts on her phone. "Yeah, you're a dancer now, Kyle Branch. Time you got to know the rest of the team."

CHAPTER 22

"Okay … you have to tell me *EVERYTHING!*" Olivia squealed into her phone.

Morgan laughed at her friend. She was in her room, door closed, lying on her belly on her large bed. Posters with famous dancers and musicians stared at her from the pastel walls. The incomparable Misty Copeland was in at least three of the posters. "Okay, where do you want me to start?"

"Well, how you got him to be your partner, for one. I was there when you asked him. He was *not* into it. How did you convince him?"

"Oh, that." Morgan shifted on her bed, and her eyes darted left and right as she thought about how to answer that delicate question. "Well, I went over why I thought he'd be good … and, uh, I guess I convinced him that it would be in his best interest to give it a try."

"No!" Olivia said with a chuckle. "Come on. That's it?"

Morgan pursed her lips and thought before she answered. "Well, maybe he wasn't ready to hear it the first time I talked to him."

"Okay, I guess." There was silence on the line as Olivia considered her next question. "Oh, how did the first rehearsal go?"

"Actually, really good," Morgan said with a laugh, as she rolled on her back to look at the ceiling. She started laughing and covered her mouth. "Oh my God! You should have seen him."

"What? What's funny?"

"Well, I asked him if he ever did a box step before." She laughed again. "So he gets in this stance, lifts his hands, and starts actually boxing!"

Olivia cackled on the other end of the line. "No way! That's hilarious." They both laughed for a minute.

"Ugh!" Morgan said with a wrinkle of her nose. "Then there were the sweaty palms."

"His hands were sweating?"

Morgan covered her eyes as she spoke. "Yeah, I had to grab a paper towel from the sink and put it in his palm before I could put my hand in there."

Again, the two teenagers dissolved in laughter. "Aww, the big fella was nervous," Olivia said.

"Weird, I know," Morgan said, still smiling. "There were some good things."

"Like what?"

"Okay, the guy picked up the box step, fast! It was amazing how quick he learned the steps and the frame."

There was silence on the other end. "That *is* surprising," Olivia finally said. "I wouldn't have figured him for a guy that would be good."

"I'm not surprised at all," Morgan said, sitting up on the bed. "I told you he could move his feet."

"You called it," Olivia confirmed.

"The guy is built, too."

"Really?" Olivia said with a giggle. "Do tell!"

Morgan laughed at her boy-crazy confidant. "Yeah, he always wears those big sweatshirts, so he looks like a big fleece marshmallow."

"He took it off to dance, didn't he?" Olivia guessed.

"Kind of had to," Morgan said playing with her ponytail. Her eyes narrowed as she thought about it. "He's covered in muscle, and he has a nasty scar on one of his arms. The right one, I think."

"Well, that must have been a pleasant surprise."

"It was … I guess." Morgan started twirling the end of her hair. "He's warm to the touch, too. Very warm."

"Hmm, I might have to stick around to watch your next rehearsal. Has he got a girlfriend?"

They both laughed at her question. "Subtle," said Morgan. "I don't think so. I don't think he has anything."

"Huh?"

"It got weird at the end. I asked for his number so I can text him."

"Let me guess. He wouldn't give it to you?"

"No, he doesn't have one," Morgan explained.

"No! *NO* phone?" Olivia said, scandalized.

"He doesn't have a land line, either."

"Nobody could survive without a phone. Does he live in a cave somewhere?"

Morgan laughed. "He might. He gave me an address, but said it wasn't his home, just where he lived."

"That is weird," Olivia agreed. "Are you … you know, interested?"

Morgan sat straight up. "What? In dating the guy?"

"Yeah," said Olivia, and laughed.

"Uh, no!" Morgan said, shaking her head.

"Not your type?"

"Definitely not!"

"Well, what is your type? Do you even have a type?" Olivia asked.

"My type? Not Kyle is my type," She chuckled, but soon stopped laughing. "Olivia, are *you* interested in the guy?"

There was silence. Morgan thought she could hear stifled laughter. Olivia cleared her throat. "Maybe a little. I like 'em big and dumb." Both the teenagers giggled at her audacity, and it was some time before Morgan could compose herself.

"Knock yourself out," she said with a grin. "He'll be sitting with us at lunch tomorrow."

"Oh *really!* You think so?"

"Yes," Morgan said with her chin set. "He has no choice."

CHAPTER 23

The cafeteria was alive with eating, laughing, and lots of talking. Hector and Tonisha were sitting in their usual spot. Lucas was sitting down when Morgan and Olivia arrived at the table. Tonisha moved a perfect braid out of her eyes and grinned at them. "Heeey! It's Betty and Veronica," she said, with a gleam in her eye.

Morgan made a face and shook her head. "Ha, ha."

"No, I like it," Olivia said. "Any Riverdale reference is great with me." Then she looked around, scanning the cafeteria.

"Looking for somebody?" Lucas asked.

She didn't look at him, just smiled. "I sure am. And there he is!" She sat down quickly and pointed at Morgan. "Well, time to work your magic, Veronica."

Morgan took a deep breath and stood up. She searched the food service area, and it didn't take her long to see Kyle in the crowd. He was head and shoulders taller than most of the other students, and he was picking out a drink. She was surprised to see that he wasn't wearing his usual hoodie, and was wearing a plain white t-shirt. *Same baggy track pants,* she thought to herself.

"Well?" Olivia prodded, as she took a bite of her sandwich.

Morgan shot her a dark look and turned her gaze back to the other end of the cafeteria. When she saw Kyle was on the move, she stood tall and waved frantically at him. She forced a smile as she saw him look up.

He looked at her, then quickly looked away and sat in his usual spot. The dancers covered their mouths and tried to subdue their amusement at her failure. Her face colored red, and she sat down hard with a scowl. "Maybe he didn't see me."

Lucas grinned at her. "Oh, he saw you all right." He put his elbows on the table. "How will the fearless Morgan Laflamme handle this indignity?"

She glared at him and drew a breath. Suddenly she stood up and started putting everyone's drinks on their tray.

"Chica! What you doin'?" Hector protested.

Morgan grabbed her own tray and looked at all of them. "Let's go," she ordered, and marched down the cafeteria.

The dancers all looked at each other, and Lucas suddenly stood up. "I'm not missing this!" he said with a laugh. The others saw it his way and followed their friends down the aisle.

Morgan strode to Kyle's table, which had emptied when he sat down, and slammed her tray down in front of him. "Hi, Kyle," she snapped. "I thought we talked about you sitting with the dance team at lunch?"

He didn't look at her, but took a big bite of his odd-looking sandwich. "Must've forgot," he mumbled with his mouth full.

Her eyes blazed, and her face colored again. She was about to say something regrettable when Lucas bounced to the table. "Hi, Kyle. Can we join you for lunch?" Tonisha, Hector, and Olivia came behind him and gave him a smile.

"Sure," he mumbled, and gestured to the empty seats nearby.

Olivia hustled over and plopped herself right beside the big teenager. Her eyes tracked up and down his bare arms, lingering on the deep scar on his forearm. She gave an appreciative nod to her friend. She approved, though she grimaced when she saw the grime under his nails.

Hector and Tonisha introduced themselves to Kyle, and they shook hands. Morgan, meanwhile, looked down at her food.

"So, ballroom dancing. How's that going for you, big fella?" Olivia asked, touching his arm with a playful pat.

Morgan smirked, watching her pretty friend work her magic on her unsuspecting quarry. Getting attention always came easy for Olivia.

Kyle shook his head, and they could barely hear his reply. "Too early to tell," his low voice rumbled.

"We've only had one rehearsal, Olivia," Morgan reminded her.

"Still," Lucas said with a grin, "it's enough to make you part of the dance team. Welcome aboard." He looked over his shoulder to the other side of the cafeteria. "Y'know, I like being far away from where the football players sit. We should have thought of this a long time ago."

"One rehearsal, it's a start," Olivia said. "It's great of you to help Morgan out. She won nationals last year. Did you know that?"

"Yeah, she told me," he said, and took a drink of his carton of milk.

The dancers all looked at each other. Their newest member didn't seem too keen on his new station in life, or the person he was working with. For Morgan, it was mutual.

"I'm sure it'll all work out," Lucas said with a kind smile. "Rehearsal conquers all."

"That reminds me," Morgan said, as she fished a pen and paper out of her backpack. She wrote down her address and handed it to him. "We're rehearsing tonight. Be at my place at 6:30. Okay?"

Kyle took the piece of paper and looked at it. "I'm not working, so ...."

"So you'll be there?" Morgan interrupted.

His blue eyes blazed as he looked at her. "Yeah, I will." he said as he stood, nodded goodbye to the other dancers, and walked out of the cafeteria.

"*Oowweee!* That was cold," Hector said.

Olivia stared after the big teenager. "Morgan, that boy does not think much of you."

Morgan shrugged and took a drink from her flask. "As long as he does his job."

CHAPTER 24

That night, Morgan stood in her living room, looking out the enormous windows at the driveway. They were covered with sheer white curtains that provided a measure of privacy. The lights were low, so nobody could see in but she could see out. She alternated between pacing and standing with her arms crossed, biting a nail. Occasionally, she would glance at the clock on the mantle. It was getting closer and closer to 6:30.

You'd better show, mister! she thought to herself.

"Whatcha doing?" a young voice behind her asked.

She jumped and turned around. "Don't sneak up on me!" she snarled at her sister.

"Okay, sorry," Taylor mumbled. "But what are you doing?"

"Ugh! I'm waiting for my new partner, okay?"

"Oh! Is he cute?" Taylor asked with a grin. "Do you like him?"

Morgan looked at her with her mouth hanging open. "Oh my God, Taylor. You're not going to embarrass me, are you?"

Taylor grinned from ear to ear. "You *do* like him, don't you?"

Morgan rubbed her eyes and let out a big sigh. "No, Taylor. I do not 'like' my new dance partner. I wish I didn't have to work with him at all. But he's all I've got, and we have a lot of ground to cover before nationals." She looked at the clock: 6:30. Her eyes were caught by a flash of headlights in their driveway. The Volvo with the grey primer had rolled to a stop.

"Oh, is he here?" Taylor asked, and craned her neck to try and see over her sister.

Morgan shooed her away. "Calm down, Taylor. You can greet him, and then you have to leave him alone so we can work."

Taylor nodded and stood beside her sister, waiting. "Does Mom know?" she whispered.

"Yes. *Now shut up!*"

There was a predictable knock on the door. Morgan took a deep breath and opened it up. "You're late," was all she said.

Kyle stood there in his usual baggy clothing and worn sneakers. His face was impassive as he stared at her. He frowned, looked at his watch, and raised an eyebrow. "I've got 6:30. You said that was when you wanted me here."

Morgan rolled her eyes. "If rehearsal is at 6:30, that's when it's supposed to be underway. You don't show up that second."

He shrugged his wide shoulders. "Then you should have asked me to be here at 6:20."

Her mouth opened and her eyes grew hostile. Kyle held up a hand to stop her. "Look, do you want me to come in and we can start, or do you want to argue about time on the front step?"

She let out a growl and stepped back, beckoning him in. He took a couple of strides inside.

"Kyle!" Taylor exploded, and started clapping.

His face of stone cracked into a smile, and his blue eyes softened. "Hey, tiger! What's up?"

Taylor rushed forward and made a fist, holding it in front of her. He laughed and bumped her fist with his own. She giggled and grinned. "We're waiting for Morgan's dance partner, and ..." Her eyes bulged. "No! Wait ... you ... are *you* her dance partner?"

"Yup," he said with a small nod.

The young girl looked from Kyle to her sister and back again. "That is so cool!" she burst out, and held both arms over her head. "I didn't know you were a dancer too."

He shook his head in disbelief and gave a hard look at Morgan. "I am now."

"What's all the noise about?" Mrs. Laflamme's voice called from the kitchen. "Is your partner here? Don't leave him standing in the foyer."

Morgan drew a finger along her lips and glared at her sister. "Now zip it!" she whispered, as she gestured for Kyle to follow her. "Leave your shoes on. We're rehearsing by the pool."

Kyle shrugged and walked behind her while Taylor trailed, bouncing as she followed. They entered the bright, spacious kitchen, and Kyle blinked as his eyes adjusted. Mrs. Laflamme was scooping powder out of a container with some measuring cups. She flashed a bright smile and waved. "Hi there, Kyle. Make yourself at home. Are you hungry or thirsty?"

"Sorry, Mom," Morgan said. "We're going out to the pool deck to practice some stuff. We don't have time."

"Very well. I'll ask again when you're done. You might feel differently after a workout."

"Thanks anyway," Kyle said softly. "You have a lovely home."

"Oh, wait until you see the pool!" Taylor said, as she pushed by her sister and grabbed Kyle's hand. She dragged him toward the sliding door at the back of the kitchen.

Morgan looked at her mother and mouthed the words, *help me*! Her mother chuckled and called out to her youngest daughter. "Leave them be, Taylor. You can talk to our guest when they're finished working."

"Aww …" Taylor moaned, and stomped through the kitchen and up to her room.

Morgan threw her mother a scandalized look. "Now the little pimple is going to be just *waiting* for us to finish. Is that the best you could do?"

Mrs. Laflamme pointed a kitchen knife at her eldest. "Hey, she lives here too. At least I bought you an hour of peace. Go enjoy it."

"Come on, Kyle," Morgan muttered, and led him onto the deck. The deck furniture had been moved to one side, and that left a sizable space for them. She hustled over to a couple of speakers that were plugged in and connected her phone.

He looked around at the large pool, the immaculate stainless-steel barbecue, and the Tiki bar in the far corner of the big backyard. "Must be nice," he muttered.

"Did you say something?" Morgan asked as she walked toward him.

"Never mind," he said, with a shake of his head.

"Okay, let's do this," she announced, as she brought her hands together. "The box step. You remember how that goes?"

"Yeah, just a minute," he answered. He pulled off his sweatshirt and placed it on one of the deck chairs, then turned to face her. "Okay, let's do it."

He walked toward her, stopped, and reached out. He was wearing a black tank top, and she couldn't help but stare at his bare arms and shoulders. Again, she noticed the angry scar on his right forearm, but now she could see a similar one on his left shoulder. It wasn't as thick, but it was a little longer.

"You okay?" he asked, squinting at her.

"Uh, yeah, yes," she said, blinking, and stepped toward his outstretched hand. There was no moisture in his hand this time. His grip was warm and strong, and she couldn't help but look at how his big, dirty hand held her delicate one. His other hand landed on her hip, as she had showed him to do. She placed her left hand on his shoulder, and she could feel the muscle move as he pulled her close.

"Is this too close?" he asked, looking at her.

"No," she answered, lost in his blue eyes for a moment. "No, this is about right."

"Should I start? Left foot first, am I correct?"

"Yes, right."

He let go and looked at her. "I thought it was the left?"

She couldn't help but laugh. "I mean, yes, it is the left one, and you got that right."

"Oh, okay," he mumbled. "You ready?"

"Waiting on you," she said, as they came together again. He stepped forward with his left foot and plunked it right on top of her right.

"Oww!" she said with a wince of pain, and backed away from him. "You have to keep your arms firm, so when you step forward, I move back and so does my foot."

He held up both his hands. "Oh, okay. Right. Sorry about your foot."

"You're heavy," she said with a smile, and she moved toward him. "It happens. Let's do it again."

He nodded, and they came together. He took a cleansing breath and tried again. This time, she felt him move forward, and she allowed her right foot to step back. To her amazement, they completed the box step well. When they finished, he let go and stepped back.

"Great!" she cheered. "But you have to keep doing it."

"Oh."

She ran to her phone. "I want to try this with music. Keep doing the box step, and I'll take the lead here and there to show you the movement through the space."

He put his hands in his pockets and looked back at the house. Taylor was grinning and waving at him from her bedroom window. He smiled and brought a finger to his lips to ensure she stayed quiet.

Morgan came trotting back once the music had started and noticed the change in his face. "What? What's up?"

"Nothing."

"Okaaay … ready to do it with the music?" she asked with a tilt of her head.

He pursed his lips and thought. "How do I know when to start?"

"I'll count you in." She closed her eyes and concentrated on the music. "Five, six, seven, eight, *now!*"

His left foot moved forward, his frame was solid, and they were away. While he got the footwork right, Morgan led their path in a flowing and circular motion that used every inch of the deck. They moved effortlessly and silently until the song completed. They stopped when the music did, and Kyle was the first to let go and look at her.

She smiled, and her brown eyes looked into his blue. "Yes! That was … that was good. That's our basic step that we return to when we aren't adding elements."

"I have no idea what that means."

"Well," Morgan laughed, as she thought about how to explain it. "It means that we will always come back to that step when we're not doing something specific or fancy."

"So that's good?"

She punched him playfully on the shoulder. "Yeah, big guy. That's good." Then she ran to her phone and looked at it. "We still have plenty of time, so I want to add an easy element that looks good."

"Whatever," he said with a shrug.

Morgan's face fell. She put down the phone and walked up to him, until she was standing right in front of him. "Look, Kyle. I know this isn't what you wanted, but you're doing a good job. Is there any part of you that's enjoying this?"

"No."

She put her face in her hands and shook her head. "Fine," she said, eyes fierce. "I guess I shouldn't complain, because you are putting in a good effort."

"I'm a man of my word," he answered gruffly. "You've kept yours, so I'm keeping mine. Doesn't mean I have to like it."

"Whatever," she said, and raised a hand to stop him. "Here, watch the next move we're going to tackle. I'll go alone first." Morgan held up her arms like she was in his frame and started stepping sideways, turning her hips and the direction her feet were going. Every step, she dropped a little and exaggerated the hip movement. "Watch, I'll do it back now," she warned him. She held her arms up to hold an invisible partner and quick-stepped, rotating her hips. The effect was mesmerizing.

"It's like a crossover, Kyle!" Taylor's voice called from her window.

Morgan stopped what she was doing and stared up at the source of the advice. "Taylor!" she snapped, and pointed a finger at her. "Close those curtains and leave us alone, or I'll tell Mom and you'll lose your phone for a month!"

"Fine!" Taylor shouted back. "But seriously, it's like our crossovers, Kyle."

Morgan turned to face Kyle. "Do you know what she means by that?"

"Yeah, she's talking about a warmup we do when we're on the mats. Here, I'll show you."

To her surprise, he went from one side of the deck to the other, crossing one foot over the other and swinging his hips to face both ways as he moved to his left.

"Yes!" she cheered. "Much as I hate to say it, Taylor was right." She held up a hand to stop him. "Only one difference. Drop your level to exaggerate every step, like this." She showed him how she bent at the knees with every step.

"Got it," he confirmed, and showed her that he did.

"Okay! Amazing!" she clapped her hands together. "Now when we do it together, we face opposite ways every step. It's called 'The Grapevine,' and it's an elegant move." She walked with long steps, and exaggerated her hip movement as she prowled over. "You have to sell it. Shall we give it a try?"

He beckoned her closer as his answer. She held up a finger to get him to wait, and ran back to start the music. Once it started, she ran back to him and settled into his embrace.

"Okay, we do the box step, and when I say 'Grapevine,' we bust that move out. Okay?"

"Okay. Count me in?"

"Right. Five, six, seven, eight, now!" she whispered. The two of them moved well from the start. He nailed the footwork, and she steered them in the space. After a loud drum fill, she hissed "Grapevine!" and the two of them suddenly veered in a straight line, legs alternating and hips turning to face in different directions. She eventually brought them to a stop, and to her surprise, Kyle moved forward and resumed the box step.

"Yes!" she screeched, spun away from him. She turned to face him. "That was great! Why did you do that?"

He frowned and gave a weak shrug. "The music was still playing, and you said that was the step we'd always come back to. So I came back to it."

She put her hands on her hips. "It's a shame you don't like ballroom dancing, Kyle. Because you're good at it." She walked up to him and looked at her partner. "Sooner or later, you're going to start liking this."

"Doubt it."

"Wanna bet?" she said, with a sly look in her eyes.

He never answered, as the sliding glass door opened and her mother's face popped out. "Hey, kids, I made a snack tray for you. Come eat something and get some water."

"Mom!" Morgan protested. "We have so much more to do!"

Her mother smiled patiently. "And you can do it … right after a snack. Besides, you're not going to finish it all in one night anyway."

She hated to admit it, but her mother was right. She looked at Kyle. "Break?"

His eyebrows raised. "I could eat."

"Okay, Mom, but only for a minute," Morgan called back. She turned to her partner. "Not for too long, just a snack."

"I guess I'd better hurry," he said with a smirk, and did the grapevine move all the way to the sliding doors. Morgan couldn't help but smile as she followed him.

CHAPTER 25

They had entered the kitchen and sat down at the island when Taylor came sprinting around the corner and joined them. "That was great, Kyle!"

"Thanks," he mumbled.

Mrs. Laflamme deposited a large tray with vegetables and a few assorted dips in front of the teenagers. "Here you go. A healthy snack should give you a bit of jump for your rehearsing. Do you like vegetables, Kyle?"

He nodded. "Very much, thank you." He brought a hand up and reached for the tray.

"You should probably wash your hands," said Taylor.

Mrs. Laflamme dropped a spoon in the sink, her eyes opened wide, and her mouth dropped. Morgan did the same, as they stared speechless at the youngest member of the family. Kyle drew his hand back and looked at it.

"What? It's true," Taylor explained. "His hand is filthy."

Kyle sighed and looked at the back of his hand, the dirt under the fingernails. "It is, to be honest. It's work that makes them that way."

Mrs. Laflamme exhaled in relief. "Oh, what is work?"

"I work with engines," Kyle answered, as he looked at the other hand as well. "That's a powerful grime, and I don't always have time to use the special hand-cleaner. Sometimes we run out too." He walked over to the sink and washed his hands. When he was done, he held them up to show Taylor. "See? It's not going to come off with an ordinary hand wash."

Taylor nodded her head in understanding. "Oh, well … do you want some vegetables?"

Kyle smiled and helped himself to some sweet peppers. He didn't bother to dip them in any of the spreads.

They all heard the door open, and Mr. Laflamme's voice rang down the hall. "Hello! Who's parked in the driveway?" he asked, as he came around the corner. He was in his lawyer's uniform, suit and tie matching, dress shirt crisp and pressed.

Kyle stood up and walked over to the patriarch of the family. "Hi, I'm Kyle Branch," he said, as he reached out a hand to shake. "I go to school with Morgan."

Mr. Laflamme blinked, then narrowed his eyes and shook the hand that was offered. Then he snapped his fingers. "Say, I've seen you before. You work at Jake's auto shop, right?"

Kyle smiled. "Yes, I do."

"I knew it," Mr. Laflamme said with a grin. "Jake's an old friend of mine. We usually make time to play poker every month."

"And I get to watch my favorite movies on those nights," Mrs. Laflamme said with a smile of her own.

"Jake has been good to me," Kyle explained. "He lets me work odd hours, and late at night."

Mr. Laflamme took off his tie. "So you're a mechanic?"

"No, I'm a student who happens to like working on cars. Jake lets me do the easy stuff. Maintenance and that sort of thing, and he tries to show me more complicated repairs when he can."

"Say," Mr. Laflamme said, walking over to give his wife a kiss on the cheek. "Do you know anything about changing brake pads?"

Kyle shrugged. "Sure. That was one of the first things Jake taught me."

"Really!" Mr. Laflamme exclaimed. "I wonder if you might be able to help me out."

Morgan rolled her eyes. "Daaad! We're supposed to be rehearsing."

Her father looked from Kyle to his eldest daughter and back again. "You're ... you're her dance partner? You're kidding."

Kyle shrugged again.

"He's also my martial arts instructor!" Taylor cheered. "He's nice."

"Busy guy," Mrs. Laflamme observed.

"What's the favor?" Kyle asked.

"Right," Mr. Laflamme answered. "I bought brake pads for my BMW, and I was going to try and put them on myself. But, well—"

"You don't know what you're doing," Mrs. Laflamme interrupted.

"I don't know what I'm doing," her husband said with a chuckle. He looked at Kyle. "Could you walk me through it?"

Kyle nodded. "Sure, but I have to make sure they're the right size and we have the tools to do it."

Mr. Laflamme nodded. "Now that I *did* get right. I've got the right pads and terrific tools, but not a lot of experience. I'm learning as I go."

"Me too," Kyle agreed.

Morgan lifted her hands up and let them fall on the counter. "We're supposed to be rehearsing! *Remember?*"

Her father gave her a disapproving look. "How long will it take, Kyle?"

The big teen thought about it. "About forty-five minutes for me to do it, a little longer if I have to explain how it's done."

"Well, that's the end of the rehearsal," said Morgan, and crossed her arms over her chest.

"Sorry, honey," Mr. Laflamme offered. "It's not often I get a mechanic in my kitchen. Besides," he said, with a gleam in his eye, "I can tell Jake that I did the work all by myself." He looked over at their guest. "What do you say, Kyle? Will you help me out?"

Kyle looked at Morgan. "Is it okay?"

"Fine," she muttered, and grabbed some celery from the tray. She shoved it in some of the dip and took a quick bite, wearing a scowl.

Mrs. Laflamme walked up to her husband and pointed at him. "Okay, but we're feeding him when he's done."

"Sounds good," Mr. Laflamme said with a wink. "Come on, Kyle. The garage is this way."

Kyle followed him, and Mr. Laflamme began talking cheerfully to him as they walked out of earshot.

"What was that all about?" Taylor asked.

Mrs. Laflamme sighed. "That was a guy thing."

"What?" Morgan asked, with a mouth full of vegetables.

"Maybe you haven't noticed," their mother said with a chuckle, "but your dad is kind of outnumbered in this house."

Taylor laughed. "So now he gets to do boy stuff?"

Her mother pointed at her. "Yes! Now he gets to do some boy stuff."

"Ugh! Boys are stupid," Morgan complained.

"Yeah," Taylor agreed. "Except Kyle. I like him."

Mrs. Laflamme came behind Morgan and patted her shoulder. "I like him too. Seems like a good guy."

Morgan made a face. "Mom! He's my dance partner. Like Bernie, remember? He isn't my boyfriend."

"He's not like Bernie, and I see why your father likes him."

"He does seem to like him. Why?" Morgan asked.

She looked at her eldest daughter with a smile. "Well, he's the first boy you've ever invited over that wasn't shy to meet your parents. He walked to your dad, shook his hand, and looked him in the eye. I don't know much about that big lug, but somebody taught him manners."

CHAPTER 26

The garage was big, clean, and well-organized. Every tool had a place on the peg-board and was traced in marker to make it easy to return to its home. Kyle and Mr. Laflamme worked together to position the hydraulic jack and raise the front end of the car.

"This is a great shop you've built here," Kyle said, opening a box that held the new brake pads.

"Your boss, Jake, gave me a rundown on what I would need. He takes engines seriously."

Kyle smiled. "You do know my boss. He's got a great sense of humor, too. He never jokes about repairs and cars. Everything else is fair game, but not that."

"Jake and I went to high school together. I went to law school and he went into business. Somehow we stayed in touch." He smiled at the thought. "I'm glad."

"The brake pads are definitely right," said Kyle, examining the car's underside, "and the car is safely elevated." He looked at the man beside him. "We're going to need a few things, and I'll talk you through it. You mind if I grab some of the tools, Mr. Laflamme?"

"Not at all, but please, when we're working together, call me Patrick."

"Okay, Patrick." Kyle walked to the tool wall and started picking the items he'd need. "How about I replace the first brake pad to show you, and you tackle the other ones?"

"Makes sense," said the older man. As Kyle set down the tools, he kept the conversation moving. "So where were you living before you came to Irvine?"

"A small town in Michigan. It wasn't as nice as this city." Kyle set one tool down, picked up another, and resumed working. He was careful to ensure that Mr. Laflamme could see what he was doing. His muscled arms were extended as he loosened the brake pad.

The owner of the car leaned in closer to see what was happening. "What brought you out here? If you don't mind me asking."

Kyle shrugged. "I was living with my grandmother. She passed, so I had to move out here to live with an uncle. It's actually worked out pretty well."

"I'm sorry to hear about your grandmother," Mr. Laflamme said softly. "I'm guessing you don't have any parents."

"Not anymore."

"Sorry." Mr. Laflamme cleared his throat. "So on top of school, working for Jake, and teaching at the MMA gym, you're also dancing with my daughter? How do you find the time?"

Kyle smiled. "It ain't easy. I had my hands full before, uh ..." He dropped his hands and hesitated. "Well, before Morgan talked me into it."

Mr. Laflamme chuckled and shook his head ruefully. "Sorry, she gets that from me. I think living with a lawyer has made her naturally argumentative."

"She is a tough negotiator," Kyle observed, as he removed the part to be replaced.

"You know," Mr. Laflamme started, as he handed Kyle the new brake pad, "my wife does the books for a few car dealerships. They might be able to pay you more than Jake. Could get you more hours of work too. I'm sure Jake wouldn't mind. He was doing fine before you started working there."

Kyle stopped what he was doing and looked at the floor for a moment. "Hey, that's ... that's really generous. Thanks." He turned to face the man beside him. "I can't accept, though. Jake was the only one who would hire me when nobody else would. He's teaching me a lot, and he lets me work late at night to deal with the simple stuff. The shop is getting things done and customers are happy. It wouldn't be right to walk out now. Sorry, I can't do that to him."

Mr. Laflamme smiled and nodded. "I understand. I respect your integrity. Maybe it was a little wrong for me to offer."

"No," Kyle said with a smile. "It was nice of you to try and give me a leg up. You couldn't know what Jake and I worked out. I appreciate the offer." He handed the older man a few tools. "You ready to try the next one, Patrick?"

"Uh, perhaps you could show me one more time how to do it?" Mr. Laflamme laughed. "I wasn't paying attention."

Kyle walked over to the other front wheel. "Okay, let's do it again."

CHAPTER 27

Morgan paced in the kitchen, her arms over her chest, while her mother moved things around in the cupboard. She stopped and threw her arms up. "Gah! What are they doing in there that's taking so long? Why would Dad do this to me?"

Mrs. Laflamme continued organizing her kitchen. "They're talking, honey. They like playing with cars and talking. It's like their version of a sleepover."

Morgan smiled in spite of herself. "I know Dad likes cars, but he's never had anyone over to work in the garage."

"He works hard and doesn't have much time. Kyle knows what he's doing, and he has an opportunity to learn. I don't blame him for making the most of it."

"I have a matter of months to turn that big doofus into someone who can actually dance." Morgan brought her hand to her forehead and closed her eyes. "The one thing I need to get it done is rehearsal time."

Her mother let out a sigh and put her hands on the counter. "About that. This guy doesn't seem like the type that's too keen to dance. So why is he doing it?"

Morgan quickly averted her eyes from her mother's searching gaze. She gave a quick shrug. "Oh, I just … uh, convinced him that he could do it, and that we had a chance at winning the national championship."

Mrs. Laflamme lifted one eyebrow. "Really? I think there's something else going on here."

Morgan blinked, and her heart sped up. "What? No! There's nothing *else* happening. What are you talking about?"

Her mother tilted her head and gave her a small smile. "You never could lie to me."

Morgan's eyes bulged and her mouth opened in outrage. "Ugh! Mom! I'm not lying."

"So there's no chance he's got a crush on you? Or maybe you're the one who's interested. He's not a bad-looking boy, Morgan."

There was a silence. Then Morgan threw her head back and broke out laughing. She looked at her mother and snorted.

"I'm taking that as a 'no?'" Mrs. Laflamme deadpanned.

"No! God no!" Morgan gasped before laughing again.

"Glad you find it amusing, but I still think this is weird."

They both turned when they heard the door to the garage opening, and the sound of Mr. Laflamme talking. "That was great, Kyle. We'd better wash this grime off our hands."

"No point," Kyle answered. "I'm going to the shop after I leave here. I have a couple of small jobs to finish up tonight."

Mrs. Laflamme raised a hand. "Let me give you a sandwich at least." She opened the fridge, while her husband started washing his hands.

Kyle nodded his acceptance. "Thanks."

"So we're *not* rehearsing anymore tonight?" Morgan snarled. "We're going to have to rehearse somewhere else. Too many distractions here."

Taylor thundered down the stairs. "Are you going, Kyle?"

"In a few minutes," he answered.

Mr. Laflamme finished washing up and walked over to Kyle. "Here, take this. It's the least I can do for you." He handed him a small container.

The big teenager read the label. "Hurry Clean?"

"Good stuff for grease and grime. Jake gave it to me, and I'm giving it to you."

Kyle tossed it in the air and caught it with a smile. "Thanks, I'll burn through this pretty quick." He looked at the time on the microwave. "I have to go. I have work and school tomorrow."

"When is our next rehearsal?" Morgan asked, a little too loud.

He didn't look at her as he started walking from the kitchen. "Let me know." He waved at the rest of the family. "Thanks for everything, I'll show myself out."

There was a silence after he left. Morgan turned and looked at her parents. "What happened here tonight? We came here to rehearse and it turned into a house party."

Mrs. Laflamme looked at her husband. "We'd heard about him from Taylor, and we wanted to get to know him. I'm sorry if that cut down on your rehearsal time, but did you ever consider that Kyle might have enjoyed meeting new people?"

"I give up," Morgan said, and stormed upstairs to her room.

Taylor shrugged. "Whatever. I think he's nice," she said, and she trotted up the stairs too.

Alone with her husband, Mrs. Laflamme chuckled. "What did you think of our guest?"

Mr. Laflamme came up and hugged her from behind. "Quite likeable. Honest, hardworking. But … doesn't seem like the type to be interested in ballroom dancing."

"There's more," Mrs. Laflamme added. "You notice he doesn't look at Morgan if he doesn't have to?"

"What does that mean? Is he interested?"

She shook her head slowly. "It sure doesn't seem like he is. Looks more like he hates her."

"And Morgan?" Mr. Laflamme inquired.

She spun around and took his face in her hands. "I don't know what's going on with her. She's hiding something, I can always tell." She kissed her husband. "You thinking what I'm thinking?"

He smiled. "Yeah. I'll check him out."

CHAPTER 28

Morgan guided her little convertible through the school parking lot and found a spot close to the school. She jumped out, grabbed her bag and purse, and stopped when she noticed the beat-up, grey Volvo. Only one person owned that thing.

Her curiosity won and she walked up to the car, peering in through a dusty window. To her surprise, the dark interior was immaculate. There was nothing in the car at all. Usually you would expect to find an empty cup, some papers, an article of clothing … something! She also noticed that it had a shifter, with a whimsical eight-ball where a normal handle would be. He drove a standard transmission, not an automatic. She'd heard of these types of cars, but had never actually seen one.

She pulled away from the window and started walking quickly toward the school, hoping nobody had seen her looking in Kyle's car. She saw the dance crew chatting and laughing on the stairs to the school. To her relief, none of them were aware she was coming, or that she'd peeked into her dance partner's car. She didn't want to answer any questions as to why she looked … because she didn't know herself why she'd done it.

Olivia and Morgan made their way to biology class, where Mr. Ryckman was shuffling papers at the front, getting organized. Morgan noticed that Kyle was already there, and his focus was on something he was writing. He didn't look up or acknowledge her presence.

Olivia looked over her shoulder as she sat and looked at Kyle. She tilted her head, then turned back to face forward. "Your dance partner isn't exactly the outgoing type."

"He's just quiet," Morgan answered. "He didn't say much more at my house when we were rehearsing."

"Oh, how did that go? I forgot that was last night," Olivia whispered.

"It went okay, but then my family all got in the way. They all couldn't get enough of the guy."

Olivia drew back and stared at her. "No! Really? They actually like him?"

"It's crazy," Morgan answered with a roll of her eyes. "My dad got him to fix his car, my mom made him food, and Taylor acted like a celebrity was in our house."

Olivia looked back over her shoulder. "And he won't even look at you?"

Lucas came in before the bell and waved to them as he hustled by. They both turned to watch him approach the topic of their conversation, sitting beside Kyle, who looked up and acknowledged his presence before turning back to his writing. Lucas said something, and they both laughed.

"Seems to like talking to Lucas just fine," Olivia observed.

Morgan made a face, and then she realized that he was ignoring her. In fact, he only talked to her when she talked first.

She didn't have long to dwell on the subject, as Mr. Ryckman called for the attention of the class and started handing out their last assignments. He had a quiet word for each group that included an equal measure of praise and feedback about what could improve. When he got to Olivia and Morgan, he smiled and handed back their assignment. The friends were pleased to see they'd received an A, but he still had some advice. "Nicely done, ladies! Elaborate a little more when you're writing about your method and observations. It won't take much more to take this mark higher."

They thanked him, and he moved on to the other groups. Olivia held up her fist to be bumped, and she wore a grin. "We're awesome," she concluded.

"Ah, Mr. Quintana and Mr. Branch!" they heard Mr. Ryckman say, loud enough to alert the entire class. "This was very well done. You followed the instructions to the letter, and you did an excellent job writing this assignment. It was thorough, and well explained. Well done, gentlemen! Well done indeed." He handed the paper to the two young men and went back to the front of the class.

Lucas held up an elbow, and Kyle bumped it with his own. They both wore smiles as they looked over their work.

"Well, what do you know?" Olivia whispered. "Kyle handled the writing on that assignment. Maybe not as dumb as we thought."

Morgan sat and stewed. It seemed like everyone was taken with her dance partner, and he got along with everyone in her inner circle but her. She shook it off and cleared her thoughts, trying to get back to what mattered. Sure, she liked to be liked ... but she liked to win more. Her course of action was clear.

When class was done, she marched up to the two young men who were packing up. "Hi, Kyle," she said, and didn't wait for a response. "We need to rehearse. I don't think I can get the utility room. Any ideas on where we can do it?"

The big teenager stood up and gave her a cold look. "Well, you could always come to my place."

She almost took a step back. "There's room there to rehearse?"

"Should be."

"Uh, what time?" she asked.

He shouldered his bag. "Any time after 6:30 tonight." He turned and started walking away. "You have the address," he said without a backward glance, and he was gone.

Morgan stood there, staring at the door. Olivia came up beside her, also looking at the door with wide eyes. "You're not going alone to his house, are you? You're bringing me along, *right?*"

"You better believe it," said Morgan.

CHAPTER 29

Morgan and Olivia crept along the outskirts of town in Morgan's convertible. The top was up, the doors were locked, and the girls sat silent as they looked for the address on the paper in Olivia's hand. Few of the streetlights were working, so it was darker than they were used to. They passed a few abandoned homes, boarded up, though a light in some of the windows showed that someone was squatting. They passed a car without windows or wheels, just sitting on the street. The few pedestrians they saw walked erratically, and with staring eyes that didn't focus.

"Tell me we're getting close," Morgan whispered to her friend, as if the denizens of this lost part of the city could hear her. She gripped the wheel with both hands.

Olivia's face glowed in the light of her smartphone. "According to the GPS, if the address is right, it should be … here!" She pointed toward a dark driveway. There was a thick growth of trees and weeds on either side, preventing any view of a home.

"This is it?" Morgan asked.

"Yeah, I can see the number on the curb. This is it." Olivia looked at her friend. "Well, are you going in?

"You think I should?"

Olivia looked outside the little car. "Better than staying out here."

Morgan took a big breath and let it out slowly. "Okay, here we go," she said, as she pulled into the dark driveway.

They rolled into an area that was no longer paved, and a small, squat house appeared in the headlights. The porch was sagging, and the posts that held up the roof had patches of peeling paint. There was only one light on, glowing faintly behind the sheet that covered the window from the inside. The two teenagers looked at each other; nothing was said. Olivia shrugged and stepped out of the car. Morgan reluctantly did the same.

The two of them were shoulder to shoulder as they advanced slowly in the darkness. They stepped on the stairway of the front porch, and the boards creaked as they ascended. Olivia looked at Morgan and pointed to a doorbell. "Ring it," she whispered.

"You do it," Morgan said, with a shake of her head.

"Oh, *come on!*" Olivia hissed.

They never had a chance to settle the matter, as the front door swung open, revealing the silhouette of a small man standing in the doorway. He was thin, almost bald, but had combed what was left of his hair over the top of his scalp ... fooling nobody. A stained white undershirt and boxers were all that he wore. He scratched at his three-day beard with one hand, and the other held a bottle. His most distinguishing feature was his eyes. Red-rimmed, bloodshot, with dark circles under his intense blue gaze.

He stared at them and frowned. "Whatchu girls want? You sellin' cookies?"

Olivia elbowed Morgan to get her to talk. The dancer shook her head quickly. "Uh, Kyle Branch. Does he live here?"

The man snorted. "The boy?" He lifted the hand with the bottle to point behind them. "Over there in the drive shed," he slurred, and closed the door in their faces.

They looked at each other in horror and turned to look behind them. Sure enough, there was a large wooden building in the darkness. It had two levels and resembled a barn, but the front door was unusually large. They could barely make out a light on the second story.

Olivia quietly said, "He lives ... there?"

"That's what the gross leprechaun said."

"Gross leprechaun!" Olivia chortled. "Well, let's go find him."

They walked over to the large wooden doors, and quickly figured out that they were designed to slide open. There was no bell or knocker to be seen. Morgan put her hands on one of the door frames and leaned into it. There was a low rumbling as it slid open a couple of feet.

Olivia stuck her head inside the opening and called out, "Hello?"

Her call was answered by a low bark coming from the second level. The two teenagers recoiled when they heard the dog. It sounded huge. They looked at each other and each took a step toward the car when they heard a voice from above.

"Enough, Roscoe! Give me a minute, don't move!"

The two young women froze and turned back towards the building. They heard heavy footfalls on wooden stairs, there was a pause, and then lights turned on and flooded the first level. Kyle's face appeared in the doorway, and he effortlessly threw the doors all the way open.

"Hi," he said mildly.

"Hi, Kyle," Olivia said with a relieved smile. She looked around him to see large machines. "You live here?" she asked.

He shook his head. "No, this is an old machine shop. Nobody uses it anymore. I live on the second level." He turned and gestured for them to follow.

"What about the dog? We heard a dog!" Morgan called after him.

Kyle continued up the stairs. "Roscoe? He's not going to bother getting up when he sees you. I wouldn't worry."

The two friends followed him up the stairs and rounded a corner to see an almost empty second level. Plain boards on the floor with no carpeting created a creaking sound every time they were stepped on. There was a queen-sized bed in the far corner of the room, and a bookshelf completely stuffed with books of every size. The opposite side had a small stove and a smaller fridge to serve as a kitchen. The middle of the room was large and completely empty.

"Woof!" they heard from their left. An enormous tan-colored dog with a black muzzle was reclining in an old sofa. He tried to sit up, and his tail thumped into the cushions as he gave up and his head flopped back down.

"That … that is one *big* dog," Olivia said, her blue eyes wide.

"It's also a tired and old dog," Kyle answered with a smirk. "He's a big suck. If you sit beside him, expect a lot of affection."

Olivia cautiously made her way to the big animal. The head lifted, and the tail flopped loudly on the cushions. Olivia sat her slender frame on the small amount of area available at the end of the sofa. Roscoe heaved himself up into a sitting position and leaned on the blonde beside him. She couldn't help but laugh and started to pet him.

"He's adorable! And heavy." She tried to lean back into him. "What kind of dog is he, and how old?"

"Don't know," Kyle answered. "He's not my dog."

"He's not?" Olivia asked.

"No, he belongs to the owner of this property. I have no idea how old he is, but he seems to be a cross between a bull mastiff and some kind of hound."

Morgan had walked over to the shelves and was looking at all the books. "That's not your father in the house?"

"No, that's my uncle Rick."

"Interesting guy," Morgan deadpanned, and took a book off a shelf. It was *The Grapes of Wrath*.

"I can't complain," Kyle explained. "He's the only family I've got, and he lets me live here for nothing." He gently took the book from her hand and put it back. "The guy has a problem with alcohol. Not much to be done about that." He walked away from her and went to a small fridge.

"You've read all these books?" Morgan asked, as she read the titles on the spines.

"Twice," he answered, as he pulled open the door to the fridge. "Are you thirsty? All I can offer you is some bottled water. That's all I have."

"I'll take one," Olivia answered, as she kept petting the enormous dog, who was closing his eyes.

"Sure, thanks," Morgan said, and walked over to a beat-up old guitar that was sitting in an armchair with patched arms. "You play?"

Kyle walked up to Olivia and handed her one of the bottles of water. Roscoe sniffed it to make sure it wasn't edible. "I'm teaching myself. It's going slow, but I'm enjoying it."

Olivia looked around. "You don't have a television?"

Kyle shook his head. "Only this," he said, and pointed at a box-shaped object beside his bed that was made of plastic to look like wood.

"What is it?" Olivia asked.

Morgan walked up to it and put a finger to her lips. "I think I know. Is that … is that an 8-track player?"

Kyle laughed. "Yeah, but I only use the radio."

Morgan came to the center of the room. "I don't know, Kyle. This is a pretty spartan way to live." She started twirling and whirling around the large space. Then she stopped and smiled. "But it's big enough, and we can definitely rehearse here." She walked to stand right in front of him, took a water bottle from him, and looked up into his eyes. "So let's rehearse already."

CHAPTER 30

"Okay," Kyle said, held up one hand, and reached for her hip with the other.

"Oh, just a minute!" She pulled away and ran to the sofa with her phone held high. "You're the DJ, Olivia."

Olivia nodded her agreement, as the big dog beside her leaned harder and started making a sawing noise. "Is he … is he *snoring*?" she giggled.

"Probably," Kyle answered.

"It's the fifth song on the list," Morgan instructed.

"Got it."

Morgan trotted back to the center of the room and into the embrace of the big fighter. "Okay, remember, the box step to the grapevine. You've done it before, now it's review. I'll count you in." She noticed there was no sweat in his big hands. They were clean.

"No need to count. I know when to come in. Let's do this," his low voice rumbled.

Olivia tapped on the phone as the big dog snored. "Here we go."

The music started, and true to his word, Kyle stepped forward with his left foot at the exact moment he was supposed to. Morgan couldn't help but smile as she realized that not only had he picked up the steps quickly, he'd retained them.

They finished the box step smoothly and immediately went to the grapevine. While he initiated it, keeping his frame firm as they moved their legs back and forth, she was the one who stopped the move and reminded him to return to a box step. Again, after completing the move competently, they came to a stop.

Olivia clapped from the sofa while Roscoe turned and looked at her indignantly. "That was great, guys!"

Morgan shrugged. "It's a start. A pretty good start." She walked over to Olivia and took her phone back. "We're going to learn a new skill, and review the ones we've learned."

Kyle frowned. "We're not doing it right?"

Olivia resumed petting Roscoe while Morgan walked back to her partner. "Your feet are going where they're supposed to be, and your timing is fine. The next step is to get you to accent the hip movement. You know what you're doing, but now we have to make it more artistic."

"We do?"

"We do," Morgan said with a chuckle. "Never forget that dance is a competition that is won and lost by the decision of the judges. We've got to be better than the people we're competing with. We have to be *better*."

"Okay," said Kyle. He took a step back and started trying to mimic her. "Is this *better*?"

Morgan put her hand on her chin and watched him repeat the move. "That's already better. But … try to exaggerate it, and you'll probably get it right."

Kyle nodded, trying to move his hips and exaggerate the moves.

"Yeah! That's it!" Olivia cheered. Roscoe snored, Kyle stopped.

Morgan gave her a stern look. "One coach here, Olivia. One coach."

Olivia held up a hand. "Okay, okay. I thought that looked more like what you were doing."

Morgan brought her hands together and thought. "Okay, right. Let's do the whole thing again, but try to throw in the hip movement." She smiled. "Treat it like a judo throw."

"Do I get to toss you at the end?" Kyle muttered, as she ran back to Olivia to give her the phone.

"What was that?" Morgan asked over her shoulder.

"Can we take a break at the end?" Kyle amended.

She scurried back to him, and they both got ready. "Depends if you get this right."

The music started. Kyle came in when he should, but this time the hip movement was there. The box step was fluid, and they easily transitioned to the grapevine. They glided from the center of the room to the edge and started another box step. They came to a stop and Olivia halted the music.

Morgan looked up into the blue eyes of her partner and gave him a satisfied smile. "Yes! That's something the judges would appreciate."

"I get my break?"

She sighed. "Fine. I could use some water myself."

Olivia took the opportunity to hand back Morgan's phone as she walked by to retrieve her water bottle. She looked at the big dog beside her, and then at Kyle. "You say he's not your dog?"

Kyle grabbed a bag from the tiny kitchen and poured some food into a large chrome bowl on the floor. Roscoe raised his head to look, then surrendered to Olivia's petting and dropped his head back on her lap.

Kyle smiled. "He belongs to Uncle Rick, and Rick's not reliable when it comes to feeding and walking him. I think that's why he comes here to spend time with me. He's good company."

Morgan walked over to the back wall of the building and tilted her head. "Does this actually open up?" she asked, pointing at the seam in the wall.

"Give it a try," Kyle encouraged.

She stuck her fingers in the crack between two doors and heaved. It opened a little. Kyle walked over to help. She held up a finger. "No! I've got this."

Kyle stopped dead in his tracks and folded his arms on his chest.

The tall brunette put her back into it, and grunted as she opened the doors wide. Once they had some momentum, they continued to move until almost the entire back wall was open and they could see the night sky and the glow of the city beneath.

"Wow, great view," Olivia observed.

"It's probably my favorite thing in this old place," Kyle said with a tight-lipped smile. "It's rustic to be sure, but quiet, and the stars on a clear night—it's awesome."

Olivia gave him a bright smile. "Maybe we'll come for a late rehearsal and see it one night. I'm sure Roscoe would be happy to see us." The dog lifted his head at the mention of his name, then let it flop right back down on the girl's lap with a big sigh. All three teenagers laughed at the lazy dog.

Morgan clapped her hands together to get their attention. "Okay, break's over." She strutted confidently to the center of the room and gave her ponytail a flip. "Time you learned how to initiate and complete a turn, Kyle."

CHAPTER 31

"Kyle!" Hector shouted breathlessly down the hall. He was waving his hands and beckoning for the big teenager to come to him.

"What?" Kyle bellowed back.

"It's Lucas. He could use you right now."

Kyle's eyes widened, and he ran down the hall and followed Hector down the stairs to the first floor of the school. Sure enough, Hector knew what he was talking about. A small crowd was gathered at the end of the hall, and he could hear Lucas protesting.

Kyle barreled through the hallway, bumping into a few gawking sophomores who were too focused on the entertainment to notice that he was coming. Being taller than the other students, he could see three teenagers in football jackets surrounding Lucas. One of them was holding a textbook high in the air and refusing to give it back. All three were too busy enjoying their moment of power to see Kyle's approach.

"Lucas!" Kyle said good and loud. "I've been looking for you. Ryckman's class is coming up. You ready, or what?"

The football players took a step back when they saw who was talking. It was Steve Harris holding the book. Kyle had heard that Steve was on probation for the attack in the parking lot. He didn't recognize the other two Steve had enlisted to help with his torture session. Lucas was shaking, but he wasn't backing down. He couldn't help but smile a little when he saw who had arrived.

"Mind your own business, Branch!" Steve barked back. The two football players fell in slightly behind their leader. They didn't say anything. Their faces did the talking.

The crowd watching had doubled in size, and came to include Tonisha. She came and stood beside Hector. "They at Lucas again?" she asked, with a shake of her braids.

"Yeah," Hector confirmed, "but things just got more interesting."

Steve looked left and right, and his eyes bulged a little wider when he looked back at the big fighter. He swallowed and tried again. "I told you to mind your own business. Why are you still here?"

Kyle smiled and pointed at Lucas. "That's my biology partner. He's the only reason I'm getting great marks in that class. I need him, and his biology book." His tone darkened as he growled, "So back off."

Steve's face colored slightly as the crowd murmured approval. Whispers flew, and it wasn't hard to tell that they were enjoying watching the football captain squirm. They'd all dealt with him one way or another.

The two football players behind Steve looked at each other quickly and back at their big adversary. Steve blinked a couple of times, and his face grew ugly. "Well, maybe *you'd* like to come over here and take this book," he said, as he held it high for everyone to see.

Kyle shook his head and smiled wider. "Nah, I'd rather you put it down in front of everybody, and my partner can get it himself. Then you can show everyone how tough you are by dealing with me. That *is* what you're looking for, right, Steve? To show everyone how tough you are?"

Silence fell as all three football players colored slightly, and there were a few chuckles from the mob. The two henchmen behind Steve balled their fists and glared at him.

"You might want to let your two new friends know what happened the last time you took a run at me. Have you recovered from the concussion yet? I'll bet you haven't," he added, and stepped forward. "Well, nobody's stopping you. Let's go!"

The crowd started parting as a staff member pushed through. It was the diminutive, red-haired English teacher, Mrs. Edgehill. "What on earth is going on here?" she hollered at nobody in particular. When she came to the center of the disturbance and saw the big fighter squaring off against the three football players, she put her hands on her hips. "Oh, I see now! Why am I not surprised to see you in the middle of all this, Steve Harris?"

The football captain shrugged lamely and looked at the floor. She turned her attention next to Kyle. "But you, Mr. Branch? That *does* surprise me. I thought you were better than all this."

Kyle looked right at her and nodded. "You're right, Mrs. Edgehill. Never should have happened. I'm sorry to have disturbed you." He turned and looked at Steve. "Soon as Steve gives Lucas here back his biology book, we can go to class."

The veteran teacher's eyes bulged, and she straightened her glasses to stare at the football captain. "Oh, I think I understand now. Give him back his book, right now!" she barked.

Steve gave her a dirty look and held out the book for Lucas. As soon as he reached for it, the book was dropped on the floor. "Oops," he mumbled with a snigger.

Lucas sighed and picked up the biology textbook, while Mrs. Edgehill glared at the football players as they walked away.

Kyle looked down at the small English teacher. "I am sorry about that," he said softly.

She held up a hand. "You don't have to say another word, kid." She smiled at him and tilted her head forward to look at him above her glasses. "I went to high school once too. I know how it works. Now get to class!"

Kyle and Lucas looked at each other and smiled at her. Lucas closed his locker, and the two of them moved through the hall.

"Thanks, big guy," Lucas said quietly without looking at him.

"No problem. You should thank Hector for letting me know."

Lucas started to laugh. "I like the part where you gave me credit for our biology marks. Creative!"

Kyle shrugged. "People find it easy to believe I'm a dummy. I go with it." He looked at Lucas. "Say, is that locker next to you empty? I might ask the office if I can move to that one."

Lucas gave him a warm look. "Yeah, it's empty. That would be good."

"Better for me too," Kyle observed. "I find I'm in the utility room more and more lately."

"Rehearsing?"

"Yeah, plenty of that," Kyle groaned. "Did you do the reading for biology?"

"Nope," Lucas admitted. "Did you?"

"Of course," Kyle answered with a smirk. "I'll help you in class."

"Thanks."

Kyle looked down and shook his head. "You've got to stop thanking me."

Lucas shrugged. "No, I don't."

CHAPTER 32

"It was awesome." Tonisha said with a bright grin. "Seeing Steve have to tuck his tail between his legs and run. Yeah, I won't forget that one." She was walking with Olivia and Morgan on the first floor between classes.

Olivia groaned. "I wish I was there to see it. I'll bet Kyle is all kinds of gorgeous when he's being macho."

"Ugh! You can't be serious," Morgan said, and came to a stop. Her friends stopped with her and they all faced each other, backs to the other students in the hall. "You saw how he lives, Olivia. You find that attractive? God!"

Olivia shrugged and ran a hand back through her hair. "Sure, it's kind of rough ... but I still think he might be boyfriend material. Maybe."

Morgan made a face, and Tonisha laughed. "Was it that bad?" the hip-hop captain asked.

"Oh, it was worse than you can imagine." Morgan said with a hand up, shaking her head. "The guy actually lives in a *barn!*"

"No! You lie!" Tonisha said with her mouth open.

"It's not a barn, exactly," Olivia protested.

"Oh, it looks like a barn and it smells like a barn," Morgan said, pointing at her. She turned back to Tonisha. "And there's almost nothing in it."

"Nothing?" Tonisha asked.

Morgan started counting the items on one hand. "Let's see ... a bed, a sofa, a fridge." She looked up as she thought about it. "Oh, and a pile of books, and some ancient radio."

Tonisha narrowed her eyes. "That's it? In a barn?"

Olivia raised a hand. "Excuse me! You're forgetting the guitar, and he has a sweet dog."

Morgan wagged a finger at her. "Uh-uh. The dog isn't even his, *remember*? All it does is sleep. It's more like a ... like a sloth! It belongs to the drunk, gross leprechaun who actually owns the property."

All three girls broke up laughing. Tonisha brought a hand to her mouth and struggled to breathe between fits of laughter.

"Oh, come on," Olivia said, trying to compose herself. "It wasn't *that* bad, Morgan."

"Yes it was!" Morgan said. "Besides, what are you going to do for your first date? Enjoy a lovely bottle of water? Listen to the radio? Or maybe he can take you hunting for cans in recycling bins? You might find enough of a deposit that he can afford to buy you a taco."

The three girls burst out laughing at the scenario. Olivia brought a hand to her face and turned red. Tonisha held her stomach, trying to deal with the pain from their hysterics.

Morgan took a couple of quick breaths. "Sounds like a great first date, Olivia. He's all yours!"

They were interrupted by a pale-looking Lucas. "Uh, M-Morgan ... please don't say anymore," he stammered.

"What? It's funny." Morgan said. "You know what we're talking about, right?"

Lucas closed his locker, and they all stopped laughing when they saw Kyle Branch. He was standing right there looking at them, and he'd heard every word. His eyes were hard and burned into them, but he said nothing.

Olivia turned beet red, and Morgan's eyes bulged; her mouth hung open in shock. Tonisha turned away and covered her mouth. "Oh, my God ..." she whispered.

Kyle slammed his locker, threw on the padlock, and took three steps to stand right in front of Morgan. He looked down at her, mouth grim and eyes blazing blue. "You're right about me. Everything you said about me is true." He looked at the ground, and the awkward silence lingered.

"Kyle, I ... I didn't know," Morgan started weakly.

He looked up fast. "And you? Well, you're *everything* I thought you were."

Without another word, he turned and marched away. Lucas stared as he went, with a pained look on his face. The other two females stood there, aghast. They all turned to look at their tall friend.

Morgan's eyes were wide and beginning to tear up. She stared down the hall as the big teenager walked away. Her mouth hung open, and her bottom lip began to quiver. "I think I'm going to be sick."

CHAPTER 33

Olivia sat in the cafeteria and munched on her wrap, staring straight ahead. Hector sat beside her and had his face in both hands, shaking his head slowly and groaning. Morgan was doing the same thing across from him, while Tonisha sat beside her, staring at her lunch.

"You didn't … you did *not* do that," Hector said with despair.

"I did do it. I *really* did," Morgan said through her hands.

It was at that moment they saw Lucas coming through the serving area. He was still pale, and his eyes were wide as he hustled to their table. He put down his tray and stayed standing, staring at Morgan. "How could you *do* that?"

She brought one hand down on the table and covered her eyes with the other. "I didn't MEAN to do it, Lucas! I was joking with my friends. I didn't know that Kyle was even there." She dropped her hands and looked at him. "What was he doing there, anyway? I thought his locker was on the second floor."

Lucas sat down and let out a sigh. "It was. He moved to the one beside me so the football players would think twice before messing with me."

Morgan let her face drop to the table. "Oh my God, that makes it even worse!"

"Listen," Hector began, "I understand saying things in confidence to your friends. I do." He looked down at the table and grimaced. "But why would you say those things in the first place?"

The tall dancer held up both hands. "It was all true. Well, except the part where I was making up what a first date with him would be like."

Lucas stared at her. "Is there some part of you that's a little horrified that you were making fun of an orphan who is poor?"

"Oh, come on, Lucas! I've heard you make fun of everyone, and you aren't exactly kind about it."

"That is true," Lucas agreed. "But there are places I won't go. I've never made fun of somebody for not having much money." He tilted his head and looked at her. "You know, not everyone lives in a beautiful house, Miss Laflamme."

Hector pointed at his friend. "Yeah, I don't live in a house like you do either, Morgan."

"Guys!" Morgan pleaded. "Give me a break."

"I don't think I want you to see my house now," Hector muttered, and crossed his arms on his chest. "We ain't rich."

Olivia smacked her hand on the table to get their attention. "Okay, enough!" She looked at the two young men chastising her friend. "Listen, we've all said stupid things and hurt people. Imagine something you said about someone that you wouldn't want them to hear."

The two young men looked at each other and then down. "I see your point," Lucas agreed.

"Yeah, I get you," Hector seconded.

She turned her attention to her best friend. "Morgan, you did a crappy thing. You know that."

"Olivia!" she protested. "You were *there!* You know how it went down."

"Oh, an accident to be sure. But still a really, really crappy thing to do. Right?"

Morgan nodded and looked down at her folded hands.

"Girl, you gotta apologize," Tonisha said firmly. "You gotta apologize as soon as you can."

"Yes, you must," Hector agreed. The others nodded their support.

Morgan let her head fall to the table. "Oh God! What do I say for something like that?" She brought her face up quickly. "Hi, Kyle, it's me! The girl who made fun of you, your uncle, your dog, and the way you live your life." Morgan smiled like a maniac. "Hey, sorry about that. We cool?" Her face fell, and she looked at each of her friends. "Think that will do it?"

Olivia shook her head. "I didn't say it was going to be easy. But you *have* to do it."

"I know, I know," she moaned. "I've been looking for him since I sat down. I don't think he's come to the cafeteria today."

"I wonder why," Lucas muttered.

Morgan's eyes blazed. "You know what, Lucas? I don't need this from you. If it wasn't for you, he wouldn't have been on the first floor at all. None of this would have happened."

Lucas dropped his lunch on his tray. "Hey, I don't feel like eating in the cafeteria either." He stood up and marched away from the table.

"Yeah, I ain't too hungry," Hector mumbled, and left too.

Tonisha sat back in her chair. "I swear, this is the worst drama that we've ever had to face on the dance team." She looked at the others. "I mean, I can't think of anything this crazy."

Morgan put her chin in her hand and closed her eyes. "It gets worse. We're supposed to rehearse after hip-hop practice today."

The other two teenagers winced and shifted uncomfortably. Morgan inspected the end of her ponytail and stared at the table. "Do you think he'll show?"

Olivia looked down too. "Would you?"

CHAPTER 34

"He's not going to show," Morgan said to Olivia. They were taking their last break at hip-hop rehearsal, both looking at the clock.

"He still might," Olivia answered.

Morgan arched her back in a stretch and smoothed her long ponytail. It wasn't looking good. Kyle was normally there by now, and the hip-hop rehearsal was almost done.

"One more time," Tonisha called, and the dancers finished drinking their water, toweling off some sweat before taking their first position. Tonisha started the music, and the crew moved in unison. They hit every mark and every formation without effort.

Morgan found her thoughts drifting to Kyle, but the next move and the next step kept her focus coming back to the routine.

The song ended, and they held their final pose. "That's right!" Tonisha called with glee. "Good work, everyone, that's a wrap. Go home!"

The dancers smiled at her command, and because they knew they'd completed the routine with confidence. A job well done. They gathered their things and started making their way out.

Ms. Blake was still reading papers in the corner. She looked up and scanned the room until she found Morgan. "Ms. Laflamme, are you and your partner rehearsing today?"

Morgan walked over to the teacher so nobody else could hear their conversation. "We were supposed to," she mumbled.

"But … now you're not?" Ms. Blake asked, with an eyebrow raised.

"Something happened today," she said, and wiped some sweat out of her eye.

Ms. Blake sat back. "Ah, some kind of conflict? Sorry to hear about that."

"You could call it conflict, but … it's my fault."

"I have to say, I hope this isn't the end of your partnership," Ms. Blake said, knitting her fingers together. "I had my doubts when he first walked in. I thought you were crazy. But you made me a believer. You work well together."

Morgan nodded miserably.

"I mean it," Ms. Blake continued. "You're a great teacher, and I can't believe how fast Kyle is able to pick up the steps. He's a rare athlete, and there's some talent there, I think."

The dancer looked at the clock. She could see that their rehearsal was supposed to start five minutes ago. "He's not coming," she said, and went to grab her things.

"Give him a chance," Ms. Blake encouraged. "He's only five minutes late. Maybe something came up."

Morgan came back after fetching her backpack to stand right in front of her. She brought her hands together, almost like a prayer. "Ms. Blake, I have a favor to ask."

"Ask away."

"Would it be possible to try again tomorrow after school? Are you able to do that?" She looked right into the eyes of the guidance counselor.

Ms. Blake sighed. "I didn't get as much work done as I wanted done today." She smiled pleasantly at Morgan. "But okay, Ms. Laflamme. Besides, I'm a sucker for ballroom. I love it."

"Thank you, thank you, *thank you!*" Morgan said, hopping up and down. She hurried to the door, a plan forming in her mind.

"What are you going to do about Kyle?" Ms. Blake called after her.

She stopped at the door. "I did this. It's my fault," Morgan admitted, to herself as much as the teacher. She looked up and flashed a confident smile. "I'm going to undo what I did."

Morgan parked the car in her driveway and ran into her house. Her mother was having a coffee with her father. "Hi, Mom! Hi, Dad!" she called, as she ran to the stairs and up into her room. She had to sidestep Taylor in the hall.

"Whoa!" her sister exclaimed. "What's the hurry?"

"Sorry, I've gotta grab something from my room and go," Morgan called over her shoulder. She ran into her room and right to the nightstand. She opened the top drawer, fished out a brown envelope, and opened it to check that it was what she needed. Then she stuffed it into her purse and headed for the door.

Her parents were staring as she came downstairs, keys in hand. "You're leaving? You just got home, and it's a little late," her mother observed.

Morgan stopped in her tracks. "Okay, I've got to talk to Kyle ... and he doesn't have a phone."

"He doesn't?" her father asked.

"No! No, he doesn't. So I have to find him and talk to him." She took a deep breath and looked at her parents. "It's important. I won't be long, I promise."

Her parents looked at each other, and her father shrugged. "Don't be long, okay?"

"I won't," she promised, and trotted to the door. "Thanks!" she called over her shoulder.

Her mother looked at her father. "Didn't expect you to agree with that so quickly. Is there anything I should worry about?"

Mr. Laflamme shook his head and swallowed some coffee. "I had someone check out Mr. Kyle Branch. I asked them to find anything they could."

"Any red flags?"

"None," he said with a tight-lipped smile. "Poor guy lost his father in infancy and his mother a few years ago. No criminal record, always employed. Nothing of note."

His wife took a sip of her coffee and thought. "He seemed like a good guy. He really is?"

"He really is," confirmed Mr. Laflamme.

CHAPTER 35

The little convertible slid through the night, quiet but quick. Morgan knew exactly where she was going, but that didn't make it any easier. She rehearsed what she wanted to say over and over. It never seemed like enough, and she couldn't decide what she wanted to say. Her head started to pound from the stress, and her face was strained.

She rolled into the driveway where Kyle lived and looked for the battered Volvo. It wasn't there. Morgan took a deep breath and let it out, partly relieved and a little frustrated. As much as she didn't want to apologize, she wanted it done.

Her hand reached for the ignition to turn off the car, but she hesitated. She was considering knocking on the door and asking Uncle Rick where his nephew might be. But she remembered his problem with the bottle. Not an option.

Instead she reversed the car, turned around, and headed to her next destination. Happy to be out of Kyle's bad neighborhood, she concentrated on the streets she needed to travel. She'd only been there a couple of times, and it was always following her father. Her memory served her well, and soon she glided into the parking lot of Gilmour's Auto Shop. There were no lights to be seen. She craned her neck to try and see through the large garage doors at the back: nothing.

Morgan put both hands on the wheel and let out a sigh. He wasn't home, he wasn't at work, there was no way to go to school this late … that left one possible place. The last place she was hoping to find Kyle.

She pulled into the parking lot of the MMA gym, and sure enough, there was the Volvo sitting innocently to her right. The car with the distinctive grey primer paint job. There was no doubt who owned it.

"Great," she muttered. This was the last thing she wanted. Walking into this environment and having a conversation she was dreading was bad enough. The idea of having to interrupt a class, or have anyone in earshot, was horrific. She took a cleansing breath. "Okay, Morgan," she said out loud. "You're scared to do this, and that's okay." Her face grew hard. "So you're just going to have to do it scared," she coached herself. She mentally counted to three, stepped out of the car, and walked towards the entrance. This was going to happen, and it was going to happen now.

Morgan pushed open the door and saw that the owner who normally ran the front desk wasn't there. She heard some music and impact noises from inside the gym. She kicked off her flip-flops and stepped into the training area.

Two older gentlemen in white martial arts uniforms were grappling in the corner, while reggae music played beside them. A loud "THWACK" from the far side of the gym caught her attention. Kyle was wearing shorts, boxing gloves, and a blue tank top as he punished a heavy bag that hung on a chain from the ceiling. He didn't see her as he lined up another kick that shook the rafters.

She looked down at the ground, willing herself to step forward and close the distance between them. Her bare feet padded across the mats until she was standing behind the heavy bag Kyle was working over. Her brown eyes were wide and her mouth small as she waited for him to notice her.

His blue eyes flicked her way and then right back to the bag, as he sank a low kick that almost folded it. The sound echoed, drowning out the music in the other corner.

"Hi, Kyle," she said, her voice sounding loud in her ears. He landed another kick, the impact sending vibrations through the air like thunder. He still didn't look at her.

"Okay, you don't want to talk. Okay," she continued, looking down at her feet. "I'm here because I'm the one who needs to do the talking, anyway." She took a shuddering breath in and started to unload her conscience. "Kyle, I came here to say … I'm here to say I am *so* sorry!" she finished hoarsely. Her eyes were watering, and she fished for a tissue in her purse.

He still didn't look at her, but threw a quick jab followed by a powerful overhand right. The bag swung slightly, so he had to reach out to steady it.

Morgan dabbed her eyes and kept going. "I said terrible, terrible things about you. Things that were unfair, and things you didn't deserve. I feel awful about what I did." She had to pause as she felt her throat tighten.

Kyle wound up to smash the bag again, but hesitated. He still couldn't seem to bring himself to look at her, so he steadied the bag with both hands and set his forehead against it. Sweat dripped off the end of his nose.

Her eyes widened and she held up a hand. "I had no idea you were there. I was trying to be funny for my friends. That was never meant for you, I swear, Kyle."

His blue eyes flashed at her with annoyance.

"I know! I-I know!" she stammered. "That doesn't make it okay. But I want you to know that I never, ever meant to hurt you. I want you to know that."

Kyle took a deep breath and let it out in a long sigh. He held his arms up helplessly and finally spoke to her. "What do you want, Morgan? Why are you here?"

She looked in his eyes and froze. Had they always been that blue? She shrugged and looked down as she answered. "Well, you told me there were only four places you would ever be. I checked where you live, the shop … it's too late for school, so you had to be here."

He put his hands on his hips and tilted his head with a scowl. He didn't say anything. He didn't need to.

"But … but that doesn't answer your question. I came here mostly to apologize." She took a breath and her big brown eyes pleaded with him. "I *had* to tell you that I'm sorry, and that I feel awful. I wish I could take it back."

"You can't," his low voice rumbled.

"I know," she agreed with a whisper. "I know that." She held up a finger to get his attention and dug into her small purse. She fished out a brown envelope and held it out for him to take. "I want you to look at this. Take it."

He looked at it suspiciously and didn't move to take it. She held it out and waited. After a moment, he reached slowly for the envelope with a wrapped hand, keeping distance between himself and the young woman. He looked down at the envelope and opened it. His eyes widened. "What is this?" he asked, and held up some cash from the envelope.

She gave him a tight-lipped smile. "That's the five thousand dollars I promised. I wanted you to see it."

"Why?"

"I want you to know that I really do have the money, and I'm going to pay you if you help me compete at nationals. I mean what I say." She took a deep breath and let it out. "I want you to know that I didn't lie to you then, and I'm not lying to you now." She took a couple of steps until she was standing right in front of him. "Kyle, I'm sorry about what came out of my mouth, and I want you to keep dancing with me. What do you say?"

He met her pleading eyes and took a step back with a shake of his head. "I don't get it. Why is this so important to you? Is it worth all this trouble? I mean ... why are you doing this?"

Morgan's mouth hardened into a grim line. "Because if I win this year, I can get into any dance school I want. I can write my own ticket to anywhere I want to go. But it's even more than that, I'm the 'tall girl.' You know what that means?"

"No idea."

She clenched her teeth. "It means that I get to be in the back of almost any formation when we perform. Oh, I might get to come to the front once in a while, and then right back out of sight. But when I dance ballroom ... it's me. I'm the one they're all looking at. I'm the one who gets to shine." She pointed her finger to her own chest. "I'm the star."

He nodded, understanding. "It means that much to you?"

She clasped her hands together and managed a weak smile. "It does. Not only because of what it can do for my future. Dancing at nationals, winning for my school, hearing my name, it was probably the best moment of my life."

"And you want that again?"

"I do. With all my heart."

Kyle's face softened, but he couldn't bring himself to look at her. Instead, he held out the envelope full of cash.

She slowly took it back and bit her bottom lip. "Look, Kyle, I don't have anything else that I can say. I am so sorry for what I said, and I'm asking you to keep working with me." She shook her head and gave a small laugh. "You're amazing! You're the best partner I've ever had. I still can't believe I found you."

He looked at the ground and said nothing. He slowly started unwrapping one of his hands. His movements were slow, and he didn't say a word; his face was impassive.

She held up a hand to stop anything he might say. "Look, it's a lot. I know. If you can do it, that's great for both of us. I get to dance, and you get paid. I booked the utility room tomorrow after school. If you want to keep going, I'll see you tomorrow at rehearsal." She took in a breath. "If you're not there, I'll know what you decided."

The fighter still looked at the ground, expressionless. He started unwrapping the other hand and still gave no clue as to what he was thinking.

Morgan knew there was nothing more to say. "Well, good night, Kyle." She took a couple of steps and stopped, then turned to look at him over her shoulder. "I hope I see you at rehearsal tomorrow," she confessed, and walked out of the gym.

CHAPTER 36

Morning people are the worst! Morgan thought to herself as she ate her cereal. Her day had started like any other. She woke up, showered, dressed, and did her makeup before going downstairs for breakfast. Now she had to listen to Taylor talking a mile a minute with her father. At least her mother suffered the morning in silence like she did.

The drive to school went by quickly, and she didn't remember getting there. Her mind wasn't on anything in the present. It was consumed with what would happen after school. She knew from the look on his face that Kyle hadn't decided one way or the other. If there was one thing that stressed her out, it was uncertainty.

Between her classes, Morgan searched the halls for him, and came up empty. Kyle was easy to notice in a crowd, but she didn't see him at all. She didn't have biology today, and that was their only shared class. She considered going down to the first floor, but she couldn't face a return to the scene of the crime. It was still too raw. The morning was a blur, and before she knew it, the bell rang.

She sat with the dancers at lunch, and it was awkward. Lucas was unusually silent and wouldn't look her in the eyes. Hector would talk, but kept his eyes on Tonisha. Surprisingly, Olivia didn't act any differently. She'd expected Kyle's number one fan to be a little distant, but she wasn't.

"Okay," Morgan announced, with her hands up to stop all conversation. "I want you all to know that I found Kyle after school and apologized."

"You did? Well, good for you!" Olivia said, and patted her elbow.

"Good for you, girl," Tonisha said. "That must have been hard."

Morgan snorted a quick laugh. "You know, it was and it wasn't." She linked her fingers and placed her hands on the table. "It took a lot of willpower to get out of the car and walk up to him. That was the hardest part."

"But not the apology?" Olivia asked.

Morgan shook her head, so that her long ponytail swayed back and forth. "No, I rehearsed it in my head a thousand times, but when I was looking at him … I forgot everything I wanted to say, and it came pouring out." She took a breath and let it out slowly. "That part came easy, because I *had* to tell him how sorry I was. Yeah, I had to do it."

Hector tilted his head towards her. "How did he take it?"

"He seemed to accept it, but he's not any happier. He doesn't think much of me."

Lucas sat back and gave her a hard look. "Not a big surprise. You do remember what you said, right?"

Morgan glared at him. "Of course! What is your problem, Lucas? Why can't you let this go?"

Lucas looked away from her as he thought. "You're right. I am taking this a little personally. Maybe it's because I've had plenty of people talking behind *my* back." His eyes lifted to meet her glare with one of his own. "I've been judged too."

There was a heavy silence as the dancers considered his words. There was little doubt that Lucas knew what he was talking about, and had experience with small-minded people. It was still going on.

Olivia was the one to ask the hard question. "So are you two still dancing together?"

Morgan shook her head as she reached for her drink. "We're supposed to rehearse tonight. I guess I'll find out."

The dancers were spread all over the utility room on their break, and Ms. Blake was in her usual spot completing paperwork. There were only ten minutes left in the rehearsal. That meant they would finish the break and rehearse until the end of the hour. Morgan sipped her water and toweled the sweat off her face. Olivia stood beside her, doing the same. Both were breathing hard from exertion. They made small talk, but kept looking up at the clock. Olivia couldn't help but notice. "There's still time," she managed to get out, between her deep breaths.

Morgan looked back at the clock. "Not likely."

"Okay! Back at it!" Tonisha called out to the dance crew.

They all slowly put down their water and towels, and made their way to their spots. Hector and Lucas both looked at the clock, and Lucas managed a sad smile of sympathy for Morgan, who looked down. Hector walked past and said, "There's still time, chica."

Morgan's eyes were fixed on the floor. She was trying to reconcile the fact that she'd lost a partner, but gained a purse. It didn't seem like a good trade.

"Hey, hey! You with us back there, Glamazon?" Tonisha called with a grin. The dance crew smiled or chuckled, while Morgan tilted her head and gave her friend a dirty look. She couldn't help but smile a little, but the words stuck with her. *Yeah, I'm in the back … like always.*

"Be careful at the end," Tonisha warned before starting the music. "We're not all ending at the same time. We need this right, and we need it tight!" The group laughed at yet another one of her motivational sayings, but the message was clear.

The music began, and the dance crew started their moves. Morgan continued to hit her marks and come to the front when required. Then it was a return to the back to pose, or frame the soloists in the middle. Her mind drifted. Maybe she should ask Tonisha if she could have a solo? When they first started rehearsing, she didn't want too much responsibility to take away from her ballroom work. That was looking less and less like an issue. Her ballroom days were done.

Her mind snapped back to what she was doing as the song neared its end. Tonisha had been clear, and she was listening carefully and counting to ensure precision. As the song hit its final beat, she was locked in her final pose. They all got it right.

"Very nice!" Ms. Blake called with a smile on her face. The dancers cheered and high-fived each other. Morgan stole a quick glance at the clock. The hour was up, and no sign of her partner. She took a deep breath and started walking towards Ms. Blake. It was time to tell her that her ballroom dreams were over, and not to file the paperwork for nationals. It was going to hurt to say out loud, and she hoped Ms. Blake didn't ask too many questions.

"Whoa!" she heard from the doorway, and quickly turned around. A small, red-headed dancer was on her backside, looking up at the young man who filled the doorway while her friends all laughed.

Kyle stood with a pained look on his face, reaching a hand to help her up. "Sorry. Are you okay?" he asked, looking down at her.

"My fault, I shouldn't have been running," she answered, with a mix of awe and terror on her face.

Her friends scooped her up, and they left as a pack of giggling sophomores. "Oh my God, Chloe!" one of her friends crowed as they headed down the hall.

Kyle entered the room, returning the greetings that Hector and Lucas gave him: a fist bump for each of the two dancers as they left.

Olivia ran across the room and plowed right into him with an awkward hug. Kyle couldn't help but laugh at the short, blonde-haired grappler, who looked up at him with a grin. "Glad you're still with us," she said.

Kyle gave a small shrug. "A deal's a deal."

Olivia's face clouded for a moment. "Whatever. Still nice to have you around," she said, and waved goodbye as she left the room. She sent a frown Morgan's way. It was one of her *What's going on?* looks.

Tonisha stopped to give him a sly look as she left. "Nice to have you back, *Gigantor*." she said with a smirk.

Kyle smiled at her. But there was no smile for Morgan as he moved closer. "Okay, I'm late because the principal wanted a quick chat when he saw me in the hall. I'm here. Let's not make a big deal about it."

"Okay," she agreed. She noticed he still wouldn't look her in the eyes. She would have killed for the smile that Olivia got.

Ms. Blake stood up and walked over to them. "I'm glad you two have worked out whatever it was between you." She paused a moment as she read their body language. Clearly, something remained unresolved. "You two *have* worked it out, right?"

"It is what it is," Kyle answered.

Morgan shot a look of disapproval at Kyle and turned to the teacher. "We're good! We'll be fine!" She pointed at the clock. "Time to get to work," she said, and ran to set up her phone and the speakers. Anything to distract Ms. Blake from that line of questioning.

Ms. Blake continued to look from Kyle, who was still looking at the ground, to Morgan and back. Her eyes narrowed and she opened her mouth to say something, and then she changed her mind. She held up a hand, as if to stop herself. "Okay then. I guess the show must go on."

Morgan trotted to the center of the room and held out her arms to her partner. "Thanks for being here, Kyle," she said, trying to catch his eye.

"Let's start. Can we go over the turns again?" His eyes were downcast, and his mouth was set in a straight line.

Morgan's face fell a little, as she could see that he still wanted little to do with her. "Sure, we can do that. Let me show you again."

Ms. Blake went back to her paperwork, and although she was happy to see the two youngsters working again, she had a nagging feeling. "So what am I missing here?" she said to herself, as she watched the teenagers work a turn.

CHAPTER 37

"That's right, remember to keep your hand flat for the turn," Morgan instructed. "It's a bit of a problem, because when your hand is up, it's hard for me to reach."

"Should I bend my elbow a little?" Kyle asked.

She stepped back and put a finger to her lips. "No, I think you should straighten your arm slowly and let me make space. Remember, you start the turn, but I'm the one who sells it."

Kyle nodded and initiated the turn by flattening his hand. Morgan put her own hand flat against his and completed her turn, with a hip-swinging set of steps that brought her back around into his frame. The rough calluses on his hand felt hard to her softer palms. She smiled. "That worked!"

"It's not working," Ms. Blake called from the corner.

Morgan's eyebrows raised and she regarded the teacher. "I thought that worked well."

"No, the whole thing," Ms. Blake explained. "You two. It's not working." The teacher put her hands on the top of the desk and pushed herself to her feet. She shook her head as she approached the two teens, her eyes on the ballroom champion. "Do you know what I mean, Morgan?"

"No, not really."

Ms. Blake pointed a hand at each of them. "This is not working. Think about what the Rumba is supposed to be."

Morgan spread her hands out, not understanding.

The teacher moved her glasses higher up her nose and gave her a small smile. "The Rumba is one of the most romantic and sensual dances in ballroom. It's meant to show a connection between two dancers."

The teenagers looked at each other awkwardly. Morgan shrugged. "Bernie and I never had any 'connection' and we did okay."

Ms. Blake held up a hand. "I am in no way saying that a couple should be romantically involved. I don't want to lose my job!"

They all laughed at that.

"No," she explained, "you and Bernie didn't have an inkling of interest in each other." She smiled at Morgan. "But you could fake it for the judges."

"We're just getting started," Morgan countered.

"True," Ms. Blake agreed. "But realistically, you have a three-minute song, and I think you're about a third of the way through this thing. You've got a couple of months to figure this out, and while your dancing is going well, you two are miles apart on a personal level."

Morgan folded her arms over her chest, looked at Kyle and back at Ms. Blake. "So you think we should quit?"

"Goodness, no! I'm offering to help."

Kyle and Morgan exchanged a glance, then looked back at the teacher.

"I don't get it," Kyle murmured.

The guidance counselor put her hands together and looked at both. "Okay, I don't know what's bothering you two, but that's in the past. We need to build some mutual respect and goodwill, right here and right now."

She had their attention. Both teenagers were hanging on her every word.

"I propose a simple exercise that neither of you should find too painful," Ms. Blake said.

Morgan looked at the ground, up at Kyle, and then back at the teacher. "Okay, I guess."

"Depends … uh, what do we have to do?" Kyle asked.

Ms. Blake smiled at him. "It's easy. First thing, face each other."

The two dancers looked at each other and slowly turned until they were face to face. Morgan had her hands folded over her chest and one hip out, looking away from her partner. Kyle had his hands jammed in the pockets of his track pants and was looking straight at the ground.

The guidance counselor almost laughed at their reluctance. "Okay, Morgan, uncross those hands. Kyle, hands out of your pockets."

The two dancers realized their posture was not helpful and composed themselves. Now they were standing tall and looking each other in the eye, albeit uncomfortably.

"Very good," the teacher encouraged. "Now, Morgan."

The teen looked at her with her brown eyes wide. "Yes?"

"I want you to look Kyle right in the eyes and say something nice about him."

Morgan looked at the floor as her mind raced.

"It can be anything," Ms. Blake added quickly. "Something you admire, a quality, even something that he has done for you or somebody else."

"Why am I going first?" she grumbled.

"Because someone has to," Ms. Blake answered. "Come on, you can do it. There must be *something* about your partner you appreciate."

Morgan took a deep breath in and let it out slowly. She looked up into her partner's eyes and said the first thing that came to mind. "You're noble."

"Good! That's a good quality." Ms. Blake said. "Explain what you mean."

Morgan shifted her feet and continued. "You're nice to Lucas, and you stood up for him when he needed it. You're honest and you aren't afraid to do what's right, even when that's kind of dangerous."

Ms. Blake nodded her understanding. "That is a good quality. I'm glad you could see that in our Mr. Branch." She turned to the young man standing in front of Morgan. "Okay, Kyle. Now that you've seen how it works, it's your turn."

Kyle looked at her quickly and then at Morgan. Her brown eyes locked with his, and he looked down at her. There was an awkward silence as he said nothing. Nothing at all.

Ms. Blake's eyebrows went up. "Um, Kyle? Can you please say something nice about Morgan?"

Kyle looked at the guidance counselor quickly and back at the dancer in front of him. Her brown eyes were hostile as he struggled to find the words. Was it that hard?

"She's ... uh ... she's ..."

"You can do it. Say what comes into your mind."

Kyle let out a sigh. "She's, uh ... clean."

Morgan recoiled and her mouth twisted into a scowl. "*Clean?* That's the only thing you can think to say after what I said?" She threw her hands up in disgust and marched to the other side of the room. She put her back to both and put her face in her hands.

Ms. Blake watched her go and her shoulders slumped. This was not going well. She looked at Kyle, who hadn't moved a muscle. "Can you explain why you used that word? Why is she 'clean,' Kyle?"

He shrugged. "It's not one thing. It's everything. When she gets close, I can smell her brand of soap, but it's much more than that."

Morgan brought her hands from her face and folded them on her chest. She still wasn't facing them, but she was instead listening intently. Where was he going with this?

Ms. Blake raised an eyebrow, intrigued. "Explain, Kyle."

He nodded. "Not a hair out of place, always well-dressed, and her makeup is always enough. She looks like she fell out of a magazine."

Morgan, sulking on the other side of the room, looked over her shoulder, but still faced away from him.

He rubbed his chin as he thought. "But it's not just her appearance, it's every move she makes. When she takes a step, it is right *where* it should be, *when* it should be. Every move she makes is immaculate. It's perfect in execution. When she does the hip-hop stuff. She makes it look so easy, but I bet it's hard. Even when she walks across the room it's smooth."

Morgan turned around to face him, her eyes wide. She unfolded her arms and went back to stand in front of him and look up into his face.

"Go on, Kyle," the teacher encouraged.

"Yeah, it's not that she's pretty. It's everything about her. So precise, determined, immaculate … every single move is *clean*. Very clean," he finished, raising his arms helplessly. He looked from Morgan to Ms. Blake. "I'm sorry if I did this wrong. I've never done anything like this."

"No, it's okay," Morgan said, her eyes soft. "I get it. That was nice of you to say." She poked him in the shoulder playfully. "I'm clean? It's weird, but I guess I can live with that."

He shook his head and the corners of his mouth moved into a smile. "Yeah, not my best answer."

Ms. Blake gave him a pat on the arm. "You did fine, young man." She went back to the other side of the room and sat down at her paperwork. "Okay, Mister Noble and Miss Clean, I think you can start rehearsing again."

Morgan grinned and looked up into the blue eyes of her partner. "From the top?"

He met her eyes. "Yeah, sure."

CHAPTER 38

Morgan sat in front of her vanity and finished applying her makeup. It didn't take long, as she didn't like to use much. She inspected herself when she was finished and liked what she saw. "Clean," she said with a grin.

She double-checked her ponytail—perfect—and came down the stairs for breakfast. Taylor was already there, laughing with a mouthful of cereal at something her father had said. He could always make her laugh, and seemed to delight in doing it while she ate.

Her mother was grinning too. "Oh, hi sweetie," she said, turning to her eldest daughter and looking her up and down. "You look nice today."

Morgan did a full turn to show off her black leggings and plain white sweatshirt. Her long, dark ponytail hung to the base of her spine.

"Very nice," her mother repeated. "You might need a haircut soon."

"Yeah," Taylor added for no good reason.

"Nope," Morgan said, pulling the ponytail in front of her for inspection. "It's kind of my trademark. It's clean."

"Well, I hope it's clean," her father said with a smirk. "You're costing us a fortune in shampoo."

"Ha ha," Morgan deadpanned as she grabbed a bowl and some cereal.

Taylor took a good look at her sister. "You're in a good mood this morning … for once."

Morgan ignored her and poured the milk into the bowl. Her parents looked at each other, and something unspoken went between them. "I take it school and dance are going well?" her mother asked.

"Mmm-hmm," Morgan mumbled with a full mouth.

Taylor's eyes grew mischievous, and she offered her own theory. "I think it's her dance partner. Morgan is crushing on Kyle!"

Her older sister shot her a dirty look. "*As if!*" she managed, once her mouth was empty.

"You *do* seem happier since he started working with you," her father mumbled, taking a sip of his coffee.

"Not you too, Dad!" Morgan protested. "If you'd seen the way he lives, you'd know that he is *not* my type."

Her mother frowned. "What's wrong with the 'way he lives?'"

"He lives on the second story of a barn," Morgan said, grimacing. "All he has is a bed, some books, and an old guitar. Even his dog is defective."

Her parents looked at each other, and she saw her father's jaw set. "Morgan, I expect better from you. Are you looking down your nose at the guy because he isn't well-off?"

Morgan put down her spoon and thought about that. "Not that he doesn't live in a mansion, but he lives in a barn. I mean, come on!"

Her father came closer and set his coffee cup down beside her. "Honey, I want you to listen to me." He looked at his younger daughter. "I'm glad you're here to get this too, Taylor." He paused as he gathered his thoughts. "Your mother and I work hard to provide for you, and we made some good choices along the way, but a lot of it is luck."

"Luck? Really?"

"Absolutely," her mother confirmed. "We always worked towards what we wanted, but we were lucky that nothing changed our course. It wouldn't take much."

"Like what?" Taylor asked.

Her father looked down, and then at both his daughters. "So many things. An illness, an accident, a bad investment, someone dying." He took a deep breath and let it out. "If your mother or I got really sick, that would have taken a lot of our money away. Maybe all of it."

Their mother nodded her head. "If your father didn't come from a family that could help pay for his education, he would not have been able to become such an accomplished lawyer today."

"You would not be living where we're living now," Mr. Laflamme explained. "And ... no convertible," he said with a wink at Morgan.

"Yeah, okay, but a barn?" Morgan countered.

"Let's look at that," her father said, pointing at her. "He probably doesn't pay much rent for it."

Morgan shrugged. "He says he doesn't pay anything."

Her father's eyes widened. "That's even better." He stood up and poured himself another coffee from the carafe. "Living like that allows him to bank every penny he makes at work. He's not lazy, he's making sacrifices to save money. Smart guy."

"Can I live in a barn?" Taylor asked.

"Taylor, *be serious*," Morgan admonished her.

Her little sister stuck her tongue out.

"Taylor, stop that. No, Mr. Branch is not a slob or a lowlife," her father explained. "He lost his father when he was young, and his mother perished not long after that. He lived with his grandmother until she passed away this year. He's had little help from anyone, and he's doing the best he can. No criminal record, either. It would have been easy for a guy like him to make some bad choices, but he didn't."

Morgan put her hands on the table, her eyes bulging and her mouth hanging open. "You're not guessing about this!" She pointed an accusing finger at her father. "You had him checked out, didn't you?!"

Her father chuckled and took a sip of the hot coffee. "A big MMA fighter like that? Dancing with my darling daughter? You bet I did."

There was a heavy silence as that confession sunk in. "I'm out of here," Morgan growled, and she leapt out of her chair, grabbed her backpack and keys, and headed for the front door.

Her family watched as she left, thinking better of saying anything. When they heard the front door slam, Taylor turned to her father. "Did you actually pay someone to investigate him?"

Mr. Laflamme nodded.

"That is *so cool!*" she gushed, grinning ear to ear.

Her parents laughed. "Come on, I don't want you to be late for school," her mother said. Taylor went to get her things, while Mrs. Laflamme gave her husband a warm embrace. "I think it's kind of cool, too."

He laughed. "And Morgan?"

"She'll get over it." She looked at the front door and then back at him. "One day."

CHAPTER 39

Morgan and Olivia were walking to biology class, students filing by on either side of them as they strolled. Morgan was filling in her friend on the morning adventure at her house. "Can you believe that?" Morgan finished.

"Actually, yeah," Olivia answered.

Morgan looked down at her. "That doesn't surprise you?"

"Nope. You remember Rhonda Miller, the pretty redhead that was a senior last year?"

"Yeah, I do. Why?"

Olivia opened her blue eyes wide. "Well, when her father found out she was dating the school drug dealer, Arnold Baker, he had him slapped with a restraining order."

"No way!" Morgan said with her mouth hanging open.

"Oh, yeah. I kind of understand it."

"Wow," Morgan mumbled as they walked.

"Say, how's rehearsal going with that big hunky partner of yours? Are you two getting along any better?" Olivia asked.

Morgan considered telling her about Ms. Blake's exercise and Kyle's unique compliment, but she hesitated and decided not to. It was weird. They shared everything, but she wanted that moment to be her own. "We're doing better."

"Are you talking about the dancing or getting along?" Olivia asked as they got to class.

They walked into Ryckman's classroom and looked around at the other students, who were seated at the large black tables that made up the science room. They saw that Lucas and Kyle were already sitting and Lucas was talking to Kyle. When the two young men saw them enter, they all greeted each other. Morgan, Olivia, and Lucas waved, while Kyle gave them both a solemn nod.

"Both," Morgan said as she sat on her stool.

"Oh, I'll meet you in the cafeteria," Olivia whispered, as the teacher entered the room. "There's something I have to do. Save me a seat."

Morgan entered the cafeteria, and found she was alone. The tables were all full of chattering students, some eating and others facing each other in conversation. The noise was an ocean in her ears that gave her pause. Nobody from the dance team had made it to lunch yet. That created a challenge. Did she sit where Kyle usually sat, and the dancers would join him? Or should she sit where the dancers sat all year and hope that Olivia came there first?

Almost in answer, she heard someone from the football team shout, "Hey, Laflamme! You still looking for a man?" Mocking laughter came from the other players.

That made her decision for her. She shot a dirty look at the group of young men, which only amplified their amusement, and strode to the other end of the cafeteria to sit closer to the food service area. Olivia would have to find her. She sat at the large, grey-topped table where Kyle usually sat, and there were plenty of seats.

As it was, Lucas and Hector were the first members of the dance team who found her. "Hey, chica," Hector offered with a smile, as he sat with her. He wore his usual jeans and clean white t-shirt.

"Hey, Morgan," Lucas said, as he sat on the other side of the table.

"Hi, guys," she returned. It was easy to smile now that the drama was over. But it was then that she saw Olivia, and she wasn't alone.

The pretty blonde was looking up at Kyle, chattering away as he carried a tray of food. He was wearing the same baggy workout gear, and Olivia was much more fashionable in her black skirt and blue sweater. When they got to the cashier, she pulled out some cash and paid for everything on the tray.

When Hector and Lucas saw Morgan's wide eyes, they looked where she was staring, and Lucas turned back to her and grinned. "Looks like our 'Betty' is interested in our new buddy. I wonder how 'Veronica' feels about that?"

Morgan snapped out of it and looked down at her lunch. "None of my business. Why should I care?"

Hector looked at Lucas and raised his eyebrows. "I think it's *romantic*. Yes! That's the word I was looking for."

"Romantic, yeah." Lucas echoed.

"It won't work, losers," Morgan said, as she took a bite of her sandwich.

The two young men couldn't help but laugh. "Forgive us, Morgan," Lucas chuckled. "You're such a together person, we don't have much chance to mess with you."

"True," Hector agreed, "we were trying to stir it up."

Morgan shrugged and looked up as the couple arrived at their table. Olivia was smiling and Kyle wore a pleasant expression. They sat and greetings were exchanged. "I was talking with Kyle, trying to get him to invite us back to his place," said Olivia.

"You're trying to get more time with Roscoe?" Morgan guessed with a tilt of her head.

"Who's Roscoe?" Hector asked.

"Kyle's dog."

"He's not actually my dog," Kyle protested.

"Doesn't seem like he knows that," Olivia said, and started taking food off the tray she shared with Kyle.

Morgan gave her best friend the "what gives?" look. Olivia picked it up and kept talking. "I made a deal with Kyle," she said, patting the big teenager's shoulder.

Morgan stiffened with her choice of words. "What do you mean?"

Olivia's blue eyes danced. "Oh, I wanted to chat with him and get to know our new member of the dance team a bit better. I offered to buy him a roast beef sandwich and a drink for his time." She gestured to the food in front of Kyle. "He accepted. Isn't that great?"

Hector and Lucas shrugged. "Sure, I guess," Lucas said, playing along. Morgan stared at her best friend. Where was she going with this?

"Okay, Kyle. My first question! Did you say you don't have to pay anything to stay where you live?"

Kyle nodded. "Yes, my uncle lets me stay there for nothing. He travels a lot, and I look after the place while he's gone."

"That's a good deal," Olivia said, with a quick look at Morgan.

"Your own place? No parents?" Hector asked.

Kyle nodded.

"Pretty sweet deal," Hector said.

Kyle shrugged and took a quick sip. "My parents passed away years ago. He's the only family I have left. Not much choice."

Hector winced. "Oh, sorry, hermano. I didn't know."

Kyle waved a dismissive hand and shook his head as he took a bite of his sandwich. "Old news," he mumbled with a full mouth.

"That is *so* sad." Olivia said, looking at her best friend. "That's sad, right, Morgan?"

Morgan took a breath to calm herself. "Yes, I'm sorry to hear that."

Olivia didn't seem to care about her answer. "And you work, right? At a garage, I think?"

"Jake's Auto," Kyle confirmed. "Good guy, good work."

"Hmm," Olivia hummed as she thought. "Well, if you don't pay rent, what are you doing with the money you earn?"

"I bank it for college," he answered, as he finished the sandwich.

"Oh, that's cool," Lucas encouraged. "What do you want to study, biology?"

Kyle snorted. "No, English. I love reading and writing."

"You're good at biology, too." Lucas said.

"Thanks, but that's to keep my average up. Without good marks, I'm not getting into any school."

"One more question," Olivia said with a grin.

"Shoot."

"Do you have a girlfriend?" she giggled.

Morgan rolled her eyes and looked disapprovingly at her friend. Could she be any more obvious?

Kyle blushed slightly as Lucas and Hector choked on their laughter. "No time for any of that," he explained. "School comes first." He stood up. "Thanks for lunch, Olivia. I've got a meeting with Mrs. Edgehill. I have to go."

"Your English teacher?" Hector asked. "I thought you were good at English?"

Kyle smiled. "I am. I want to make sure I understand our assignment. I need to keep that mark up most of all." He looked at Olivia. "Thanks again."

"You're welcome," she said with a bright smile. "Great talking to you!"

He waved and walked away. "Interesting guy," Hector said with a smirk. "There's a brain on top of all that brawn."

"Yes, I'm sure he has lots of interesting things to say," Olivia mused, looking at Morgan as she said it.

Morgan stared back, her eyes hard and her mouth set in a grim line.

Hector and Lucas exchanged a glance. They knew there was more to this, but it was not for their ears. Lucas put his hands on the table and stood up. "Excuse me too," he said, looking at Hector. "I'm meeting Tonisha in the lab."

Hector stood up too. "I've got a couple of things I gotta do. Hasta luego," he announced cheerfully. The two dancers left together without a backward glance.

When they were out of earshot, Morgan gave her friend a hard look. "Alright, out with it. What are you up to?"

Olivia sat back and folded her arms over her chest. "It's interesting. When Kyle said that he had some kind of deal with you, that got me to thinking."

"What? What are you talking about?" Morgan said, exasperated.

Olivia pointed a finger at her. "You forget that I was there when he turned you down flat. It was done. His answer wasn't 'no,' it was never."

Morgan sat back and folded her arms, mirroring her friend. "So? He changed his mind."

"No, there's more to it than that. I asked him when we were in line if he liked dancing with you. He said he thought it was okay, but it wasn't like he had much choice."

"I have no idea why he said that," Morgan muttered.

"I asked him what he meant," Olivia continued. "Know what he said?"

"No."

"He said that I should take it up with you," Olivia replied.

"It's nothing. I asked him again to dance, told him why, and he agreed," Morgan said. "That's it."

Olivia looked at her. "We've been friends a long time, right?"

"A long time," Morgan confirmed.

"You're a good friend, Morgan, but you've always been crap at lying."

Morgan stood up and looked down at her, eyes blazing. "Olivia!"

Olivia stood up too and looked up at her friend. She pointed right at her. "Don't worry, Morgan. I'll find out what *really* happened. I always do." Then she turned on her heel and walked out of the cafeteria.

Morgan stood there blinking, watching her leave.

CHAPTER 40

"That was good," Morgan said, as she and Kyle finished their routine and the music ended. "Very good!"

He let go of her and nodded his head.

Ms. Blake was in her usual spot, but instead of poring over papers, she had a laptop on the desk. She would occasionally look up to watch the dancers.

Morgan brought her hands together. "Okay, we're pretty solid on the Rumba. Might be time to look at the next dance." She pointed both fingers at Kyle. "I'm thinking about Salsa next."

Kyle tilted his head at her and narrowed his eyes. "Hey, you said we were only going to do one dance. One! That was the deal."

"Well," Morgan answered, looking sideways, "there's a little more to it than that."

"Like what?"

"Well, we have to learn five styles of Latin dance and—"

"FIVE!" he interrupted. He shook his head and raised a hand to stop her. "I'll never learn five of these well enough to compete at a national championship."

Morgan walked to him and put her hand on his shoulder. "You can. You can do it!"

"No, he can't," said a voice from the side. Both students turned around to see that Ms. Blake had left her desk and was walking up to them.

Morgan stared at her. "I think if we double our rehearsal time—"

"No, it's not about him learning the steps." Ms. Blake walked up to Kyle and smiled pleasantly at him. "You have impressed me, young man." She turned and pointed at Morgan. "And you've been an amazing teacher. But there's no chance of winning a national championship like this."

Morgan stared at her, as if she'd been slapped. "You think we should give up?"

Ms. Blake held up both her hands to stop her. "You misunderstand. You can still learn, you can still compete, but not like this."

"You're right, I don't understand," Morgan answered.

The guidance counselor took off her glasses and smiled at them. "Even if Kyle learns all the steps, and you go compete, you're not making the top three with what you've got now."

Morgan crossed her arms and shrugged. "Why not?"

Ms. Blake continued to smile. "You work well together, but there's no connection. There's no passion."

Kyle held up a hand. "Whoa! We're not going to do another one of those things where we have to say something nice, are we? I embarrassed myself enough last time."

The two women broke up laughing, and Kyle had to chuckle. "No," Ms. Blake reassured him. "We're not doing that. But honestly, I thought you did a fine job."

"What are you suggesting?" Morgan asked.

Ms. Blake brought her hands together. "Listen, if you can't succeed competing in Latin, go another direction."

"You're thinking American Smooth?" Morgan asked with a frown. "I don't see that being any easier. And we still have the issue with time."

"That's why I'm not suggesting American Smooth." She looked from Kyle to Morgan and smiled wide. "I have one word for you. Cabaret."

Kyle scowled. "I have no idea what that means."

"I do," Morgan said in a small voice. "Cabaret ... of course." She looked at Ms. Blake and shook her head. "But they don't offer that for the eighteen- and under dancers at nationals."

Ms. Blake wagged a finger at her. "Ah, but I checked their website. Says they're offering it for the first time this year."

"No!" Morgan almost shouted.

"Yes!" Ms. Blake answered back, with a shout of her own.

Kyle shook his head and held up both his hands. "What's going on?"

Morgan laughed, leaning on one hip as she looked at him. "It's one dance, and the rules are different."

"There are lifts, and it's much more theatrical," Ms. Blake explained.

"Kyle's big enough to lift me, and we can explore all kinds of tricks," Morgan said, her mind already working.

Ms. Blake pointed at her to show she was right. "And although I don't know what's keeping you at odds with each other, it won't matter if you use that in the dance."

"Tell a story—one of two people who are in conflict," Morgan agreed.

"Yes! And you can do so much more with the costumes. It opens up many new possibilities," Ms. Blake added.

There was silence as Morgan considered it. "Yeah, it might work."

"And it's only one song?" Kyle asked, an eyebrow raised.

Both women nodded.

"Then I'm all for it," Kyle said with a grin.

The teacher and the dancer laughed. Morgan ran to grab her bag. "Rehearsal is over. I have a lot of research to do tonight." She looked at Kyle and Ms. Blake. "Can we do this again tomorrow?"

"I can," Ms. Blake answered. "I can't wait to see this come together."

Kyle rubbed his chin. "I can go to work now so I can make up the hours. Yeah, I can be here tomorrow."

"Okay then," the tall dancer announced. "Tomorrow it is!"

CHAPTER 41

"Higher!" Morgan grunted, as she spread her arms and looked at the ceiling with a graceful arch in her back.

"Okay, okay," Kyle muttered, and straightened the arm in the middle of her back, taking her closer to the low ceiling. His other hand tightened on the ankle he held for control. A twinge of pain distracted her.

"Ow! Easy on the grip!" she squealed.

"Sorry."

Ms. Blake looked up from her paperwork. "That's it! A beautiful lift."

"Down!" Morgan commanded, and Kyle lowered her to the floor. She rubbed her ankle. "That's going to be a bruise." She glared at Kyle. "I thought you lifted people up all the time."

He smirked. "I do. Then I throw them on the floor. We can always do that if you like."

Morgan stood tall. "And you'd enjoy that?"

There was silence as he considered the question. His eyes grew cold. "Wouldn't lose any sleep over it."

Morgan's eyes widened, and her hands balled into fists. "Oh *really!* So that's the way you'd like it to go?"

Ms. Blake suddenly appeared between them. "Okay, both of you take a breath. You've been working hard and you're getting punchy." She playfully tapped Kyle's shoulder. "You're doing well with this. I know it's new."

Kyle's face softened, and he thanked her quietly.

The teacher turned to the fuming dancer. "Morgan, you're still doing a great job teaching. You couldn't see what I saw. You gave him all the important points, and that lift was impressive."

Morgan shifted her weight and relaxed. "Thank you."

"It's not just the height," Ms. Blake explained. "It was the pose you struck. It's going to stay in the judges' minds." She looked at her watch and clapped her hands together. "Okay kids, I have to make a phone call, and I'm going to grab some more paperwork. You're going to be on your own for a bit."

"You want us to keep rehearsing?" Morgan asked.

The guidance counselor smiled. "No, I want you to talk. I want you to talk it out and stop bickering, because it's going to keep you from succeeding. You're a striking couple, and you can get it done. It would be a shame if some bad feeling kept you from reaching your potential."

The two teenagers looked at each other sheepishly, and then at the floor. Morgan folded her arms over her chest, while Kyle stuffed his hands in his pockets.

Without another word, Ms. Blake walked to the door as she fished her phone out of her pocket. She pushed it open and was gone. All that remained was an awkward silence.

"Well?" Morgan said, still looking at the ground.

"Well what?"

"Well," she said, and let out a sigh. "Are you going to tell me what your problem is?"

He looked at her, his jaw clenched. "It's amazing. It's like you're not aware of anything you've done."

Her eyes flashed. "Come on, Kyle! I apologized for those things I said. You know I was being outrageous. I didn't mean any of it."

He shook his head and looked up in frustration. "So you're not going to consider the fact that you blackmailed me into doing this? Of course you won't."

"Look, if you had a problem with it, you wouldn't be here."

He took a step closer to her and folded his arms. "You think I should have chosen jail time and a criminal record over ballroom dancing?"

Her eyes goggled. "Jail?"

"Yeah, assault with a weapon." He took a step closer and looked down at her. "Those liars were more than willing to say that knife was mine, and if a witness was good enough to come forward, I wouldn't have had a worry in the world."

Morgan lifted her chin defiantly. "A witness *did* come forward."

"Only if she got what she wanted first. Because she only cares about what *she* wants."

"That's … that's not true," Morgan stuttered, as her face colored red.

Kyle turned his back to her and walked away. "Oh, that's true all right. No surprise to me. Pretty typical for your kind."

"My *kind*?" she snarled. "What exactly do you mean when you say that?"

"Rich, spoiled kids," he replied with a shrug. "Nothing new."

Morgan's mouth opened in outrage. "That is *not* who I am!"

"It isn't?"

"NO!"

He turned to face her, and a slow smile came over his lips, but his eyes were fierce. "Then why don't you tell me what you do for other people?"

She frowned. "What?"

"Go on," he said, pointing at her. "Tell me what you do for anybody else. Or is it always all about you?"

She stared at him. "I … I do things for other people."

"Like what?"

"I, well, I …" Her mind raced, but she didn't come to an answer.

"See? If you actually did anything for anyone but yourself, you would be able to tell me in a second."

Morgan let out a sigh. "Okay, I'm well-off. I admit it. So what?"

He walked up to her again. "You're rich, and you have everything handed to you, and you look down your nose at someone like me." He snorted a laugh. "The irony is that you don't know what you don't know."

"Oh?" She stuck out one hip and put her hand on it. "Why don't you give me an example?"

"Sure," he answered. "You see that car I drive around in?"

"Yeah, what about it?"

"You think it's junk. It's a heap, right?"

"It needs a paint job and it's a Volvo," she answered, making a face. "What is there to know about that?"

He pointed a finger at her. "You don't know that I swapped the engine for a smaller Ford six-cylinder engine and rebuilt the interior."

Morgan blinked. "So?"

He chuckled. "So it's reliable, easy to work on, parts are cheaper, and it rarely breaks down. It's also comfortable. That's more than you can say about that little lemon you drive around."

She glared at him. "I love that car. You're jealous because you can't afford one."

"No," he said with a smile and a slow shake of his head. "If I *did* have a father who could buy one for me, I wouldn't get it. Mine's better."

"I could buy that car for half of what mine cost," she countered.

"Yeah, your *father* could," he replied. "So it doesn't mean anything to you. I've worked for mine. It drives smooth and it's great on gas. But more than that, I have pride in what I've created and it has meaning. Your car, and most things in your life, are disposable."

She stared at him, not knowing what to say.

He pointed to himself. "And I'm disposable too. If my well-being mattered to you at all, you would have gone right to the principal or the cops and told them what you knew."

Morgan shrugged. "I saw a way to get a partner and help you. I figured it was good for both of us."

"You still don't get it. You live in your beautiful house with your awesome family, and things are just handed to you. And still you take advantage of a guy like me, and I don't have any of that."

Morgan ran her hands through her hair and smoothed her ponytail. She let out a sigh, looking her partner in the eye. "So that's it? What I did to get you to dance with me, and the fact that I'm just another 'rich kid?'"

He nodded. "Yeah, that sums it up."

"Okay, I get it. But now you're doing what you accused me of doing."

"How's that?"

"You call anyone with money a 'rich kid' and think we're thoughtless and selfish. Maybe I do have some things to learn, but did it ever occur to you that I didn't have a choice either?"

He rubbed his chin as he stared at her. "What do you mean?"

She walked closer and looked up at her partner. "Did you ever consider that I didn't have any more choice in the matter than you did? Rich kids don't have any more choice about their situation than poor kids. You're as judgmental as I was. You judged me by what I have, and I judged you by what you don't have. It's the same thing."

Kyle's eyes opened wide. He looked left, then right, but he never answered her, as their conversation was interrupted by the door opening.

"Uh, guys?" a voice came weakly from the door. They turned to look at the speaker and froze in shock.

There in the doorway stood a small figure, covered in blood. He had some crumpled paper in one hand and clutched the doorknob with the other. His teal dress shirt was torn, and his khaki pants were spattered with blood and water.

"LUCAS!" Morgan screamed, and brought her hands to her mouth.

Kyle ran to the door and caught him as he fell.

"I'm … I'm sorry," the dancer said faintly, as he held up the papers and passed out.

"Oh my God!" Morgan moaned.

"Look for Ms. Blake!" Kyle snapped. "Is she there?"

She quickly stepped around Lucas and felt sick as she saw the blood on the tiles. Looking left and right, she came back, shaking her head. "No sign of her."

Kyle hefted Lucas into his arms. "He needs a hospital *right now!*" he barked. "Grab your bag and my hoodie from the table. We're going to take him."

CHAPTER 42

"No! We should call an ambulance," she protested as Kyle stood up. "There's no time! He's hurt bad, and we're talking about a head injury here. Let's go!" he commanded. He shouldered open the door and hustled down the hallway, carrying the unconscious young man.

Morgan ran ahead of him and opened the door to the parking lot. Kyle charged down the stairs and through the nearly empty lot. When he stood beside the grey Volvo, he paused. "The keys are in my hoodie," he called to Morgan.

She started fumbling through the pockets, found the silver keys, and frowned. "Where's the remote?"

"Find the key with the round end. Put that in the lock and turn it," he said.

She found the right key and inserted it in the driver's door. She turned it the wrong way, realized her mistake, and got it right. She saw the door lock rise with a thump and opened it wide.

"Good work. Now reach around and lift the passenger lock."

"*Gah!* How old is this car?" she snarled, as she hurried to get it done.

"Old," he answered as she opened the rear passenger door. "Hold the door open for me."

She did as she was asked, and Kyle leaned in with the unconscious teenager in his arms. He laid him down carefully and reached a hand back. "Give me the hoodie."

Morgan didn't think as she gave him the hoodie. She stood with her eyes wide and her mouth slightly open, her heart racing.

She saw Kyle place the hoodie gently under Lucas's head and retreat slowly until he was standing beside her. He took the keys from her and pointed to the other side of the car. "Get in."

Morgan looked at the blood all over her dance partner's shirt and arms. There was a stain on his chin. She paled and grew dizzy.

"Morgan!" he barked. "Get in the car. I need you to help get me to the hospital."

She snapped out of it and ran to the other side of the car. She tried to open it, but it was locked.

"Just a minute," Kyle said, as he sat in the driver's side. He effortlessly reached across the front seat and pulled up the lock on her side.

Morgan opened the door and sat down quickly. Out of habit, she closed the door and put on her seatbelt. A coppery, sticky and salty smell filled her nose, and her stomach felt queasy.

He fired up the car, grabbed the shifter, and worked the pedals. The tires squeaked as he reversed hard, and protested more as he shifted gear and jumped forward. The grey Volvo flew through the parking lot.

"The smell …" Morgan said, bringing her hand to her mouth and nose.

"That's the smell of blood," Kyle explained. "It's distinct. Smell it once and you never forget it. Which way do I turn?"

"Right," she said and pointed.

The car turned quickly and thundered down the road. Kyle effortlessly shifted the gears. This was his car, and he knew exactly how to drive it. She suddenly understood everything he liked about it. It was unique, and performed well.

They were lucky at the next light, but had to slow for a red. "We're not waiting for this," he warned her.

"What? You can't—"

He ignored her as he came to a stop, looked both ways, and spun the wheels, jumping through the intersection. A few angry honks came from the other drivers waiting for their turn.

"Are we close?" he asked.

"Y-yeah, next left turn," she stammered.

He jammed hard on the brake and turned equally as hard. She felt like they were on two wheels as they rounded the turn, but they could see the hospital in the distance.

"Great," he said with a grim smile. "Listen, I'm going to pull right into the emergency parking, and they're not going to be happy about that."

"What do you want me to do?"

"Don't take 'no' for an answer, and give me time to get Lucas out and into the hospital. After that, nothing else matters."

"Okay."

They approached the entrance of the semi-circle meant for ambulances, and he rolled right up to the enormous sliding glass doors. Kyle released his seatbelt and jumped out of the car.

As he'd predicted, a portly security guard hurried up to them. He looked Kyle up and down, seeing the blood on his shirt, face, and hands. "Excuse me! You can't park there!"

Morgan hopped out of her side of the car as Kyle moved to open the rear passenger door. The guard approached Kyle, but she hurried to intercept him.

"No, it's okay!" she said with her hands up.

The security guard looked in her wide brown eyes. He blinked and shook his head. "No, miss. This is for ambulances only."

Kyle had opened the car and delicately removed Lucas, carrying him like a child.

When the guard took one look at the amount of blood on Lucas, he had a change of heart. "Oh my God," he muttered, and nodded his head. "Okay, follow me, young man. Can you carry him on your own?"

"I've got him," Kyle replied. "Let's go!"

The guard pushed by Morgan, Kyle right behind him. Morgan's eyes were still staring and wild as she followed them.

They went through the sliding glass doors, and the security guard called to the triage nurse. "We need a gurney fast. This guy is in trouble!"

The blonde nurse stood up, and her eyes goggled when she saw the condition of Lucas and the athlete who carried him. She grabbed the phone, and a couple of orderlies arrived with a gurney and a doctor in tow.

Kyle gently lowered the inert Lucas onto the white gurney, and blood stained the pillow as he removed the hoodie from under his head.

A tall doctor with glasses and short hair came and started pulling on some blue rubber gloves. "How did this happen?" he asked Kyle and Morgan.

"Don't know," Kyle said. "We found him like this."

The doctor nodded as he rolled back Lucas's eyelid and shined a small light into his eye. "Are you family?"

"No," Morgan answered.

The doctor nodded again. "You'd better call them and get them down here," he said to the couple. He turned to the orderlies, "Take him." They started rolling Lucas down the hall.

Kyle and Morgan were moving to follow when they were stopped by a nurse. She held up a hand. "Sorry, kids," she said, in a voice that was kind but firm. "That's as far as you go."

"Is he … is he going to be okay?" Morgan asked.

"That's not up to us," the nurse replied. "Can you get his family here? That's important."

"Hector!" said Kyle. "Do you have Hector's number? We can call him and let him do the work."

Morgan nodded and fumbled in her bag for her phone. She pulled up Hector on the contact list and called him. "Please answer," she prayed.

A moment later, she heard a click and Hector saying, "Hola, chica! What up?"

"Hector! Lucas is in the hospital. Me and Kyle drove him here."

"Whoa! What happened?"

"He was beaten up," Kyle growled, a dark look on his face.

Morgan looked at him and then at the ground. "Kyle thinks he was beaten up. There's blood everywhere." It was then that she noticed the blood on Kyle's shirt; his arms and the hoodie were soaked in it. "So much …" she trailed off.

Kyle gently took the phone from her. "Hector! Can you get in touch with Lucas's family?"

"Damn straight!" Hector replied.

"Good. Call anyone you can and get them down here. This can't wait for anything."

"So it's bad," Hector asked.

"Yeah, real bad. Get them here, buddy."

"Yo, hermano … is he gonna make it?"

"Don't know. Don't know anything," Kyle answered.

"Damn. I'm saying goodbye. I'll find the family. I got this!"

"Thanks, brother," Kyle said with a grim, tight-lipped smile. He ended the call and handed the phone back to Morgan.

His hands were covered in blood, and she noticed some was on the phone. "So much blood …" she almost whispered.

Kyle's eyes searched hers. "Morgan, are you okay?"

She didn't answer him, so he put his hand on her shoulder and gently turned her towards a seating area. "Come on, partner," he encouraged, as he slowly walked her over and sat her down. He sat beside her.

Her eyes were tearing up. "Oh my God. Poor Lucas!"

The security guard approached them, and he had a partner now. "Hey, that car has to move. We need room for the ambulances!"

Kyle tossed him the keys. "Park it wherever you want, guys. I need to stay here with her." He gestured with his head towards Morgan, who was wearing a thousand-yard stare.

The security guards looked at each other. The new guard shrugged, and then they both looked at the young woman. The first guard sighed. "Okay, cool." They turned and walked away.

Kyle turned his attention back to Morgan, throwing a big arm over her shoulders to reassure her. "You did great, Morgan!"

"What?"

"No, you were awesome. We did what we had to do. We got him here as fast as we could, and now it's out of our hands. The doctor is taking care of Lucas, and Hector will get his family here. I know he will."

"So now what?" she asked.

He gave her a kind smile. "Now I take care of you."

She sniffed back some tears, held up her hand, and said, "No, no, I'm okay. I'm okay. It's just … so much *blood!* I can tell you've seen this before, but it's new to me."

"Yeah," he agreed. He took her hand in both of his and looked her in the eyes. "You know, Morgan, it's alright not to be okay with this."

Morgan held his blue-eyed gaze. She let out a sigh and leaned into him. The tears came and she started to cry.

He pulled her closer and clenched his jaw as his own vision clouded.

"Are you mad?" she asked.

"Yeah, I'm mad," he confirmed. "But mostly I feel awful for Lucas. Poor guy."

"Me too," she agreed. The two teenagers sat in the waiting area, him holding her and she letting him. Neither said a word. They didn't need to.

CHAPTER 43

Half an hour later, Hector arrived with a small, older woman on his arm. She was crying, and he was talking to her in Spanish.

Kyle pointed them out to Morgan, and the two teenagers stood and approached them. Hector steered the distraught woman toward the pair, and the second the older woman saw the bloodstains that had darkened brown on Kyle's shirt, she erupted. "Dios mio!" she cried, and Hector comforted her.

"This is Lucas's mother," Hector explained, as Morgan hugged him and Kyle gave him a fist-bump. "Guys, what the hell happened?"

Morgan and Kyle looked at each other. He waited for her to do the talking.

"We were rehearsing and he walked in, covered in blood," she said with a shudder.

"You think he got beat up?" Hector asked.

"Yeah," Kyle answered. "That wasn't an accident." He flexed a big fist in front of his face. "I have a pretty good idea who did it, too."

Morgan grabbed his arm. "Kyle, don't do anything crazy, okay?"

He nodded his agreement, but his eyes burned.

"Oh, man. Let me explain it to his madre," said Hector. He turned to the unfortunate woman on his arm, speaking in Spanish and gesturing at the two teenagers in front of him. She asked a question of her own and pointed at them.

"You guys brought him?" Hector asked.

"Yeah, together," Kyle answered.

Hector spoke to the woman for a moment, and she suddenly reached out a trembling hand to shake theirs. Morgan placed her delicate hand in the older woman's gnarled, arthritis-ridden paw. She shook vigorously and then reached for Kyle. His big mitt enveloped her entire hand and some of her arm.

"She's grateful and thanks God for you," Hector explained.

"Don't thank us yet," Kyle said grimly. "Come on over and help her talk to the nurse. I have to get Morgan home."

"My parents were expecting me a while ago. They'll probably start worrying." she admitted.

They walked over to the triage nurse, and Hector translated for Lucas's mother. Kyle looked at Morgan and gestured with his head toward the door.

"We have to go. Thank you so much for coming, Hector," she said with a pat on his arm.

"No, it's cool. I'll take it from here. I'll see you guys at lunch tomorrow and fill you in," he promised, and turned his attention back to the nurse.

They found the car after asking the security guard where he'd planted it. Turned out he parked in an employee spot he knew would be open, so they didn't have to pay any parking fees. They thanked him, and he commended them for helping Lucas.

When they got to the car, Kyle held up a hand. "Give me a minute." He reached in and fired it up, then wound down the driver's window and walked around the car to do the same to the passenger side. "That's as good as it gets now."

Morgan got in slowly and looked at the dark stains on the backseat. "Your car ..."

"Is just a thing. I'll try and deal with the stains tomorrow," he reassured her. "Let's get you home."

He backed the car up. "Maybe you should text your parents and let them know that you're alright," he said as he started forward.

"Good idea. I'll make sure they know that we had to go to the hospital, but we're okay." She grabbed her phone and started texting.

"They're going to be a little freaked out. We're going to have to calm them down."

"You think?" Morgan asked.

When they arrived at her house, her entire family was waiting on the front lawn.

Kyle grinned. "There's your answer."

She couldn't help but laugh. "Maybe you should get out slowly. You're a mess."

"I hear that."

She got out of the Volvo and her family walked toward her. "Are you okay?" Taylor burst out before anyone else had a chance to talk.

Morgan held up both hands to stop them from saying any more. "I'm fine, and so is Kyle."

"What were you doing at the hospital?" her mother asked.

"As I tried to explain in my text, another dancer got hurt." As she tried to reassure them, Kyle stepped out of the driver's seat.

"Oh my God!" Taylor shrieked when she saw all the blood that had dried on the young man. "Kyle! What happened?"

He too held up both his hands to slow her down. "None of this is from me. I'm fine."

"Well, somebody isn't," her father said.

"You got that right."

Morgan explained that they'd been rehearsing when the bloodied Lucas came through the door, and that they'd taken a wild ride to the hospital.

Her mother hugged her. "I am so proud of you."

She smiled in spite of herself. "It was a team effort. Kyle and I did it together."

Kyle gave her a small smile. "I couldn't have done it without you. No way." He looked at her father. "Mr. Laflamme, I was thinking you and I could go pick up Morgan's car. It's probably still in the parking lot."

"Oh! I completely forgot," Morgan said, and brought her hand to her forehead. "I can go with you, Kyle."

Her father placed a hand on her shoulder and gave her a kiss on the cheek. "You've done enough for one day." He took the keys from her and looked at Kyle. "You don't mind giving me a lift there?"

"Not at all. It's on my way home."

"Just a moment," her father announced. "There's at least one thing I can do for you." He went back in the house and they watched him go.

"You sure you're okay, Kyle?" Taylor asked, her eyes wide.

Kyle put a big hand on her shoulder. "Don't worry, tiger. Nobody touched me."

"Here," their father called, as he jogged back out of the house. He held up a blue t-shirt. "It's the largest one I have. I hope it fits." He tossed it to Kyle.

Kyle turned it over in his hands and held it up to examine it. "Looks good, thanks." But he stared at the ground and didn't make a move.

Morgan's parents looked at each other, wondering what was bothering him. "Aren't you going to put it on?" Taylor blurted out.

Kyle sighed. "Yeah, why not." He set the blue shirt on the grass and peeled off the bloodstained shirt that would never be clean again.

The Laflamme family couldn't help but stare at the muscles on the tanned young man, but there were deep scars on his torso. One on his flank, under his left arm, and another across one pectoral muscle. They were identical to the thick scar on his forearm and shoulder.

He quickly put on the new shirt, and the family had nothing left to shock them. He looked down at himself and nodded. "Good fit. Thanks again."

Mrs. Laflamme embraced her daughter and steered her towards their home. "Come on, honey. Your dad will fetch your car." She turned to look over at Kyle and mouthed the words, *thank you.*

Kyle smiled and waved his hand to accept her gratitude. Taylor waved too, and got a wink in return.

Mr. Laflamme clapped Kyle on the shoulder. "Come on, big guy. There's a convertible to retrieve."

"Hop in, but keep the window down. It's not a pleasant smell in there."

CHAPTER 44

The wind blew loudly through the open windows as the old Volvo glided down the road. The sun was thinking about setting, while the pre-dusk sky darkened into a deeper blue. Mr. Laflamme looked over at the teenager guiding the car down the road. "I can't thank you enough, Kyle."

"Uh, okay, for what?"

The older man smiled. "You can't know this because you aren't a parent. We'd like to shield our children from this kind of violence, and we know we can't always succeed. I'm glad you were there when it happened. Morgan isn't used to that level of cruelty." He rubbed his chin as he thought. "I have a hunch that you've seen a lot more in your life than she has."

"That's for sure," Kyle answered with a tight-lipped smile.

"You probably have an idea what I'm going to ask next," Mr. Laflamme said with a sigh as he looked out the windshield of the car.

"The scars?" Kyle asked, with a quick glance at his passenger.

"Yes, the scars." Mr. Laflamme let out a sigh. "That's from a knife, isn't it?"

Kyle looked at him again. "Yeah, how did you know?"

"I'm a lawyer. I've seen all kinds of evidence. What those scars look like and where they are suggested a knife fight."

Kyle snorted a laugh. "A knife fight? It might have been if I had one. As it was, I was trying to stay alive. I was attacked when I was in eighth grade. Someone who I beat up when they tried to rob me came back looking for revenge."

"Would you say he got it?"

"Well, it depends how you look at it," Kyle said with a smile. "He managed to leave his mark on me, but he got a worse beating and jail time. Hard to pick a winner in that one."

The lawyer smiled too. "I've heard it said that nobody ever wins in a fight."

"Ain't that the truth," Kyle laughed.

Mr. Laflamme nodded his agreement. "I have to tell you, this business with Lucas Quintana has me concerned. Who would do such a thing?"

Kyle's jaw clenched, and he gripped the wheel a little harder. "I've got a pretty good idea who would want to do that."

"You do?"

"Yeah, the same guy who *always* takes a run at Lucas. It's a coward named Steve Harris who gets my vote."

Mr. Laflamme nodded his head and watched the road. "Do you have any evidence? Or is that conjecture?"

Kyle leaned back and took one hand off the wheel. "No evidence. Since I've been at Southwood, there's only ever one guy who gives Lucas the gears. I think he went too far this time."

"That's unfortunate, because young Mr. Harris is well connected. His uncle is the mayor," the lawyer explained.

"Oh, great."

"I wouldn't worry," Mr. Laflamme said. "I'm pretty well connected myself. If Lucas wakes up and can identify his attackers, I'll do my best to make sure they get the book thrown at them."

Kyle smiled maliciously. "Now that I'd like to see." He suddenly pointed ahead, where their car was rapidly approaching the school. "Here we are. Let me find Morgan's car."

The Volvo crept into the parking lot, where the little convertible was one of two cars remaining. Kyle took the parking spot right beside it. Mr. Laflamme stepped out of the car and leaned down to talk to the driver. "Thanks for the ride. There's ... there's something else I wanted to tell you."

Kyle raised an eyebrow. "Go ahead."

"Kyle, I know about your dad's death."

He shrugged. "Of course. I told you."

The lawyer gave him a sheepish look. "When I knew you were going to be spending time with my daughter, I had someone check you out."

"I see," Kyle said quietly. "I guess I don't blame you."

"Anyway," Mr. Laflamme continued, "I want to say I'm sorry that you went through that."

Kyle looked down. "Me too." He looked up at the older man. "Do me a favor? Don't tell Morgan. It's not something I'd like to be common knowledge."

"I give you my word. I won't say a thing."

"Thanks, Mr. Laflamme. I know you won't. Have a good night."

The Volvo pulled away, and Mr. Laflamme waved goodbye. "You too, young man," he said to himself.

CHAPTER 45

Though the cafeteria was buzzing, the mood was somber. The football team were not as energetic as usual. Steve Harris was back in school, but had been quiet after being put on probation for attacking Kyle. The court case was pending, and he was keeping his head down.

The whole school had learned of what had happened to Lucas. There were many theories, but one thing was unanimous. Most students had no trouble accepting who he was, and even those who had a problem with him being gay were not happy. It was wrong, it never should have happened, and whoever did it should pay for what they did.

Hector found Morgan in the food service area. "Hey, chica! I have a lot to tell you. Is Kyle joining us?"

She thought about that. She wanted him to. He'd been a tower of strength during that emergency, and she was grateful. But she also didn't want to get her hopes up. "I don't know."

"Well, we should sit where he usually does so he can find us. He'll want to hear what I have to say." He had to hurry to keep up with the tall dancer's long strides. "Where's blondie? You know she wants to know what's up."

"Sad, but true." She frowned as she answered. Olivia was getting on her nerves. Their friendship was strong, but sometimes a little space was a good thing.

"Okay, just saying," Hector said. He knew better than to ask too many questions when the ladies were feuding.

They paid for their lunch, and to their surprise, they found Kyle already seated and unwrapping his lunch at the usual table. He was wearing an old white t-shirt with a couple of small holes in the back. His usual baggy track pants and old sneakers completed his look. Nobody else was brave enough to sit at the table. Morgan and Hector looked at each other, then went to sit with Kyle.

"Hey, hermano!" Hector said with a grin. "I've been looking forward to talking to you."

"Hi, Kyle," Morgan offered, not knowing what else to say.

He offered Hector a fist bump and looked at Morgan. She caught her breath as his blue eyes looked right into hers. Normally, it was a quick glance. But this was … this was *different*. He looked her in the eyes, and there was something warm in them that she liked.

"How's Lucas?" he asked immediately.

"Wait, here comes Olivia and Tonisha. You know they want to hear this," Hector said.

"That's for sure," Morgan muttered.

They greeted their friends, and Olivia and Morgan delivered a short and awkward nod. Friends, but still at odds.

"Okay," Hector said, his eyes dancing. "Lucas had extensive head injuries, and the doctor told his mother that if he didn't get to the hospital fast, he might not have made it." He looked at Kyle and then Morgan. "You two probably saved his life. I mean, *damn*. That's a hell of a thing!"

Morgan and Kyle looked at each other and there was relief, understanding. They'd acted fast, worked together, and probably saved their friend.

"Shouldn't have happened," Kyle growled.

"No, no! You can't escape that easy," Olivia said with a laugh. "You're awesome, and we love what you did."

"Not just us," Hector said with a grin. "Lucas's mother is dying to see you two again. She knows what you did. Pretty sure everyone will."

Kyle winced. "Well, I can do without the attention. But I'll probably see her after school. I'm going to visit him. Is he awake yet?"

Hector grew somber and shook his head. "Not yet, and they don't know if he'll be the same after that damage. Won't know until some time goes by."

There was silence as they all digested that reality. Kyle cleared his throat. "Well, I had an interesting meeting with Ms. Blake today."

Morgan sat up straight. "Oh my God! I totally forgot about her. She must have come back to find us gone."

"Yeah, and a pool of blood at the doorway," Kyle said.

The friends erupted in shocked laughter, and Olivia covered her mouth to keep food inside.

"She probably thought you murdered our Glamazon!" said Tonisha.

Kyle couldn't help but laugh too. "Her face … man, she was worried. I explained it to her and she went from relieved to really, really upset."

"Ms. Blake is good people," Hector said. "I hear she's retiring this year. Too bad."

"She is good people," said Kyle.

"There's another problem for the Quintana family," Hector said, looking down at the table. "Insurance."

Tonisha scowled. "Oh, right! They're going to have medical bills. *Serious* medical bills."

"That could ruin them," Olivia observed.

"No … no, it won't," Morgan answered.

"What're you saying? Of course it could ruin them." said Tonisha.

Morgan shook her head and looked at each of them in turn. "We're going to have a fundraiser."

"One of those online things?" Hector asked.

"Nope," Morgan answered. "A good old-fashioned fundraiser. A dance!"

"A dance! *Yes!*" Olivia cheered. "But where will we have it?"

"You know the school won't have it here," Hector pointed out.

"We … we could rent a hall?" Morgan suggested.

"No good," said Tonisha. "We'll lose half of what we raise to the rent."

"You can have it at my place," said Kyle, taking a sip of milk. "My uncle is away for the next couple of weeks."

They all turned to look at him. "The barn?" Olivia asked.

He looked at each of them as he spoke. "Open-air dance outside the drive shed. If it rains, we can move into the bottom floor. I'll move the machinery out."

Kyle went back to eating his sandwich while the dancers all looked at each other. "Yes, yes!" Morgan agreed, her eyes wide.

"I know many people that I train with who can provide the security," Kyle added.

"That's it. That's all we need. We can handle everything else," Morgan said with a smile.

"This is going to be amazing!" Olivia cheered.

Morgan looked at her dance partner. "Kyle, we should probably talk to Ms. Blake. Tell her about Lucas, what we want to do, and see if we can hang some flyers. You want to go after we finish lunch?"

"Sooner is better," he agreed. "Right after we eat."

The teenagers continued to eat and plan. Olivia wanted to handle refreshments, while Hector could get turntables and act as a DJ. Tonisha knew that her uncle had all kinds of outdoor lighting he wasn't using. They all agreed that people could donate whatever they wanted to gain entrance to the dance.

"We can totally do this," Morgan said with a grin. She looked at her dance partner. "You about ready to go find Ms. Blake?"

He organized the garbage on his tray and stood up. "Let's go."

Morgan stood too and followed him as he dumped the garbage, and she did the same. She fell in step beside him as he walked across the cafeteria. "This is going to be great! Thanks so much for letting us run it at your place."

"No problem," he answered.

They walked by the football players, and before they made the door, they heard a familiar voice call out to them. "Nice shirt, Branch! What is this? Some kind of white trash, trailer park fashion show?"

Kyle looked over his shoulder and saw Steve Harris fist-bumping one of his teammates. His hands balled into shaking fists, his jaw clenched, and he tried hard to focus on the promise he made to Morgan. When he looked her direction … she wasn't there.

Morgan stormed up to the seated football player and, without breaking stride, landed a punch right on his nose with a loud crack. Steve's arms flailed as he fell backwards, and he landed flat on his back. He stared at her with wide eyes, and covered his nose with both hands. Blood was leaking between his fingers.

Morgan stood over him and pointed a finger right in his face. "Steve, just … *just shut up!*" she screamed at him.

The entire cafeteria, including the other football players, erupted in laughter and cheers as she turned away from the stunned bully and marched up to Kyle. "Come on!" she snapped, grabbed his arm, and led him from the cafeteria. He could still hear the applause as the doors closed behind them. A smile crept on to his face as he followed the furious dancer.

CHAPTER 46

"*Ow, ow, ow!*" Morgan complained as Kyle gently put an ice pack on her hand. "I didn't know that punching Steve would hurt me too."

"Well, it was a pretty hard shot," Kyle answered, as he wrapped her hand in a tea towel. They were sitting on a bench in the office, waiting to see Ms. Blake. "Your hand is like a birdcage, and you slammed it into an ivory helmet. No contest." He inspected the wrap job and leaned back.

"I've never punched anyone before. I always thought you punched them and that was all there was to it," she said, wincing as she placed her hand in her lap.

"It was well-placed." Kyle grinned as he looked at his shoes. "Maybe you should be the MMA fighter, and I'll be the dancer." He looked back up, right at her. "Why did you do that? What were you thinking?"

Morgan laughed. "I wasn't." She rubbed her hand and looked at him. "I didn't like what he said. It wasn't nice, and there was no need for it."

"That's all?"

Morgan sighed and looked down at her lap. "No. It reminded me of what I said when you overheard me. Truth is, before I got to know you, I would probably have said something like it."

"Well, thanks. You didn't have to do that."

"No, I did." She turned a little to look at him. "Kyle, you were right about me. I did look down my nose at people who don't have as much as I do. I see that, and I'm trying to change."

The big fighter took a deep breath in and let it out slowly. "Since we're being honest, I wasn't completely right about you. And you said something that I've never considered."

"Really? Care to explain?"

He rubbed the inside of his palm with his other hand as he spoke. "Yeah, well … I don't ever think I'm going to forget how you roped me into this, but you aren't what I thought you were."

"No?"

"You stepped up for Lucas when he needed it, and now you're stepping up to help his family. That's not something a spoiled brat would do."

She gave his shoe a light kick. "That's nice of you to say."

"There's more," he said, sitting back and crossing his arms over his chest. "It's not your fault that you have an awesome family, and that you were born into money. It wasn't your choice, and you don't deserve to be resented for it. I mean, what are you supposed to do?"

"Kyle—"

He held up a hand to stop her. "Look, it's easy for someone, well … in my situation to have a hard time not holding a grudge when someone else has so much more than I do. But you're right. It isn't any better than thinking less of someone for being poor. It's not like you took it from someone."

Morgan pulled her long ponytail over her shoulder and played with the end with her hands. "Thanks, Kyle," she said quietly, not looking at him. There was an awkward silence, as neither was sure what to say next.

She chuckled. "You think I'll get suspended for punching Steve?"

"No chance," he answered. "Harris isn't going to run to the principal. That would be more embarrassing than the punch if everybody found out. He'd never live it down."

Ms. Blake came around the corner. "Hello," she greeted them. "Morgan, you've hurt your hand! What happened?"

"I wiped out in the hallway. I don't think anything is broken, it just hurts."

"I see," the older woman said. "What is it you wanted to see me about?"

Morgan looked at Kyle and then back at the teacher. "We're holding a dance off school property to raise money for Lucas Quintana's medical bills. We were hoping to get permission to make some announcements and post a few flyers. Would that be okay?"

Ms. Blake smiled. "I think that's wonderful. The flyers are no problem. If it's appropriate language and subject matter, you're welcome to post on the bulletin boards and halls. I don't think we're allowed to make any announcements. It's not school policy to advertise something off campus, but I'll see if they might make an exception." She tilted her head. "Can I come to this fundraiser you're having? I can cut a rug."

The teenagers couldn't help but smile. "It's an all-ages event for everyone in the community. Of course you would be welcome."

"Great, when are you two looking to rehearse again? Tomorrow after hip-hop?"

The two students looked at each other, and Kyle nodded. "Tomorrow would be great." Morgan answered.

"See you then," Ms. Blake said, and turned to leave. "Oh, Morgan?"

"Yes?"

"I hope that hand of yours doesn't interfere with your dancing— however you hurt it." Ms. Blake gave her a wink before she walked away.

Kyle grinned, while Morgan stared. "Do you think she believes me?" the tall dancer asked.

"Not a chance," Kyle said with a laugh. "She *is* awesome."

CHAPTER 47

Nothing about the day was working for Morgan. Olivia was still avoiding her, snooping into what was going on between her and Kyle. And something hung on her shoulders like a weight. Every time she started to feel good about the fact they were getting along or dancing well, the feeling of unease came back into her mind. If everything worked out, if Kyle made money, did it matter how they got there? The answer wouldn't come.

She took refuge in her schoolwork, attacking assignments, answering questions, and focusing on any reading that had to be done. Morgan had always been a good student, and this was the perfect way to get the things that weighed on her to slide to the back of her mind.

Finally, lunch arrived, and she wasted no time getting to the cafeteria. The dancers always sat at Kyle's table now. Nobody acknowledged it, but there it was. They wanted to be around him. She wanted to be around him.

Tonisha and Olivia were already seated and talking. "Hi," Morgan offered as she sat down. They both greeted her, but Olivia didn't show much enthusiasm.

Hector hustled to their table and put the tray down hard. "You hear what's going down?" he whispered with wide eyes.

"Hello to you too, Señor," Tonisha teased. "No idea what you're talking about."

He sat down and looked at each of them. Then he leaned closer and whispered, "Blake and the principal took Kyle out of class this morning, and they all went to the office for a talk."

Olivia's eyes lit up. "Wow, do we know what it was about?"

"Oh, there's more. Guess who I hear was waiting in the office to speak to him," Hector said, scanning all their faces.

"Tell us already," Morgan said.

"Okay," Hector said with a wink. "A couple of police officers."

That was it for Morgan. "Hector, this is *not* cool. You're making it sound like Kyle's broken the law. That's not how we talk about our friends."

Hector grinned and shook his head. "That's not it. Not at all. All of this happened after what happened last night." He held up both his hands and let it spill. "Last night, Lucas woke up!"

"Shut *up!*" Olivia exclaimed.

"No way!" Tonisha said. "Is he okay?"

"Hard to say, but he's talking."

"When did this happen? Last night?" Morgan asked.

"As I hear it from my cousin, who talks to Lucas's cousin," Hector said, looking at her, "it was when Kyle was visiting."

"He was there when Lucas woke up? That's amazing!" Olivia squealed.

Hector laughed. "I guess Kyle walked in, and Lucas's mother started fussing over him and hugging him. She was babbling in Spanish, and Kyle was trying to calm her down."

"And Lucas woke up?" Tonisha guessed.

Hector pointed a finger at her. "Yeah, I guess she was going on, and Kyle was saying he didn't do anything. You know, typical Kyle."

They all looked at each other and smiled. "Yeah, that's him," Olivia giggled.

"Anyway," Hector continued. "Kyle is trying to get out of the spotlight, and they hear a quiet voice from the bed. Lucas says, 'He's lying, Mom.'"

The dancers broke up laughing. "He actually said that?" Morgan asked.

"Yeah!" Hector said as he caught his breath. "Those were Lucas's first words."

Tonisha raised a hand. "Okay, what happened next?"

"My cousin told me that all hell broke loose," Hector explained. "Doctors, nurses, all kinds of people go running in the room."

"Well, him waking up is a big deal," Olivia pointed out.

Hector laughed. "His mamacita sure thought so. She fainted dead away, and Kyle had to catch her."

The dancers erupted into laughter again. "Poor Kyle!" Morgan exclaimed. "The guy goes for a visit and then all this happens? He's not very lucky."

"Funny, I was thinking the same thing. He has no luck at all," Olivia said, with a look at her friend.

Morgan glared back, and Olivia looked away and took a bite of her wrap.

Tonisha shook her head. "Okay, but that doesn't explain why Kyle was called to the office."

Hector nodded. "Well, apparently Lucas had more words to say. Told quite a story, as I hear it."

"Oh my God!" Morgan said, eyes huge. "Did he say who did that to him?" They all hung on his answer.

"I hear he did," Hector said. "And it must have something to do with Kyle, but I don't know what."

"Ugh! I'm dying to know," Olivia moaned.

"Well, I have to admit that I feel the same, chica," Hector agreed. "I was thinking about taking a walk by the office to see what I see. Anyone want to join me?"

The dancers walked together out of the cafeteria, down the hall, rounded the corner, and stopped dead. Their eyes were wide, and their mouths hung open as they took in the scene.

Kyle was being talked to by the principal, Mr. Hayes, and Ms. Blake had both hands up as she stepped in front of him. They could only see Kyle from behind, but it was clear who he wanted to get to.

At the other end of the hall, two uniformed police officers were escorting a handcuffed and sobbing Steve Harris. His face was red, and tears flowed as he looked down at the ground. Students gathered at either end of the hall, and there was a low murmur as they watched the captain of the football team walk in shame.

Morgan could see Kyle towering above the two adults in front of him. She couldn't see his face, but she could imagine the look on it.

The big fighter raised a hand to point at the football player as he grew closer. His voice was so loud that there wasn't a doubt that every student heard him. "YOU COWARD! YOU COULDN'T COME AT ME, SO YOU BEAT UP A FRIEND?"

Ms. Blake and Mr. Hayes kept themselves between Kyle and the police as they drew closer. Morgan recognized one of the officers as the one who'd interviewed her. Officer Gatlin looked at Kyle as they passed and held up his hand. "Stand down, son. We have him."

Kyle seemed to calm down, and Ms. Blake was still talking to him as the police continued down the hall. He turned from her and had one more thing to say. "YOU GOT OFF EASY, HARRIS!" The words echoed down the hall, and the crowd fell silent. Then he held up his hands, as if in surrender, and walked away from the situation. The guidance counselor and the principal watched him go. As he neared the crowd at the end of the hall, the students parted to let him pass. They gave him a lot of room.

"Wow," Hector said, stunned. "I didn't expect to see *that*."

CHAPTER 48

The hip-hop crew was on fire. Hot and blazing. Every move was fierce, and they were in complete synchronization. There was a conspicuous space that Lucas usually occupied, but nobody was complaining. Tonisha had addressed it before they started. "Let's do this for the guy who can't be here today, so he can jump right in tomorrow," she said, with a sparkle in her eye. She was greeted with cheers, and everyone brought a little more to the rehearsal.

Ms. Blake noticed, looking up from her paperwork from time to time with a small smile. Her foot would occasionally move to the beat, or her head would move up and down a little as she wrote.

About ten minutes before rehearsal was done, Tonisha called for a water break. The dancers had started moving when the door opened and the frame was filled by Kyle Branch.

He still had a fire in his eyes, but it was more subdued than what everyone had seen as Steve Harris was escorted out. The dancers couldn't help but stare. A few waved nervously at him, and he nodded to return their greeting.

"Kyle," Ms. Blake said with a gentle smile as she stood up. "Come on over and sit with me. The hip-hop isn't done, and it's a pleasure to watch." She gestured to the desk beside her. "Come on over."

Kyle nodded again, and the dancers quickly moved out of his way. A couple of sophomores watched him pass and started whispering. "He's not bad looking, but those clothes!" a brunette with short hair said to the redhead beside her, and they both giggled.

Morgan stiffened and slammed her water bottle down on the desk behind them. They jumped and turned to stare at her.

She glared at them, her eyes fierce. Her next words were for the room, but she kept her eyes on the two dancers. "Tonisha, can we get back to it? I'm getting kind of tired of the small talk around here."

Tonisha flashed a grin. "You got it, tall, dark, and gorgeous." She looked around the room. "You heard her! Take your places."

The two sophomores scuttled away from Morgan's glare, more than happy to take their places and escape her focus.

Morgan looked over at Kyle and Ms. Blake. They were talking quietly to each other, and to her surprise, it was Kyle who was saying the most. She burned to know what they were talking about, but she couldn't overhear anything. Tonisha started the music, and the dance crew went to work.

The front row moved while Morgan posed with the back row. When it was their time, she put a little more into what she did. They all did. It is the nature of the artist to shine in front of an audience, and Kyle had unknowingly become popular among the dancers.

The dance never paused for a moment. Everyone hit their formations, solos, and transitions seamlessly. Tonisha had guided and teased them to greatness.

When the song ended and the crew stopped in perfect unison, Ms. Blake turned to Kyle with a smile on her lips. "So? Didn't I tell you?"

He nodded and looked at all the dancers, his eyes resting on Morgan. "Yeah, that was amazing. Really great."

The dancers beamed, and Tonisha pointed a finger at the big fighter. "Damn right!"

"Language, young lady," Ms. Blake admonished, while the dancers laughed. The teacher stood up and said, "Okay, hip-hop rehearsal is over, but I believe there's a quick meeting about the dance that's happening tomorrow night."

"That's right," Morgan spoke up. "I have flyers for you to put up around the school. I think the word has already spread, but this gives people an address and a few more details." She started handing out bright yellow flyers with bold type. "Put these up everywhere!"

Hector turned the page over in his hands. "We're calling it 'The Friends of Lucas Quintana Dance?'"

"That's right," said Morgan. "It's an alcohol-free dance, where people can donate whatever they want to help pay for his medical bills."

"I'm taking care of refreshments," Olivia announced. "I'm making smoothies that are going to blow your mind."

Hector raised a hand. "I got the turntables and sound system. My cousins and I are running the music. Be dressed to move."

"I got the decorations from my uncle. We're good," Tonisha offered.

"I don't know the address," one blonde sophomore observed. "Is this a house?"

Morgan smiled at her. "Kind of. It's going to be an open-air dance. Kyle is providing us with the location and the security. It's a great space. Wait and see."

Ms. Blake held up a finger. "Aren't you going to need some kind of permit for this?"

Morgan nodded. "Yes! My father is calling in a favor. We should have one tonight or tomorrow."

"I wouldn't worry too much," Kyle said with a shrug. "There aren't many neighbors around, and the ones close by aren't likely to complain."

"Still, I can keep the volume right. Loud enough to enjoy, but not enough to disturb," Hector said to them all. "We're looking to help somebody out, not cause any trouble."

There were murmurs of agreement. Ms. Blake raised a hand. "I think it's wonderful what you're doing. I'm sure the Quintana family won't forget this." She turned to Morgan. "I guess that's it. Are you ready to get on with your rehearsal?"

She looked quickly at Kyle, then back at the teacher, and nodded. "Very ready."

"Okay then," Ms. Blake said, bringing her hands together. "Everybody out! Hip-hop is over, and Cabaret is starting!"

"Okay, I have a lot to tell you both," Morgan said with a big grin as the last dancer left the utility room. She pointed at Ms. Blake. "You were right.

Dance is about telling a story, and I'm planning on telling one that's never been told. This is my last year, and I want to show them something they've never seen."

Ms. Blake raised her eyebrows and sat down, putting her chin in her hand. "This I have to hear."

Kyle folded his arms over his chest and narrowed his eyes at her. He cocked his head to one side. "What do you mean?"

"Right, okay," she said with excitement. "All the performances I reviewed tell a story of a couple in love, or a woman being rescued, or something romantic like that."

"Every time?" Kyle asked.

"Yes, every time," Morgan answered.

"Every time," Ms. Blake confirmed. "So what story are you going to tell?"

"Well," Morgan began, "I'm going to tell a story of a couple at odds. A conflict, something that hurts and ignites when they are close."

"Interesting," Ms. Blake said. "Do you think the judges will be down with that presentation?"

"If we sell it," Morgan answered. "If we show them a dynamic dance with a happy ending that resembles what they're used to, I think it could make an impression."

Nobody said anything for a couple of seconds. Ms. Blake turned to the young man standing in the center of the room. "Kyle, you haven't had much to say. What do you think?"

He shrugged. "I don't know. I get the idea that it's got to stand out, but if it's really out there, won't they hate it?"

Morgan bit her lip. "It's not going to be 'out there.' We're still going to have elements of the style. We're going to give them some amazing lifts. It's just … it's just going to be different in the way we come together and the way we separate."

"I get it," Ms. Blake said. "I think I see where you're going with this. You couldn't sell the idea of romance, so you're using what you have." She leaned back in her chair. "Although you seem to be getting along a bit better lately."

The two teenagers looked at each other quickly, and Morgan leaned toward Kyle and bumped him with her hip. "Yeah, we are."

"Good," Ms. Blake said with a bright smile. "You two are going to dwarf the other dancers, and you're going to stand out. You've got all the tools, and you could show them something new." She pointed to the center of the room. "Get to it!"

Kyle smiled while Morgan chuckled and ran to get her phone. "I'm going to show you the first lift."

"Okay, sure," Kyle said.

She returned and pulled the video up on her phone. "Okay, I actually initiate this lift by coming toward you, and I jump up when you get hold of my hips."

He nodded.

"Right, I have to stay straight and spread my arms like wings. You have to extend your arms to get me as high as possible."

Kyle leaned in to see closer. "Okay, what's the footwork on this one? Can you show me again?"

"Sure." She took the phone close and backed it up. She brought it where they could both see it. "See how he spins as he takes her momentum?"

"Yeah, I got it."

Morgan ran and put her phone down. "Okay, moment of truth." She let out a big sigh. "You ready?"

He stood looking at her with a faint smile. "Bring it."

She laughed and started moving toward him quickly. He put a leg back and reached forward, and the second his hands touched her hips, she leapt. Kyle took her weight and easily hoisted her over his head. She lifted her chin and extended her own arms.

"Good!" Ms. Blake called. "Kyle, can you get her any higher?"

He answered by straightening his arms, and Morgan's eyes bulged as she found herself rising in the air.

"Okay, okay! Down, please!" she laughed nervously.

Kyle set her down effortlessly and took a step back.

"Okay, that was perfect." She gave him a grin. "Now, you're going to love the way you get to put me down."

"Oh yeah?"

"Oh yes! We're fighting, remember?"

He laughed. "I'll try to remember that."

CHAPTER 49

"The flyers are everywhere!" Olivia cheered at lunch. "Everybody knows."

"But will they come?" Morgan mumbled, as she ate her sandwich.

"Oh, for sure," Tonisha said with a dismissive wave. "I wouldn't worry."

Hector smiled. "Lucas has a lot of family, and they're excited about this. It's all they're talking about. They'll be there."

Kyle walked up to their table, and was greeted by the dancers. He nodded, as was his way, and sat down.

Morgan noticed that he didn't have his usual serving of milk, but a smaller carton instead. She wondered if that was because it was cheaper. That bothered her, and that it bothered her was confusing. Why should she care? But she did.

Without a word, she stood up and strode quickly into the food service area. The dancers watched her go.

"What's with our tall girl?" Hector asked.

"Who knows," Olivia said with a shrug. "There's something going on with her, but I can't figure it out. I will, though."

A couple of minutes later, she returned and plopped a larger carton of milk on Kyle's tray. She sat down with a satisfied smile and resumed eating.

Kyle fixed a glare on her and held up the carton. "What's this?"

Morgan made a face. "It's milk. What do you think it is?"

His blue eyes grew cold. "So why is it on my tray?"

The dancers gave each other an uneasy glance. They knew the makings of a fight, and it wasn't a spectator sport.

Morgan shrugged. "I figure if I'm going to keep asking you to lift me over your head, you're going to need a lot of energy. Don't make a big thing out of it."

Kyle stood up and gathered his lunch back into the paper bag. He removed the milk from his tray and set it on the table in front of Morgan. "I like to be asked." Without another word, he turned and walked out of the cafeteria.

"What's his problem?" she growled at his back.

The dancers all looked at each other, but Hector was the one to speak up. "Why did you do that, Morgan? What were you thinking?"

She shrugged. "I know he always drinks a lot of milk. I figured he didn't have the money for what he wanted, so I bought it for him. Is that so wrong?"

Hector gave her a gentle smile. "Your heart is in the right place, chica. Really, I mean that. The thing about being poor is, well … it doesn't bother you until somebody reminds you that you're poor."

Morgan looked down at the table and crossed her arms. She sighed, understanding.

Tonisha patted her arm. "Don't worry about it, honey, he doesn't hold a grudge." She stood up and gathered the trash from her lunch on her tray. "Maybe ask him next time," she said, as she left the table.

The other dancers started gathering up their lunches as well. Morgan sat and stewed, unwilling to move.

"See you at the dance tonight. Can you give me a ride home after?" Olivia asked.

"Sure," Morgan mumbled.

"Catch you later," Hector said. "I've got some great music ready for tonight."

Morgan gave them a small wave and remained sitting where she was, still. She was angry at Kyle, angry at herself, and hurt. But for the life of her, she couldn't figure out why.

Morgan pulled up to Kyle's home after school. There was a large chain strung up across the driveway, so she parked on the street. There were a few cars parked, and she noticed that the neighborhood seemed much nicer in the daylight. It was still a little sketchy, but she didn't feel unsafe. The two homes on either side of Kyle's driveway seemed abandoned. He was right—there was little chance of a neighbor complaining.

She grabbed a small, metal box from the passenger seat in one hand and went up the driveway. She easily stepped over the chain with her long legs and walked up to see what was happening. There were many things on the go.

Tonisha was on a ladder, hammering in a nail and hanging some bright patio lanterns. Hector was standing at a table on the top floor of the drive shed, wearing headphones. Clearly, that was where the DJ would play the music and watch the dancers.

Olivia was to one side of the big structure, setting up a blender on a table that was covered with sliced fruit and vegetables. There was also a large drum that was probably filled with water.

She heard a loud *THUMP* from inside the big shed and walked over to investigate. The big tan dog was lying down beside the door. He lifted his head and made a half-hearted attempt at barking.

"Hi, Roscoe," she said, and bent down to pet him. His tail flopped, and then he rested his head back on the ground.

As she reached the door, Kyle came out, wearing a tank top and sweating profusely. He was taking off a pair of work gloves. "Oh, hi Morgan," he said, looking down at the gloves.

"Hi, Kyle," she mumbled, and looked down at her feet. "Listen, about lunch today—"

"Forget it," he interrupted. "We've got bigger things to talk about. Did you bring the lock box?"

She held up the small box in answer. "Yup. I have money in there in case anybody wants change or something."

"Smart," he said with a smile.

Olivia came walking over. "Hi Morg! This place is looking pretty good, am I right?"

The tall dancer gave her a look. "I told you. My name is *Morgan*." She looked around and smiled. "But yeah, it does look pretty good. I hope it doesn't rain."

Kyle shrugged. "The forecast is pretty good, but check this out." He slid open the large doors to open the bottom of the drive shed. The two young women walked in and looked around.

"This is big. This is really big!" Olivia laughed.

"Where did the machinery go?" Morgan asked.

"There's a patch of grass behind this place. I moved it there for tonight."

Morgan turned and stared at him. "By yourself? Some of that stuff was pretty heavy."

Kyle smiled and looked down at his gloves. "No kidding. But it needed to get done."

Olivia rubbed her chin. "We could always start the dance outside and move in as the night goes on."

Kyle nodded. "It'll be warmer as the temperature drops, and quieter for neighbors who might like to complain."

Olivia started walking toward the door. "I'll see if Tonisha has any lights that might work in here."

Morgan let out a big sigh and looked at her partner. "I hope this works. Not for me, but for the Quintana family and Lucas."

"That's out of your hands. You've got a good place for the dance, you've let everybody know. There's nothing left for you to do. Wait and see."

She nodded and started chewing on a nail. "Still, I'm nervous. I want this to go well."

"It would be weird if you weren't a little worried. I think calling the dance 'The Friends of Lucas Quintana' was brilliant."

"Really?"

He smiled. "Yeah, I do. I think Lucas has more friends than you know."

She brought her hands together in front of her. "I sure hope so."

"I think you're in for a surprise tonight." He shrugged again. "It'll be something you'll always remember."

Morgan didn't know how right he was.

CHAPTER 50

The dance started slowly, but never stopped. The first arrivals were a dozen athletes from the MMA gym, all wearing red t-shirts that had their martial arts club logo. It was a smart move, because it clearly identified who they were and why they were there. Morgan had never seen such an intimidating crew. Some were larger than Kyle, while others had cauliflower ears or scars on their faces. Yet they had a friendly confidence. All were willing to shake her hand and smile as Kyle introduced them.

The owner, Paul Stewart, was there, and he assured Morgan that there wouldn't be any trouble. Looking at his merry band of goons, she had no doubt.

After the introductions, she looked at Kyle. "That is a scary-looking crew."

Kyle smiled. "Yeah, but they're perfect. They're taught how to fight, but they're also taught not to fight."

"I don't get it."

"Well, if someone wants to start trouble, they're going to de-escalate and be polite. If it goes to the next level, these guys can win without hurting the troublemaker. They're that good."

Morgan nodded. "They actually seem like nice guys. Thanks for asking them to volunteer."

"My pleasure."

The next wave that came were the dancers and their relatives. Some brought tables and food to put out for the people attending the dance. Lucas's mother arrived with a small army of relatives, who all brought Mexican food. The spices mixed into a mouth-watering scent. She kept hugging Morgan and Kyle, crying happy tears.

Kyle was not comfortable with the attention. He was polite, but his eyes were wide as he looked for an escape. His training partners were laughing it up, and Olivia had to chuckle. "Oh! He looks like he wants to die."

It wasn't long before the dance was looking like a happening event. Hector started playing music and setting the volume levels. Tonisha turned on the lanterns that glowed faintly in the dusk. They'd put out more light as the sun went down. Tables of food and drink surrounded the dance area, and a table was set up at the entrance of the driveway to collect donations. There were always going to be at least two dancers at the table, and two red-shirts from the MMA club to watch over them.

About a half hour before the dance was to officially begin, Morgan called everyone to the center of the dance floor. She brought her hands together. "I wanted to take a moment to thank everyone for helping out." She pointed at Kyle. "Thanks to our friend, Kyle, for giving us a place to hold this event."

As the applause rose, he pointed a finger at her. "Your idea."

She pointed back and then looked at Paul. "Thanks to Paul Stewart for bringing these ... guardian angels to watch over us," she finished with a chuckle.

"*Angels?*" Paul said with a snort. The fighters all laughed and looked at each other.

When the laughter subsided, she turned to the members of Lucas's family. "Thanks for coming out to help us. We're all hoping we have a successful night."

"No, no!" Mrs. Quintana said with a strong accent. "Thank *you!* Muchisimas gracias, bonita chica!"

She looked at Hector, who smiled. "She's happy."

Kyle grinned. "Thanks for the translation, hermano."

"Okay, that's it! If you need anything, find me or Kyle or any of the dancers." She paused and threw her arms up. "Let's do this!"

A line of students soon formed down the driveway, and it was a mix of all ages. Morgan, Olivia, and Kyle worked the table and explained the situation. "Donate anything you want and enjoy the dance. Refreshments and food are also free," she instructed everyone who approached the table.

It was a diverse group that came. A few of the faculty members came too, including Mr. Ryckman, Ms. Blake, and the principal, Mr. Hayes. She was amazed how much money people were donating, and everyone commended them for their efforts. "I'm so proud of you," Ms. Blake beamed.

"Well done, kids. Very well done," Mr. Ryckman praised them.

Mr. Hayes stepped up and dropped a fistful of cash into the box. "Sorry we couldn't hold this at the school. But I must say, you've done a better job here than we could have done at the gym."

"Thanks." Morgan said, smiling. "Thanks so much for coming and helping."

Kyle nodded his gratitude, and Olivia waved to them as they walked by. There was a surprise for Morgan when she saw some familiar faces. "Mom? Dad? Taylor?"

Her parents stepped up with a smile, and Taylor waved energetically at Kyle.

"Hi, tiger," he said with a wave of his own. Then he pointed to a table behind him. "Check it out."

Taylor's eyes bulged. "Churros!" she yelled, and ran past the table to the area where they were serving the South American dessert.

"I hope she doesn't eat so many of those things that she throws up," her father said.

"Wouldn't be the first time," Morgan said with a chuckle. "Thank you for coming, I didn't expect that."

Her mother stepped around the table and gave her daughter a hug. "I'm so proud of you for making this happen." She looked over at Kyle and Olivia. "You two as well."

Mr. Laflamme took out his wallet and handed a stack of cash to Olivia. "For the cause."

Olivia tilted her head and smiled at him. "Thank you so much. Have fun!"

Mrs. Laflamme grabbed her husband's arm and started steering him toward their youngest daughter. "We'd better hurry before she achieves 'churro coma.'"

Morgan waved as they went. "That was a nice surprise."

Kyle looked at her. "There are sure to be more. I'm telling you, Lucas was better-liked than you know."

Tonisha came to the table and touched Kyle's arm. "I've set up some lights inside the shed, but I need your help to power them up, big boy."

"I'll be back," Kyle assured the two dancers at the table.

"Better be!" Olivia teased.

The next half hour was spent greeting the guests and accepting their donations. They saw members of the dance crew, and sophomores who they knew attended the school but didn't know by name. They were certain that they'd seen a few teenagers that attended other schools.

"Isn't this amazing?" Olivia whispered quickly to her best friend.

"I can't believe it," Morgan said. "I'm having trouble fitting the cash in this box, and nobody has asked for any change at all."

Olivia looked up at the line, and the smile fell away from her face. "Uh oh," she murmured, and hit Morgan with her elbow to get her attention.

"What?" she said, looking up. Olivia pointed down the line. Right after the next few people coming in was a significant number of young men wearing school jackets. Football jackets.

Morgan's eyes grew wide. "Oh no …"

"I'm getting Kyle," Olivia said, and she sprinted toward the big drive shed.

One of the two young men wearing red shirts came up to the tall dancer. "Trouble?"

"I don't know," she answered. "Maybe."

The young man looked at his partner. "Get the posse."

He nodded and jogged the opposite direction from where Olivia had run.

As the football team stepped up for their turn, Morgan held up both hands. "Hold up a minute, guys."

"What," said one of the players, "you're not going to let us in?"

"What's your problem?" another chimed in.

"It depends what you want," Morgan said with her chin up. "If you're here for trouble, you can turn right around. Don't forget it was your captain who put Lucas in the hospital in the first place."

Two-Ton Tony limped up with a cane in his hand. "We want to dance. That's it."

"Thought we already did that," a voice called out. They turned to see Kyle, Olivia, and Tonisha arriving on Morgan's right, as half a dozen tough-looking fighters in red shirts arrived on her left.

Kyle glared at each of the football players, and his gaze finally rested on Tony. "How's the knee?"

The big football player looked at the ground, and then back at Kyle. "It still hurts, but I have nobody to blame but myself." He limped closer to the table and held a hand out to the big fighter, who was still glaring at him. "I want to apologize for coming at you in the parking lot. I had no idea that clown was going to pull out a knife. He told us he just wanted to rattle you. Never should have happened." He let out a big sigh. "I'm sorry, dude."

The crowd all looked at Kyle. The air seemed to come out of him, and he took the hand Tony offered. "You're right. I'm sorry you got hurt."

Tony shrugged as they shook hands. "You've got nothing to apologize for. You gave me an out and I should've taken it." He turned to Morgan and the other two dancers. "I guess you're next."

Morgan made a face. "What are you talking about?"

Tony limped closer to them, and everyone heard his clear voice spell it out. "I owe you an apology for every time the team called rude things out at you or other dancers. That was stupid, and we ain't doing that anymore." He scratched his head with his free hand and looked at the ground as he continued. "We had a team meeting after Steve was arrested, and we agreed that we were idiots to listen to him and follow his example." He looked up at Kyle, Morgan, and Olivia. "I'm captain next year, and bullying is taboo. Anyone doing it is off the team. Coach is down with that too."

Kyle's eyebrows raised. "I've gotta admit, if you're telling the truth, I'm impressed."

Tony looked him dead in the eye. "God's honest truth, brother." He reached into his pocket and pulled out a wad of cash. "If you don't want us in, you got the right to say no. But at least let us make a donation to Lucas before we go. We owe him."

There were murmurs of agreement among the football players, and they all pulled out cash and held it up.

Morgan and Olivia's eyes bulged, while Tonisha muttered, "That's a lot of cash!"

The dancers looked at each other, and Morgan looked up at her dance partner. "What do *you* think? Are they for real?"

Kyle frowned as he thought. "I think Tonisha called it. You don't donate cash if you're looking for trouble." He shrugged. "I say let them in, but it's your call."

Morgan turned to face the young men that had tormented her for years. She took a quick breath and let it out slowly. Then her eyes softened and she gave them a small smile. "Well, I guess I have to thank you for coming and for the donation. Have a good time, guys."

The football team cheered raucously and high-fived each other. True to their word, they all gave a substantial donation, and each one apologized to Morgan and her friends as they entered.

"That was a damn miracle, that's what that was," Tonisha said, shaking her head.

"No," Kyle said with a smile. "That's a bunch of guys realizing that Steve was a jerk and they had to clean up their act." He spread his hands. "They aren't bad guys, they were influenced by a bad guy."

The music was increasing in pace and volume. Morgan turned to see Two-Ton Tony shaking hands with the principal, who gave him a pat on the shoulder and a smile. Kyle was right. Tony was a good guy. It was a shame it took an injury, and seeing his captain get taken away in handcuffs, to help him figure it out.

There was nobody left in line, and it was all Morgan could do to shut the lock box. "That is a LOT of money," Olivia said.

"I guess we don't have to worry about this being a success or not," Kyle said with a smirk.

Morgan smiled back, but her face darkened when she saw a large, grey sedan parked in front of the chain. "Oh, is it a good idea that they park there?"

"No," Kyle confirmed. "I'll ask them to move."

"I'll come too," Morgan offered with a grin. "To protect you."

Kyle gave her a sideways look and snorted a laugh. "Great."

They had only taken a few steps down the driveway when they saw an older man get out of the driver's seat. He was wearing a suit, and he looked stern. He went to help someone out of the passenger side.

Morgan stopped, and her eyes goggled. "LUCAS!" she cheered, and ran down the rest of the driveway with her arms open.

Kyle grinned ear to ear and slowly strolled after her. "*No way!*"

CHAPTER 51

The older man held up a hand to slow Morgan down before she could embrace her friend. "Whoa, young lady! I'm Dr. Silverman. He's still fragile. No hugging."

Morgan stopped and covered her mouth with both hands as she took in his appearance. "Lucas! Oh my God! Are you okay?"

The small dancer had bandages on his head, some tape on the bridge of his nose, and was using a walker to move. He was a mess, but he was still Lucas. He looked up at her slowly and narrowed his eyes. "I'm sorry, do I know you?"

Her face fell. "Oh, well … yes, you do. My name is—"

"GOTCHA!" he interrupted, with a sly grin and a gleam in his eye. It was Lucas all right.

Morgan's mouth hung open in outrage. "Oh, you little stinker!"

"Good one," Kyle called from behind her. "But you didn't fool me."

When Lucas saw Kyle, his eyes softened. "Kyle, there are some things I have to say to you."

"No, man. You don't have to say a thing."

"Yeah, I do." Lucas left the walker with the doctor and took a couple of slow steps toward the fighter. "You have no idea what it means to me. You stood up for me, and you saved me."

Kyle looked down and sniffed. "Look, don't make a big deal out of it."

Lucas smiled, tears in his eyes. "No! I will if I want! You will *always* be my hero." He leaned forward and embraced him. "Sweet Jesus, I forgot how big you are," his muffled voice mumbled into Kyle's shirt.

Morgan's eyes teared up, and she brought her hands together in front of her face and laughed at what Lucas had said.

Kyle gave her and the doctor a look. "Okay, you all saw it. He hugged *me*. This is not my fault."

They all laughed at his discomfort. Lucas backed up and sniffed back a couple of his own tears. He pointed at Morgan. "And you, you big beauty! When I heard that you arranged all this, I had to come and thank you." He looked over his shoulder at the doctor. "One more hug?"

Dr. Silverman grinned and said, "You snuck the last one in, but I can give you one more."

Morgan couldn't contain her tears as she hugged her old friend and teammate. She had to bring one hand up to wipe the moisture off her cheek.

"Thanks, Morgan," Lucas whispered to her. "You have no idea what this means to me and my family."

"Come on, there are a lot of people that are going to want to talk to you," Kyle said, gesturing over his shoulder.

They slowly started plodding up the hill. "Biology was boring without you," Kyle said as they moved.

"Liar," Lucas chuckled. "You're probably getting better marks when you don't have to help me."

"Not true," said Kyle. "If you don't believe me, you can always ask Mr. Ryckman. He's here, you know."

Lucas stopped moving his walker. "No! Really?"

Morgan laughed. "Lucas, you're going to be amazed to see how many people have come to our dance. Seems you've got more friends than you know."

"That's not the weird part," Kyle said, looking down at him. "The football team is here."

Lucas looked up at him in shock. "What?"

The big fighter shrugged. "They apologized and made a big donation. Don't be surprised if they want to talk to you."

Lucas started moving the walker again, and he looked at the ground as he went. "That's going to take some getting used to."

"I hear that," Kyle agreed. "Hey, don't walk right up to everybody. Follow me, I've got an idea."

They all followed Kyle around the back of the big drive shed, past the machinery he had moved, and entered the first floor. They helped their friend up the stairs to Kyle's home, where Hector was playing the music. The DJ was moving to the beat and had his headphones on, looking over the crowd that had started to dance.

Morgan stopped their progress and snuck up on Hector. She tapped him on the shoulder and when he turned, pointed at Lucas on the other side of the floor.

"*Dios mio!*" he exclaimed, and started running toward his friend. He was halted when the headphones tore off his head, as he hit the end of their reach. He looked at his friends and started to laugh. The three teens burst out laughing at his blunder, and the doctor wore a grin.

Lucas looked over his shoulder at Dr. Silverman. "Can I hug him?"

"I've completely given up," Silverman answered with a sigh.

Hector grinned as he gave his friend a careful embrace. "Nice bandages, bro."

"You like them? I could only get one color."

"No worries, man." Hector pointed to the DJ table overlooking the crowd. "Hey, you gotta make an appearance. Let people know you're here."

Kyle held up a hand. "That's why I snuck him up this way," he said, looking at the doctor. "They can't hug him if he's up here."

Dr. Silverman raised both hands. "Listen, I'll allow him to hug people as long as they're gentle. He shouldn't stay here more than an hour."

"No problem," Lucas said, with a sly wink at Morgan as he made his way up to the DJ table.

"He's not leaving, is he?" Kyle asked.

Morgan looked at him and laughed. "Lucas is always the *last* guy to leave the party."

The rest of the dance was uneventful. The football players were as good as their word and were perfect gentlemen. Every one of them took a moment to apologize to Lucas for past wrongs and wish him well.

The members of the dance team were in their element, moving with confidence and sometimes in unison to the delight of the crowd. Kyle was the only one not dancing. He was circulating and talking with his friends from the MMA gym, and some of the football players were going out of their way to make small talk with Kyle.

Hector slowed down the music and made a quick announcement. "Okay, this next song is a slow one, and it's what you call, 'ladies' choice.' Guys, you hombres can't ask anyone to dance. It's up to the ladies to do the asking, and you can't refuse!"

The crowd laughed, and everyone looked around, wondering who would be asked and who would do the asking.

Morgan looked toward the drive shed, where she saw Kyle talking with Lucas and the doctor. A million thoughts raced through her mind. Her first thought was, *why not?* The next was, *you dance with him all the time.* No sooner did that notion enter her head then the answer came right after. *A slow dance is different.* She took in a breath to steady herself and took a step towards Kyle.

Her hesitation cost her. A flash of long, light brown hair blew past her, and she had to stand and watch as Taylor ran up to her Judo instructor, grabbed him by the arm, and dragged him to dance with her. Kyle couldn't help but laugh, and he held her delicately as they rocked back and forth. She wasn't quite up to his chest, so she had to crane her neck to look up at him as they danced.

"Damn," Morgan muttered to herself. She couldn't stay mad as she watched the mismatched couple. Taylor couldn't know that she was trying to find the courage to ask Kyle for the dance. She smiled too as she saw her little sister step on Kyle's feet. She wished she'd had a chance to ask this young man who had become so important in her life to dance, but she didn't mind Taylor having some fun.

What *did* bother her was seeing Olivia in his arms a few songs later. She figured the blonde was the one who'd done the asking. She hadn't seen Kyle ask anyone all night, and she also knew her best friend was fearless.

Olivia was taller than Taylor, but not by much. Her blue eyes were wide and excited as she chattered away, looking right into Kyle's face. When Morgan saw her arms wrapped around his shoulders, and his large hand on her waist, she had to deal with a flash of ... *what?* What was she feeling? Was it anger?

It hit her like a thunderbolt. She wasn't angry that Olivia was dancing with Kyle. She was upset that *she* wasn't dancing with him. "Oh, no ..." she murmured as understanding set in. Morgan Laflamme was dealing with the reality that for the first time in her life, she was jealous.

She couldn't take her eyes away from them. *This is stupid!* she thought to herself. But there it was. It went around and around in her head and always ended up in the same place. It bothered her to see her best friend in Kyle's arms, obviously enjoying the experience. It was a lot to feel at once.

The song came to an end, and they let each other go. She saw them talk briefly. Kyle shrugged and turned away from her. Olivia frowned and brought a nail to her mouth. She put the other hand on her hip, and was mulling something over as she looked at the ground.

Morgan watched Olivia suddenly look up and scan the crowd. Her wide eyes settled on Morgan, and she walked right up to her. "Hey," she said with no warmth.

"Hey," the tall brunette returned with a frown. "What's wrong?"

"You lied to me."

Morgan blinked. "I don't know what—"

Olivia brought a finger up and pointed right at her best friend. "Yes, you do!" She looked around. "This isn't the time, but know this, Morgan ... we *are* going to have that conversation."

Morgan watched her friend march away. Kyle was right. She would always remember this night.

CHAPTER 52

The evening ended the same way it had begun. It was well past midnight, and only the dancers and a few family members remained to clean up. Hector was packing up the DJ equipment on the second floor of the big drive shed while the other dancers cleaned up the ground.

Lucas had stayed far later than he was supposed to, but he felt the effects of his injuries and allowed Dr. Silverman to take him home. After he left, more and more people said their goodbyes, and it wasn't long until the dance had come to an end.

"So how much did we raise for Lucas?" Olivia asked, as she packed up her blender.

Morgan shook her head. "I don't know. I didn't count it before I gave the lock box to Lucas's mom, but it's a lot."

They heard Tonisha laughing, standing on a ladder and removing her patio lanterns. "Good thing I *love* to count money." She looked at them with a smile. "You've put a little over twelve thousand bucks in that box, Glamazon."

"Wow!" Olivia said with a grin.

"I think you can say your night was a success," Tonisha said.

Morgan looked at the drive shed, where Kyle was heaving a large drill press into place. "It was *our* night," she corrected. "It took all of us to do this."

"Well said," Morgan's father called as he approached them. Her mother had an arm around Taylor, and the girl's eyes were half closed.

"I hope it's enough money to cover his bills," Morgan said, wiping some sweat off her forehead with the back of her hand.

Mr. Laflamme looked at her and raised an eyebrow. "I wouldn't worry. I'm going to represent the Quintana family and sue Steve Harris to cover the rest."

"I like the sound of that," Tonisha said, flashing a malicious grin.

"Yeah, that's perfect," Olivia agreed.

Mrs. Laflamme smiled and walked closer to her daughter. "You kids have done something special here tonight."

"Her idea," Kyle said, as he approached them, pointing right at his dance partner. He was wearing a blue tank top that showed his muscular arms, and he was glistening with sweat.

"Hey, Kyle," Taylor said with half-lidded eyes. She suddenly broke into an enormous yawn. Everyone was smiling as they looked at her.

"I think it's time we took our youngest home," Morgan's mother said with a chuckle.

"What? I'm *not* tired," she protested.

Kyle walked up to her. "Of course you're not, tiger." He patted her shoulder. "But I need you to rest up, because I'm depending on you to run warm-up next Judo class. Okay?"

Taylor broke into another yawn and started laughing. "Cool!"

Kyle waved at all of them. "I'm going to move some more heavy metal and then I'm headed to bed. I'll see you tomorrow. Good night, everyone."

They all wished him a good night and watched him walking away. "That is a good guy," Tonisha said with a nod of her head.

"He sure is," Olivia said, and shot a quick look at Morgan.

Morgan's mother moved to give her eldest daughter a hug. "Well, we have to go. Don't be up too late, honey."

"I'm almost done," Morgan reassured her. "I have a couple of things to do."

"Great job, kids. Get some sleep!" called Mr. Laflamme with a smile and a wave, as they walked down the driveway.

Olivia stepped up to Morgan and looked her in the eyes. "I'm ready to go home now, if you don't mind giving me a ride."

Morgan saw something behind Olivia's eyes. Something unsettling. Clearly, Olivia had something to discuss. She was hoping she could put off this last errand a little longer.

"Go ahead," Tonisha said with a wave of her hand. "I can help Hector, and I think that should do it. Go home!"

"Okay, then," Morgan said, looking at Olivia. "Let's go."

"What's on your mind?" Morgan asked, as the little convertible slid through the quiet streets of Irvine.

Olivia sat in the passenger seat, glaring straight ahead, as her blonde hair whipped in the wind. "Kyle let something slip after we finished dancing, and I think I know how you made him change his mind."

Morgan gripped the wheel a little tighter. "What did he say?"

"It was weird. We were dancing and making small talk. When we finished, I said that I thought it was great that he was dancing with you. He kind of nodded and said something under his breath as he turned away. You know what he said, Morgan?"

Morgan took one hand off the wheel, and she shot a scowl at her passenger. "Uh, no, Olivia. Why don't you tell me?"

Olivia turned to face her and crossed her arms over her chest. "He said, 'better than jail.' Isn't that odd? But it got me thinking. I think I know what you did, Morgan."

Morgan stared straight ahead. Her breathing started coming faster and her mind raced. "What are you talking about?"

Olivia turned back to face the road. "Okay, enough is enough. I'm going to ask you one more time. How did you make him dance with you?" She turned and gave Morgan a hard look. "I don't want any lies or half-truths. Tell me what you did!"

Morgan took in a deep breath and let it out. The fight she witnessed, how Kyle was arrested, and finally, the bargain she struck.

Olivia's eyes bulged, and her mouth hung open. "Morgan! Oh my *GOD*! You … you *blackmailed* him!"

"He's making five thousand bucks too," Morgan said, as they pulled into Olivia's driveway. She shut the engine off and looked at her outraged friend. "It's not all bad news."

"Morgan, the money doesn't matter. That's so you can feel okay with what you did. It's not for him!"

Morgan scowled at her. "No, that's not true. I figured he could use the money, and I tried to make it a better deal."

Olivia shook her head and her eyes were wild. "This is not okay. This is *not* okay, Morgan! He's a *person*, and you used his situation to make him do what *you* want. You should have told the principal what you saw. I know nationals mean a lot to you, but this? Is this even legal?"

"What is your problem, Olivia?" Morgan said, with her own fire. "Why do you care? I've been your best friend since we were in elementary school. You're going to give me a hard time over this?" She made a face. "Is it because you've got a crush on the guy?"

Olivia jumped out of the car and slammed the door shut. "No! It's … it's because it's all my fault," she said, as all her fury left her face.

"What are you talking about?"

"Morgan, the day that Kyle got in the fight, you remember it all, right?"

"Yeah, so what?"

Olivia raised her hands in frustration and let them fall at her sides. "Morgan, I was the one who called the cops. It was *me*."

Morgan's eyebrows went up and she stared at her friend. "You? You were there?"

"Yeah, I was hanging around waiting for you." She took a deep breath and slowly released it. "I knew you were going to have to bow out of nationals and tell Blake. I figured you could use a shoulder to cry on."

"Oh my God," Morgan said, looking down. "I never thought that it could be you. How is it that the police don't know? Why did you call them?"

Olivia gave her a small smile. "When I saw Steve and his idiots walking up to him in the parking lot, I was worried for him." She looked at her shoes and crossed her arms. "When I saw that knife come out, I was scared. I ran into the foyer of the school. You know the old pay phone right inside the doors?"

"Yeah, why?"

"Well, when you call 911 on those, it's not like using your home phone or cell. I never identified myself because I didn't want to get involved. I didn't want Kyle to die, but I didn't want to get the attention of the football team. So I made the call and took off." Her eyes welled with tears. "I had no idea that Kyle could take them apart. I thought I was doing the right thing, but I was a chicken and because of me, *you* were able to blackmail him!"

There was an awkward silence as Morgan absorbed it all. "What's done is done, Olivia. What do you want me to do?"

"Let him out."

"What?"

"You heard me. Let him go. And I'll tell you another thing. Either you're going to tell Ms. Blake what you did, or I *will!*"

"Olivia!" Morgan exclaimed.

Without another word, Olivia retreated up her driveway, wiping tears away as she disappeared through the doorway.

Morgan's heart was racing as she fired up the engine and backed out. She was in a trance as she glided through the streets toward her home. One thought echoed in her mind. *What am I going to do?*

CHAPTER 53

Mrs. Laflamme woke up in the middle of the night. She'd been restless when she went to bed, and she was having trouble quieting her mind to sleep. She put on her robe, walked by her youngest daughter's room, and looked in on her.

Taylor was snoring softly, her hair in her face. The covers were twisted like she had gone down in a fight. When she was sleeping, she always ended up in a pose that looked like someone had pulled the batteries out of her. She had a pretty busy night. Her teachers were in for a treat the next school day.

She walked further down the hall and looked in on Morgan's room. Her bed was empty. Moreover, it hadn't been disturbed in some time. Concerned, she walked down the stairs and into the kitchen. She looked over at the table and saw her oldest daughter, sitting in the dark.

In one hand, Morgan held a glass of milk, and the other was placed on the table. She was staring straight ahead, and her eyes were puffy and red.

"Morgan!" her mother said quietly. "What is the matter, honey?"

The teenager started to cry and brought a hand to her face. "Oh, Mommy … I've done something terrible and I don't know what to do. What am I going to do?"

Her mother held up a hand to stop her, hurried across the kitchen, and retrieved a box of tissues. She hustled to the table, plopped the box in front of her daughter, and sat down. "It'll be okay. We just have to talk it out." She took a deep breath and folded her hands on the table. "So, tell me what happened. Start at the beginning and tell me everything."

Morgan talked and talked. From the first day she laid eyes on Kyle to her fateful conversation with Olivia, she didn't leave anything out, and she never tried to minimize her mistake or defend herself.

Mrs. Laflamme listened to it all and tried hard not to show any emotion or judgement. She couldn't help her eyes widening when Morgan described the way she'd held Kyle's future over a barrel, and tried to sweeten the deal with the allowance she had saved up. Finally, Morgan finished.

"Okay, wow," her mother said when it was her turn. "I'm not going to lie, Morgan. I'm shocked and more than a little disappointed that you would take advantage of that young man's misfortune. The right thing to do would have been to go right to the principal and explain that Kyle was only defending himself."

"I know, I know!" Morgan moaned, putting both her hands over her face.

"That choice is gone, and we must live with the choices you made," her mother counseled. "Do you believe that Olivia will tell Ms. Blake what is going on?"

"Yes, she will. She's pretty mad."

"Okay, so you're not going to like this part," her mother said, patting her hand.

"Oh, no. What now?"

"Morgan, we're going to have to share this with your father."

"Share what?" they heard from the kitchen. There Mr. Laflamme stood, bleary-eyed in his bathrobe. "What's going on?"

"I'll make you a coffee. I need you to sit down and listen to your daughter." She pointed a finger at Morgan. "Go on, tell him everything."

"Everything?" she asked in a small voice.

"Everything."

She laid out the whole situation, and every decision she had made. When she finished, her father's eyebrows shot up. "Wow! Wow, Morgan. Did you consider the legal ramifications of what you've done?"

Morgan sat up straight. "No, did I break the law? Olivia said what I did is blackmail."

"No," he corrected. "Blackmail is when you threaten to reveal information and take payment in some form. What you did is technically extortion."

"Extortion?" she asked.

"Yes, you threatened to withhold information for payment, or in this case, a service. And yes, it is a serious crime that can result in a fine as much as a hundred and fifty thousand dollars. Or four years in prison."

She swallowed nervously. "Oh my God!"

Mrs. Laflamme gave her husband a disapproving look. "But that's not going to happen ... is it, dear?"

A smile tugged at the corners of her father's mouth. "No, I'm sure that we can avoid all that unpleasantness. At the end of the day, you *did* tell the authorities the truth, and the only indignity the young man suffered is, well, ballroom dancing."

"What do I do?" Morgan moaned. "I wish I'd never done it, but I can't undo it."

"No, you can't undo it. But you can make it right," her father said.

CHAPTER 54

Ms. Blake came into the office after first bell and greeted her secretary, Ms. Hoover. "Good morning, what's on the table for today?"

The secretary smiled back and handed her a piece of paper. "You've got a phone conference in about five minutes with Arnold Baker's family. They're hoping to get him back in school."

Ms. Blake shook her head and grimaced. "Mission impossible, I'm afraid."

"Oh, one of the dancers is waiting for you in your office. Seems pretty upset."

"About what?"

Ms. Hoover shrugged. "Wouldn't say. She says she'll only talk to her guidance counselor."

"Of course," Ms. Blake said with a chuckle. "Ah well, that IS my job."

"And you're good at it. We're going to miss you around here," the secretary said with a warm smile.

The guidance counselor held up a hand. "Don't make this harder than it already is. Thanks for the heads up. Might as well get to it." She grabbed an armful of files and made her way to her office. The door was open, and she was surprised to see Morgan sitting in the chair.

"Good morning, Morgan," she said, with a small smile that left her face when she got closer. The dancer's eyes were puffy and red. She was pale, and she was the picture of misery.

"Good morning," Morgan mumbled.

"Goodness gracious! I don't know what's bothering you, but I know we can find an answer. I've got to make a phone call. Can you wait about fifteen minutes? You're welcome to leave and come back if you like."

"I can wait."

Ms. Blake nodded and plopped the files on her desk. "Okay, then. I'll make the call in another room. Confidentiality, you understand."

"I do," Morgan said.

The guidance counselor left, and Morgan found herself alone. She considered taking out her phone, but there was nothing she wanted to read or watch. She looked around the office and saw old pictures of Ms. Blake and the dance teams over the years. There was a coffee mug with her name on it, and a few family pictures. Everybody was smiling.

Her gaze wandered to the files on the desk. They were all different colors, and some had labels. Her eye strayed to a battered manila envelope with a familiar name. "Kyle Adam Branch" was written in blue ink on the tab.

She sat back on the chair, and stole a glance at the door. Ms. Blake had said she would be gone for at least fifteen minutes, and that was two minutes ago. She looked back at the file, took in a deep breath, and let out a sigh. "Probably can't get in more trouble than I'm already in," she muttered.

Morgan stepped out of the chair and grabbed the stack of files. She carefully put the half on top of Kyle's folder to one side, so it would be easy to put it back the way it had been. She slowly sat back in her chair and opened the folder. It was Kyle's school record.

She went right to the pictures in the back. There he was, a young five-year-old Kyle. He had the blue eyes, tanned skin, and dark hair, but he wasn't smiling. His eyes had a faraway stare that wasn't focused on anything. He was a cute little boy, but not a happy one.

The other pictures showed him growing up, and gradually the confidence in his gaze grew to what she was used to now. His middle school pictures sometimes showed him sporting a split lip or a black eye.

The tall dancer turned back to the first few pages: his report cards and notes from teachers, doctors, and other professionals. They talked about "trauma" and were worried about "long-term consequences." She noticed that his marks were always quite good, particularly his reading and writing. Every teacher wrote about what a nice boy he was, but they were all worried about the way he kept to himself. The words "painfully shy" came up more than once.

When she made it to the last page of the file, she noticed it was different. It wasn't any kind of an official document. It was a photocopy of a news story about a homicide in a small Michigan town.

Her brows furrowed. What was *this* doing in a school record? Apparently, somebody thought it was important. "KNOWN DEALER MURDERED," the title shouted. She read the first line: "Known drug dealer Adam Branch was gunned down in front of his five-year-old son …"

Morgan's eyes widened and she leaned closer to the article. Adam Branch? She was reading about Kyle's father! When she was finished reading, she slapped the page back in the file and stared straight ahead. "Oh my God. Oh, Kyle," she sobbed, and put her face in her hands. She grabbed some tissues from the corner of Ms. Blake's desk and wiped her eyes. Then she quickly put the file folder back where it was, and put the half she'd moved back on top. It looked exactly as it had before she read her partner's file.

Timing is everything, and Morgan had only covered her tracks when Ms. Blake came back to her office. She was struck by the dancer's appearance. "Oh, honey, there's no need to cry. We can work it out, whatever it is."

Morgan took a cleansing breath, looked at the woman she admired, and started with the truth. "No, Ms. Blake. It's not going to be that easy. I've done something wrong. Something REALLY wrong, and I'm going to need your help to put it right."

The seasoned guidance counselor was intrigued, but cautious in her approach. "Okay, Morgan. Start at the beginning. Tell me what's going on and we'll figure it all out."

For the next twenty minutes, Morgan laid it all out, including a play-by-play of how Kyle took apart his attackers. She wrapped up by explaining who it was that had called the police, and how she had taken advantage of the fact that she was the only witness. The final subject involved the five thousand dollars she had thrown in to ease her own guilt. Through it all, she was clear who was at fault, and she didn't sugarcoat a thing.

Ms. Blake's mouth hung open, and she kept shaking her head as the tale unfolded. When she was finished, she took off her glasses and started cleaning them. "My goodness," she said quietly, as her mind absorbed the implications.

"So you see," Morgan concluded. "Kyle was accused of committing a crime, but it was actually me who broke the law. I … I didn't know that I was doing it, but that's no excuse. I committed extortion." The tears started flowing and she grabbed some more tissues. "What you must think of me," she sobbed.

The guidance counselor put her glasses on. "Oh no, honey! You've been in my dance crew for years, and I am SO proud of the woman you've become. Have you already forgotten what you did for Lucas and his family?"

"That doesn't make what I did okay."

"That's true. However, you weren't wrong about anything, but the way you went about it."

Morgan slumped back in her chair. "I don't get it. What was I right about?"

"You said that Kyle was the perfect answer, and you were so right. You and that boy are a perfect couple, and he learns fast. I think you don't understand how much being a part of something has changed him. He's a shy boy, misunderstood. I think he's grown because of this. I know you have."

Morgan sniffed back a tear. "You think … you think I've grown?"

"You have," Ms. Blake said. "Without a doubt. You were always a good student, always stayed out of trouble, but it was all about you. Everything was about what YOU wanted."

"I guess I was kind of selfish."

"No, that's not what I said. You were more self-centered, sheltered, than anything else. But I've seen you reach out for others. You stood up for Kyle in the cafeteria, or so I'm told."

Morgan sat up and stared. "Oh my God. You know about that?"

"Are you kidding?" Ms. Blake chuckled. "That was a big discussion in the staff room. Most of the staff loved hearing about you punching that bully."

Morgan and Ms. Blake shared a laugh over that. The guidance counselor stood up and walked to the doorway. She told the secretary she was going to need some privacy and then closed the door. Then she went back to her seat and let out a sigh.

"Morgan, when I was in high school, I was focused. I had great marks, made good friends, and life was easy … until I took physics. Oh, I liked science and math, but not when you put them together. I went for extra help, and I got a friend to tutor me. No matter what I did, my marks were low. Barely passing, actually. You know what I did?"

Morgan shook her head.

"I snuck in some formulas, and some answers I was able to buy from someone who'd attended the class the year before. I figured that the teacher wouldn't change the final exam too much, and I was right."

"You … you cheated?" Morgan asked, incredulous.

"I cheated."

"That doesn't seem like you at all!"

Ms. Blake laughed. "The same way extortion doesn't seem like you. Morgan, I rationalized it the same way you did. I told myself that I wasn't going to major in physics anyway, and I did need a good average to get into college. But what I did was wrong, and there's no denying it."

Morgan was fascinated, and had stopped crying. "Why are you telling me this?"

The teacher leaned on her elbows. "It's the way the story ends that matters most. I went on to have a great college education, and I became a teacher to help students. Later, I became a guidance counselor, and I've had a terrific career. Mostly because of amazing young people like yourself."

"You are great," Morgan confirmed.

"Thanks, kiddo! I tell you the story because I, like you, did the wrong thing. I don't think I'll ever forgive myself for what I did. I wish I didn't do it, but it never defined me. It made me who I am today. It made me better, and I think the same can be said for you."

Morgan looked down at her feet and back at the woman behind the desk. "Thanks. That helps more than you know. I've got to believe I can make this right, and I'm asking for your help."

"Anything," Ms. Blake said.

Morgan took a deep breath. "Okay, I need you to quietly approach each dancer and ask them to do one simple thing. And I need this done today."

"Today! That's not much notice."

"You're right, and I'm sorry for that. Trust me when I tell you that I've got to deal with this immediately."

Ms. Blake raised an eyebrow. "Is this for him, or for you?"

"Both," Morgan said. "You'll understand when I tell you what I want you to do and what I'm going to do."

They talked at length, and Ms. Blake found herself nodding and smiling the more she learned. Morgan passed her a piece of paper from her bag, and Ms. Blake inspected it.

"I like it. I think this is the right thing to do. I'll photocopy this and track down each dancer this morning. Is that it?"

Morgan stood up. "Yes, that's everything. Thanks so much. I'll find you after school to see what you could collect. Have a good day."

As she started moving toward the door, Ms. Blake spoke up. "You have a good day too, young lady. And Morgan, I hope you're right."

Morgan looked down at the floor and back at the teacher, with hopeful eyes and a sad smile. "Me too."

CHAPTER 55

The meeting with Ms. Blake had taken longer than she thought. The lunch bell had rung, and the halls were filled with students making their way to their lockers or the cafeteria. Morgan could only do the same.

She didn't have to go to her locker, as her lunch was in her bag. She walked in the cafeteria and heard her name being called.

"Hey, Laflamme!"

She stopped and looked at the football players, where Two-Ton Tony was waving at her.

"That was a good time last night," he said. "Thanks for giving us a chance." The other football players nodded, or waved a hand of their own.

"You guys were awesome," she said with a smile.

Tony frowned when he saw how red her eyes were. "Hey, Morgan, looks like you been crying. You okay, girl?"

She shrugged. "I will be. Thanks, Tony." Walking down the center aisle, she approached the table that had become the dancers' table. Her friends were already there. Tonisha, Hector, and Olivia were looking tired, but still smiling. Last night's dance was a success, and they knew it.

Morgan braced herself and went into the fray. "Hi guys," she said as she approached, and sat right across from Olivia. They all greeted her, but the blonde only gave her a wave and looked away.

"Olivia, I told Ms. Blake," Morgan said, looking right at her. "I told her everything."

Blue eyes snapped up to look in brown. "You did? Wow, well … now what?"

Morgan smiled and looked down. "The first thing I have to do is thank you."

"*Thank me?* Now that I didn't expect."

Morgan grinned at her shock. "It's not easy hearing things you don't want to hear, but friends will tell you what you *need* to hear. Now I can do what needs to be done."

"I'm lost," Hector mumbled.

"Yeah, me too," said Tonisha.

Morgan turned to them. "Sorry, guys, I'm not ready to share yet. I will. I think that's a part of my punishment. There's something that I have to ask you to do."

Tonisha and Hector sat back and looked at each other. Tonisha wore a sly smile. "Now I *really* want to know what's going on!"

"You will, I swear," Morgan assured them. "Hector, do you know where Kyle is?"

"Yeah, I do. He's taking the day off school to help out his boss and make some money. Sounds like the shop is swamped."

Morgan sat back and let out a sigh. "I was hoping to talk to him at his place, or his gym, but if it has to happen at the auto shop, so be it."

Olivia and Morgan walked down the hall, silent. Someone had to talk, and they were both waiting for each other.

"Listen, Olivia," said Morgan. "If you've got feelings for Kyle, I would totally understand—"

"Nope," Olivia interrupted. "I mean, I *did*." She looked up at her friend. "I like him, and he's definitely boyfriend material, but it isn't mutual."

"He's not interested?"

Olivia shrugged. "Well, not in me, anyways. There's no spark there." She lifted an eyebrow. "I think I kind of lost interest when I saw that my best friend was starting to get more and more attached to the boy."

"*Me?*" Morgan squawked. "We're dance partners. That's all."

"Yeah, okay," Olivia said. "Whatever you say. I'm sure you're not thinking about him all the time."

"I hate you," Morgan whispered.

They came to a corner in the hall, and they had to part ways. "Hey, Morgan, good luck tonight. I hope the conversation goes well."

"Thanks, Olivia. I wish you could be with me for this one."

"Nope, this one you have to do on your own."

CHAPTER 56

Morgan applied some eyeliner while she looked in the mirror. A little lip gloss applied perfectly, and she blinked at her reflection. She inspected her high ponytail for the fifth time and gave herself a small smile. "Clean," she murmured.

She walked over to the full-length mirror to make sure everything was in the right place. Her dark blue dress with small white polka dots hung just right, and she had selected the perfect purse and shoes.

Morgan let out a sigh. It was now or never. She grabbed a stack of papers and an envelope from her dresser and headed downstairs. Her mother was making a smoothie in the kitchen, her father was reading at the table, and Taylor was on the sofa looking at her phone.

"Going somewhere, dear?" asked her mother.

"Yes, I am. I'm going to see Kyle."

Her father looked up and gave his wife a glance.

"Is it a date?!" her sister screeched from the sofa, sitting up to look at her with a grin.

Morgan smiled in spite of herself. "No, I'm going to talk to him."

"About what?"

"Taylor, this isn't any of your business," her mother admonished.

"But I want to know!"

"It's okay, I'll tell you tomorrow," said Morgan. "You might learn something. I know I did."

Her mother walked over to her eldest daughter. "I'm proud of you, honey."

"You are?"

"Yes. You made a mistake, and now you're doing the right thing."

"What's she doing?" Taylor moaned as she moved closer. "Aw, tell me!"

Morgan smiled without showing any teeth. "Tomorrow, shorty." She looked at her parents. "I've got to go. I'll see you later."

"Morgan," her father said, as he put down what he was reading. He looked like there was something he wanted to say, but instead, he sighed. "Good luck."

Morgan parked her shiny little convertible in the lot of Gilmour's Auto. She turned off the engine, swung her legs out the door, and walked with her head held high. She didn't want it to happen here, but here was where it would happen.

She pushed open the door and saw a man with a dark beard behind the desk. He had a manual in front of him, and he was consulting a computer screen. Grime was smeared on his hands and on his grey t-shirt. His blue eyes turned her way, and he gave her a gentle smile. "Sorry, miss. We're closed now."

"Aw, come on, Jake. You can't spare a minute to talk to me?"

He squinted and pointed a finger at her. "Say, you're Pat Laflamme's girl, right?"

"Morgan," she confirmed.

"Right," he said, as his smile broadened. "Car trouble?"

"I wish," she said with a roll of her eyes. "Jake, I need to talk with one of your employees."

"I've only got one," he said with a chuckle. "He's fixing a car on the lift. You're welcome to go talk to him. I'll be checking on a few parts here, so you'll have some privacy."

She smiled. "Thanks. I hope you beat my dad the next time you play poker."

"Damn straight," he said, as he turned back to the computer screen.

She walked past the desk and through the glass door that led to the back of the shop. As soon as she pushed it open, she heard some old rock music coming from a small player on a work desk. She saw a big pair of boots that belonged to an equally large body, wearing dark coveralls and looking up into the wheel well of an old Mercedes.

Morgan walked over to the desk and shut off the music. Then she turned, leaned back against the desk, and waited.

She saw the boots walk around the car, and Kyle came into view. He had grease to his elbows and a little on his forehead. His eyes opened wider when he saw her. "Morgan? What are you doing here?"

She gave him a sad smile. "I have to talk to you. It's important."

He frowned and took a step closer, grabbing a rag and starting to take the worst of the grease off his hands. "Are you okay?"

The tall brunette looked down and gave a small laugh. "Everybody is asking me that today."

Kyle came closer and searched her face. "It's in your eyes. You've been crying."

"I have," she confirmed. "But I'm done doing that now. I have some things that I need to say to you. I only have one request."

"Okay. What is it?"

She turned her brown eyes up to his blue. "I don't want you to interrupt me, and I don't want an answer tonight. I want to say my piece and go. Can you let me do that?"

He nodded and his eyes narrowed.

"Okay," she said, and took a deep breath. She looked at the ground. "What I did to you was wrong. I saw what you can do, and I saw the answer to all my problems. When I was the only witness to what went down in that parking lot after school, I used that as leverage to make you do what I wanted."

Kyle continued to look at her, his eyebrows raised.

She looked up at him with watery eyes. "That's called extortion. You didn't commit any crime when you were defending yourself, but I did when I made you choose between a criminal record or dancing with me."

"Morgan—"

The dancer raised her hand to stop him. "I'm not finished." She took another breath and let it out slowly to steady herself. "So I'm setting you free."

She took the envelope in her right hand and shook it in front of him. "This is the money I used to make myself believe that what I was doing was okay." She placed it on the work desk and turned to look right at him. "It's yours. All five thousand dollars." She looked down at the ground again. "You shouldn't have that hanging over your head, and you've earned it ten times over."

Morgan turned the stack of paper in her hands. "Okay, here's the second part." She set the papers down on the desk beside the envelope. "I'm going to ask you to continue dancing with me. But it's not about me this time." She looked at him with pleading eyes. "Kyle, you're good! I'd keep you over my old partner, even if I could get him back."

She picked up the stack of paper and let it thump back on the desk. "This is a letter from every dancer on the team."

Kyle rolled his eyes and shook his head, but Morgan held up a hand to keep him from saying anything. "I'm still not finished." She crossed her arms on her chest. "They were asked to write about how their lives have changed since you joined the team." She looked at him and smiled. "I even gave one to Two-Ton Tony. He wrote a great letter. Might be my favorite. Mine is the last in the stack."

She started walking away from him and stopped at the door. She didn't look at him as she spoke. "I don't know when it happened, but you mean a lot more to me than being my dance partner. I know I've blown it with you, Kyle. I have nobody else but myself to blame." She looked up, tears in her eyes. "I'll never forgive myself for what I did to you, but maybe, just maybe, you could find it in your heart to forgive me ... one day."

Without another word, she walked to the glass door, pushed it open, and left.

Kyle stood there, staring after her. He turned to the desk and picked up the envelope. Sure enough, it was filled with cash. He picked up the letters and started turning through the pages.

The door opened again, and Jake walked in. "Well, that was a nice break for you. Do you understand what just happened?"

Kyle shook his head. "Only some of it."

"You think she dressed up like that for no reason? That girl has it bad for you, you big dummy." Jake laughed as he clapped his employee on the shoulder. "Get back to work. That'll give you time to figure it out."

Kyle watched the headlights from the convertible pull away. "*Damn,*" he muttered to himself. "Now what do I do?"

CHAPTER 57

Nobody likes waiting, and there's nothing worse than waiting for an answer that might be hard to hear. It's worse when there's no way to know when the answer is coming. Morgan's anxiety was high as she made her way from homeroom to biology class. She was dreading seeing Kyle. Admitting that she'd mistreated him was like a weight lifted off her shoulders. She wasn't ready to admit to herself that her dreams of dancing at nationals were probably over.

She walked into the classroom and saw Olivia waiting for her. She stole a quick glance at where Kyle and Lucas usually sat.

"He's not here," Olivia said with a shrug. "He must have had a late night at work. Or he's avoiding you."

Morgan gave her a stern look. "You can stop being too honest now."

Olivia laughed. "Okay. But you've got to tell me, how did it go last night?"

She put her face in her hands and moaned. "Oh, it was so weird. It was all I could do not to cry, and I swear if I stayed any longer I was going to start begging him to keep dancing."

Olivia scowled. "Yeah, that does sound awkward. Did he quit?"

Morgan took her hands away from her face. "I don't know. I told him I didn't want an answer that night, but to tell me the next day."

"I wonder what he'll do."

"With Kyle, you never can tell," Morgan said with a sigh.

Mr. Ryckman walked into the class and ended their conversation. He ran a good class, but Morgan didn't learn a thing.

Olivia and Morgan, walking from the food service area of the cafeteria, joined Hector and Tonisha at their usual spot. "Hey guys," Tonisha said with her mouth full. "Hear the news?"

"No," Olivia said. "Tell me, tell me!"

Hector grinned. "I talked to Lucas, and he's cleared to come back to school tomorrow."

The two teenagers smiled and looked at each other. "That *is* news," Olivia agreed.

"There's more," Hector said, holding up a hand. "He also told me he'd be able to dance at nationals."

"Yes!" Tonisha said, raising both arms. "We need him."

Hector picked up a water bottle and had a sip. "It's amazing how much money was raised for the Quintana family."

"Twelve thousand is a lot of money," Olivia agreed. "I hope it's enough."

"Seventeen thousand," Hector said, with a shake of his head.

Tonisha bristled. "No, I counted it, and it was twelve thousand dollars."

"Well, it was," Hector said with a shrug. "Lucas tells me that Kyle came over and gave him some money that came from latecomers. Five thousand bucks."

Morgan's eyes goggled and her mouth fell open. "Did you say Kyle gave Lucas five thousand dollars?"

"Yeah, what about it?"

She looked at Olivia and gave a small laugh. "Like I said, with Kyle you can never tell." She let out a sigh and looked down at her hands, folded on the table. "Well, I guess I have my answer."

Hip-hop rehearsal had wrapped up, and the dancers were drinking water and breathing hard. Morgan had gone through the motions, completely distracted. She looked at Olivia. "You were good today. Really good."

Olivia smiled ear to ear. "Thanks! You too."

Morgan snorted a laugh. "No, I wasn't. But thanks for lying."

Olivia gave a laugh too, and her eyes turned sympathetic. "Kyle on your mind?"

"Yeah, I guess I'd better tell Ms. Blake the score. At least she'll be glad I did the right thing."

Olivia gave her a pat on the shoulder. "That's the spirit!"

Morgan laughed and sipped some water. "Here we go," she said, as she wiped her forehead with the back of her hand.

She walked across the utility room to where Ms. Blake sat and read the work in front of her. "Ms. Blake? Do you have a moment?"

The teacher looked up and gave her a smile. "Always." She gave the dancer a sideways look. "Is Kyle coming to rehearsal today?"

Morgan looked down and shook her head.

"You talked to him?"

"I did, and it was hard," Morgan said, bringing a hand to her forehead. "I had to do it, and I'm grateful for the letters you collected from the dancers. Thanks."

Ms. Blake waved a hand at her. "Oh, it was no trouble at all. Every single one was excited to do it. That young man is a natural leader, but he doesn't know it." She gave Morgan a grin. "Kind of like you."

Morgan smiled too, then turned to go and get her things. She was throwing her bag on her shoulder when the door burst open and Kyle walked in.

"Sorry!" he announced, breathing hard from running. "I was catching up with my teachers on the work I missed today. Lost track of time."

CHAPTER 58

Morgan's bag fell off her shoulder to the floor and her mouth hung open. "Kyle!" she exclaimed. Nothing more would come out. She stared at him and blinked, speechless.

Ms. Blake stood up and smiled at him. "You're right, school comes first. I can only give you kids about half an hour. Do you still want it?"

"YES!" Morgan said far too loudly. Kyle and Ms. Blake turned to stare at her.

"Okay, then," Ms. Blake chuckled. "Back to the paperwork for me. Get to it."

Morgan walked up to Kyle and looked in his eyes. "I did *not* expect to see you today."

Kyle shrugged. "Yeah, well, I'm here. Want to practice what we've done or work on a new lift?"

"Both!" She ran over to grab her phone and accessed it as she walked back to him. "I have a video of a lift I want to use in our routine. I figure you'll probably only need to see it a couple of times." She went right beside him as she cued up the video, playing it for him and tilting her head to rest on his shoulder. "Thank you, Kyle," she whispered.

"No problem."

The video finished, and she stepped away from him. "What do you think?"

He nodded. "I get it. When she steps in, it's that raise of her leg that starts the momentum. He uses it to start the big movements. I need to have an underhook, though. That's important."

She laughed. "An under-what now?"

He smiled. "It's when my arm is under yours and comes up. I have your right leg, but my arm must be under your left armpit. That's what will keep you from falling as you lay on your side. Make sure you throw that leg up with some authority. If I muscle you up, it's not going to look good."

She raised an eyebrow and pointed at him. "Oh, you don't have to worry about me or my leg. Think you can handle the balance when I transition to lay on my back?"

"I guess you're about to find out."

Morgan smirked and took two steps back. "Right leg, coming up. Ready, big guy?"

Kyle turned sideways and gestured for her to come with his back hand.

Morgan took a couple of quick steps and threw up her right leg while keeping her spine straight. Kyle brought his arm under her leg and grabbed her at the knee. His other arm went into her left armpit. He used the momentum she had created and hoisted her high until his arms were straight.

"I'm going to lay back now, okay?" she said with a strained voice.

"Yeah."

She lay back until she was parallel to the ground. Kyle held her easily and started to spin slowly. He abruptly stopped. "I forget how to get you down."

"Oh! Bring me back down to your shoulders."

He did as she asked. "And now?"

"I'm going to roll and reach for the hand under my armpit. You need to grab that, or I'm going to hit the ground *HARD*."

"Just go slow, Morgan. I've got you."

She took a deep breath and closed her eyes. She turned slowly to her side and reached for his hand. Her heart leapt as she felt herself descending towards the tiles, but relief flooded over her as she felt Kyle's grip on her hand.

She continued rolling and came to a stop, inches from the ground. She looked up at Kyle and smiled with wide eyes. "Yes! That was it!"

"Wow!" Ms. Blake called from the corner. "That's how your routine starts? Where does it go from there?"

Kyle lowered Morgan slowly to the floor, and she popped up and started walking towards the guidance counselor. "Oh, this is going to be a dynamic routine. I'm going to need you to record us sometime so we can watch it and see if we're putting everything together. Do you mind?"

"Not at all," Ms. Blake said with a nod. "If you're going to start with such a dramatic lift, how on earth are you going to end it?"

Morgan chewed a nail as she thought. "I know, right? I'm confident with the lifts I've picked. I mean, we're already two lifts in, and it's going great."

"But you need a finale. Something the judges are going to remember, right?"

"Yeah," Morgan said. "That's the one thing I'm missing."

Ms. Blake stood up and reached for the teen's phone. "Well, want me to record that lift for you?"

"Yes, please," the dancer handed over the phone. "Pretty sure I can do a better job with my arms." She turned to Kyle. "Ready to do that again?"

"Sure."

Ms. Blake held up the phone. "Ready when you are."

Morgan took her position, and Kyle turned sideways and called her on. She didn't hesitate to step in and throw the leg. She was amazed at how fast Kyle positioned his hands, and she found herself elevating towards the roof. Kyle spun her slowly, and she didn't say a word as she initiated her lean back. She didn't need to.

Kyle responded wordlessly as she flattened and extended her arms gracefully.

"Showtime," she announced, and Kyle let her roll. Morgan felt his iron grip find her hand as she rolled to a stop, inches from the floor.

He eased her down to the tiles, and she jumped right up.

She smiled and ran to grab her phone. "Oh, that felt right!"

Ms. Blake handed her the phone, and they both watched the lift again as Kyle waited patiently in the center of the room. The two women smiled as they watched the video, and looked at each other when it was done.

"Perfect!" Morgan cheered.

"Great," Kyle announced. "Let's do it again."

They walked side by side down the hall. Morgan was still riding the good feeling that came with his return, but she couldn't stay silent.

She looked up at him as he walked beside her. "Kyle, why?"

He gave her a sideways look. "Why what?"

She stopped walking and he followed suit. She rolled her eyes and laughed. "So many questions!"

He laughed and gestured for her to continue.

Morgan looked at him and cocked her head. "Okay, why did you give the money you earned to Lucas?"

"Ah! Well, that money was nothing but a problem for you, and for me as well. I couldn't feel good keeping it, so I gave it to someone who needed it a lot more."

Morgan thought about that and nodded her agreement. "Okay, but I thought that meant you weren't going to keep dancing."

"Why?" he said with a frown. "One thing has nothing to do with the other."

"Well ..." She put a hand on her hip. "I guess I figured that was a total rejection of me, and everything to do with me."

"You're weird."

She couldn't help but laugh. "You think that's a weird way to interpret that?"

He laughed with her. "I seem to remember a dancer crashing into my workshop, demanding I say nothing, and laying down a hell of a speech."

"Oh my God! It sounds so stupid when you say it like that."

He folded his arms over his chest. "I also seem to remember that the same dancer told me not to speak, and refused to take an answer until the next day."

She covered her face with her hands. "I did that. I totally did that." Then she brought her hands down. "I thought that was the 'Kyle way' to send me a message."

"No."

She closed her eyes and laughed again. "Okay, I get that now. May I ask ... why *did* you decide to keep dancing with me?"

Kyle thought about that. "A few reasons. I mean, we've come pretty far on this thing, and I think I kind of understand what you're trying to do. Seems dumb to quit now."

Morgan nodded and wore a tight-lipped smile. "Okay. Keep going."

He raised an eyebrow. "You need more?"

"You said a couple of reasons. That was one." She held up her index finger and grinned at him. "One! I can count to one."

Kyle smirked and snorted a laugh. "Okay, okay. Another reason is that I liked getting to know the dance team. I've kind of stuck to myself for a long time. Other than training partners, not much in the friend department." He scratched his head and looked away from her. "I wasn't lonely, but this is ... I don't know—"

"It's better?" she interrupted.

"Yeah. It's ... better."

"Okay," she said as she stepped closer to him. "Any other reasons?"

He looked down at his feet and let out a barely audible sigh. "Another reason that I chose to keep working with you is that *you* are different."

Morgan stepped back and her eyes widened. "How am I different?"

Kyle looked her dead in the eyes. "When I met you, it was all about you."

"And that's changed?"

He nodded and still held her gaze. "Yes, you've changed. That dance you arranged for Lucas, that clumsy attempt to buy me milk. Not the same girl who shook me down at our first meeting."

She looked down and her cheeks colored. "Yeah, our first meeting wasn't good. I think you said I was a 'pretty princess' who was used to getting her way. Or something like that."

He smiled. "Yeah, but now you're pretty on the inside too."

Her brown eyes darted up to the big teenager in front of her. "Is that a compliment?"

"Yeah," Kyle chuckled. "It is." He looked up at the clock in the hall. "I've got to get going. I have work tonight." He turned and walked away from her. "I'll see you at rehearsal tomorrow." he called over his shoulder.

"See you tomorrow," she agreed. Morgan stood and watched him walk away as she considered everything he had said. "Wow," she whispered to herself as she hustled down the hall. Tomorrow couldn't come fast enough.

CHAPTER 59

"Chico grande!" Mrs. Quintana chuckled, as she wrapped the tape measure around Kyle's chest. Lucas and Morgan sat on the couch, smiling, as they watched his measuring.

"Is this going to take much longer?" Kyle growled, staring straight ahead.

"Much longer if you don't stay still." Lucas advised him.

"You want your costume to fit, don't you?" Morgan asked.

Kyle didn't answer, but he did try to be more still.

Lucas looked at Morgan. "I always forget how big this hombre is. He's not a branch, he's the whole damn tree!"

Morgan and Mrs. Quintana laughed while Kyle deadpanned, "Very funny."

Morgan pointed at him. "Well, I choose to be grateful that Mrs. Quintana is a seamstress. She sewed last year's costumes for Bernie and me. She's really good!"

"Gracias, chica bonita!" Mrs. Quintana said, as she started running the measuring tape from Kyle's shoulder. She had to step on a stool to do it.

"Measure that if you want," said Morgan, "but there won't be any arms on his costume."

Kyle gave her a scowl. "Why show my arms? All the dancers I've seen in the video don't have clothes like that."

"Because they don't have arms like yours," Morgan answered.

"I don't like it."

"Is it the scars?" Morgan asked, no longer smiling.

"Well, yeah. I'm not ashamed of them, but it's not like I want everyone to see."

"I think it's kinda hot," Lucas offered, with a gleam in his eye.

Kyle gave him a withering look. "Not helping, buddy."

Morgan stood up and walked over to him. "You're going to need a little more patience. We have two more stops to make."

He frowned at her. "What? When you picked me up at my place, you told me we had to come here and get ready for nationals."

"No, I told you we were *going* to get ready for nationals. I never said it was a one-stop deal," she corrected.

"Finito," Mrs. Quintana announced.

"Good!" Morgan said as she fished for her keys. "Thank you so much, Mrs. Quintana. I'll send some sketches home with Lucas tomorrow." She looked over at Lucas. "You're back at school tomorrow, right?"

Lucas knocked on his head with his knuckles. "All better. Not looking forward to the homework waiting for me."

"I can get you past the biology you missed," Kyle offered. "You know Ryckman is going to be cool about it."

"No more small talk," Morgan interrupted. "We have to go."

They said their goodbyes and walked out to Morgan's little car. She moved to the driver's side and unlocked the doors. Kyle sat down heavily, and the car sagged with his weight.

"What's our next stop?" he asked.

Morgan fired up the car and then looked at him. "Well, we're stopping to get you proper shoes and then a haircut."

He gave her a sideways look. "And you're paying for all this?"

"Yes."

"I'm not okay with that."

Morgan sighed and turned off the car. "Okay, here we go." She turned to face her passenger. "Let's take stock of what you've done for others recently."

"Like what?"

She started counting on her fingers. "You used your size to stand up for Lucas, you used your muscle to move the machinery out for the dance—"

"We never actually needed to go indoors," he interrupted.

"Doesn't matter! You still did it." She continued ticking her points off on her fingers. "You allowed us to use your uncle's place, or there would have been no dance. You helped my father change his brake pads when he has plenty of money to pay Jake to do it."

He dismissed her with a wave of his hand. "That wasn't a big deal. None of that was hard for me."

She smiled ear to ear. "Exactly. I was hoping you'd say that."

"I don't get it."

"It wasn't hard for you to do what you did, and it's not hard for me to pay for this. I have the money."

He glared at her and said nothing.

"Not convinced? Weren't you the guy who gave away five thousand bucks?"

He held up a hand to stop her. "That was different."

Morgan let out a sigh and put her hands on the wheel. "Look, Kyle. We can do this all day. The fact is, we need to get you better shoes, and you don't know how to pick them."

He considered that. "It's true, I don't know anything about dance shoes."

"And I *do*. Let me use the money I have to get you what you need. No more complaints. Okay?"

"Okay," he mumbled.

She smiled. "Good! You have strength and I have money. We use what we've got. Glad we came to an understanding."

He shifted uncomfortably in his seat and scowled. "Why don't you use all the money you have to buy yourself a car that's built for adults?"

She shrugged, wearing a smug smile as she started the car and turned on the music. "Let's get some shoes!"

CHAPTER 60

Morgan walked in the front door, sweaty, still wearing her leggings and shirt that she'd worn to hip-hop rehearsal. She plopped her school bag on a chair and went to the fridge, where she poured a cool glass of water and gulped it down.

"Well, hello!" her mother greeted her as she came down the stairs. "I guess you rehearsed today. How did it go?"

"Good," Morgan said, gasping after swallowing the water. "Tonisha runs things like a boss. It's going to be interesting to see where we land at nationals."

Taylor came thundering down the stairs, wearing her martial arts uniform. "Oh, hey Morgan!" she called out, and started throwing punches into the air. "I've got class tonight." She stopped punching and looked at her big sister. "I'm dangerous now."

Morgan grinned. "You've always been dangerous." Then she glanced at her mother. "You want me to take her to class tonight?"

Her mother looked at her eldest daughter. "You don't mind?"

"I finished my homework during my spare time today. I don't mind."

Mrs. Laflamme gave her daughter a smile. "It wouldn't have anything to do with a certain instructor at the club, would it?"

Morgan scowled at her and put her hand on her hip. "I thought I'd do something nice for you. Besides, I want to see what shorty here can do."

"I'm awesome," Taylor reassured her.

"Okay, then," Mrs. Laflamme said. "While you're at her class, I'll make a great dinner for all of us. There's a recipe I'm dying to try."

"Let's go!" Taylor shouted and ran for the door.

Morgan and her mother exchanged a look. "You're right," her mother chuckled. "She's always been dangerous."

The gym was hot, but not unbearable. Morgan sat with the mothers and fathers, watching their children roll around on the mats. Though she was looking at her phone, her focus was elsewhere.

Kyle was dressed in his martial arts uniform, walking amongst the children. He would stop now and again to help them with some advice or move them away from each other for safety. He looked large walking among the youngsters, but he spoke softly, and usually ended each conversation with a pat on the shoulder.

The only thing she didn't understand was something the students would call after him as he walked away. "Will you do the trick?" was repeated over and over. She couldn't help but wonder: what was the trick?

Class came to an end, and the head instructor, Paul Stewart, told them to line up. But instead, they ran to Kyle and started chanting, "The trick! The trick! The trick!"

"I hope he does it," one mother in the gallery said to the woman beside her.

Morgan didn't try to appear like she was looking at her phone. No point in pretending. She was ready to start chanting "the trick" with the kids.

Paul Stewart said something to Kyle, and they both laughed. Kyle held up both his hands to silence the chanting students, and she could barely hear him say, "Don't try this yourselves, okay?"

The students cheered and sat down on the mats to watch. Morgan looked to her right and noticed that all the parents were sitting up and watching. Every single one. She turned back quickly when she saw some movement in the corner of her eye.

Paul approached Kyle, and the teenager held out his arms. "This is a normal throw," Paul announced. He grabbed Kyle's right arm and twisted to put his back and hip into him. Then he straightened his legs and elevated the young man. He threw him over his shoulder, and Kyle soared high and landed hard on the mats. The students laughed, and Kyle was smiling as he stood up.

The head instructor held up a finger. "Now, this is a trick to deal with it." Again, Kyle stood and waited, and Paul came at him, but much faster. He grabbed his arm, turned his hip in, and started the throw, but this one ended differently. As Kyle started elevating, he twisted and cartwheeled over the instructor, landing with a bounce on his feet. It was fast, and it was spectacular. The students cheered and the parents applauded.

Morgan didn't notice any of that, as she was walking across the mats, right up to the instructors.

"Morgan?" Kyle said, surprised to see her standing in the middle of the class.

Paul Stewart wore a surprised look, and his eyes were kind. "Are you okay, young lady?"

She nodded quickly and pointed at Kyle. "Can you do that again?"

"Yeah! Do it again!" Taylor cheered.

Paul and Kyle looked at each other, and back at Morgan. "Why?" Kyle asked.

"Because I want to see it again. Kyle, *that's our finale!*"

CHAPTER 61

"Oof!" Morgan grunted, as she plopped on the mat and the air left her lungs. The gym was deserted, and Morgan had been thrown over Kyle's shoulder into a hard landing.

"That wasn't it," Taylor deadpanned.

She raised herself on one elbow and winced. "Thanks, little sister. I think I figured that out on my own."

"You okay?" Kyle asked, offering her a hand. He was the only other person there to offer. The class was over, and the owner allowed them to stay and work on the "trick."

"Just my pride," Morgan answered, as she allowed him to help her up. "At least there was nobody here to see it."

"I saw it," Taylor said with a grin.

Morgan gave her sister a glare. "Thank you for that. It's not easy, you know."

"Damn right it's not," Kyle said, as he walked to the corner of the gym. "Let's make sure you survive." He grabbed a large blue gymnastics mat and dragged it to the center of the room. "At least if you screw up, you can land on this big pillow."

"Great," she said, trotting up to him. "Let's try it again."

"Yeah! This is fun to watch." Taylor giggled.

Kyle pointed a finger at Taylor. "Not nice, tiger. Give your sister a chance." He stood facing Morgan. "Okay, partner, you've got to put your left hand down to the mat and then let your legs find the floor."

"I'll get this," the dancer growled at the fighter. "Let's go!"

She whizzed over Kyle's back and slammed down into the thicker blue mat. Taylor pealed with laughter, and Kyle had to grin. "Better!" he cheered. "Did I see your left hand touch the mat?"

"*Ugh!*" Morgan groaned, and then laughed. "Yes! I did get my hand down."

"Well, that's enough for tonight," Kyle said, and he hauled her off the mat.

"I'm not done," Morgan protested.

"Yes, you are." Kyle dragged the big pillow back to the corner. "You're turning right and touching the ground. That's a great start, and that's enough for now."

She stretched her back out and moaned. "Maybe you're right."

"I know I'm right," he said, as he came back. He grabbed Taylor as he walked by and swung her over his shoulder. She giggled and struggled as he carried her to the front door. "This one is up past her bedtime."

Morgan had to laugh as she followed them off the mats. She was sore, but she was also excited. That move was exactly what she needed to wrap up the choreography in her head. It was fast, spectacular, and sure to leave an impression.

She caught up to her sister and the martial artist at the front desk. "Say, Kyle, where did you learn that move?"

"I first saw it demonstrated by a guy named Zantaraia. He's a world-class Judoka, and he pulled that off in competition. I thought it was cool, so I worked on it until I could do it."

"It *is* cool," Taylor agreed.

"It's perfect for our routine," said Morgan. "Can we work on it again soon?"

"Soon," Kyle replied. "But not tomorrow. I have to work late."

Morgan's face fell. "Will you be able to rehearse at school?"

Kyle sighed. "Wish I could. But I have a lot to do at the shop. I'm on my own, since Jake is working the day shift."

Her face softened. "I wouldn't ask, but nationals are so close."

"You think we'll be ready?"

"I really do," she said, clenching a fist.

"Well, let me get changed, and I'll walk you both to your car."

Morgan flapped a hand at him. "Don't bother. We'll be fine."

"Besides," Taylor piped up, "I'll be there to protect her from bad guys."

Kyle walked into the changing room, laughing. "I'd better walk you out to protect the bad guys from *you*, Taylor."

The sisters looked at each other and smiled. A moment later, Kyle walked out with them. He took a moment to lock the door, and they all walked to the parking lot together. Then they separated to go to their cars. The sisters approached the little convertible, while Kyle strode toward the grey Volvo.

"Say, you ever going to paint that car of yours?" Morgan called out to him.

"Haven't picked a color for her." He held up a hand. "Good night, ladies."

"Good night," Morgan returned.

"Bye, Kyle!" Taylor called, with a frantic wave.

The cars both fired up and they moved toward the road. Morgan's convertible turned toward the nicer part of town, while Kyle turned his machine toward the other side of the city.

"Why are you sad?" Taylor asked her sister.

"What? I'm not sad. Why would you think that?" Morgan asked, her face lit up by the dashboard.

Taylor kept her eyes on the road as they drove. "Whenever you say goodbye to him, you're okay, and then you get quiet. Your face changes too."

Morgan thought about it. "I guess … I guess I am a little sad after I talk with Kyle."

"Ha! I knew it. Why?"

Morgan pursed her lips. "I wasn't nice to him. I didn't understand him and I was selfish. I guess I feel guilty after I'm done talking with him."

"Did you say you were sorry?"

"I did, but … that doesn't always make it right."

Neither said anything as they got closer to home. When she pulled into their driveway, Taylor looked at Morgan. "I don't think you should feel guilty anymore. Kyle is nice. He'll forgive you." She smiled as she bounced out of the car and ran to the front door.

Morgan stared after her. "Thanks, Taylor," she whispered to herself. "I hope you're right."

CHAPTER 62

An old Creedence Clearwater Revival song was blasting on the radio as Kyle worked on the car on the lift, replacing some corroded fuel lines with a more resilient plastic alternative. He heard a rapping, bumping sound that didn't match the drumming on the classic track.

He looked over his shoulder and saw a figure standing at the window of the big garage door, which was closed. He couldn't make out who it was, so he turned off the music and strolled over to look out the window.

When he made it to the window, he instantly recognized the person waving at him. Morgan was standing there with her long hair down and a smile on her face. The hand that wasn't waving held a Jack In The Box paper bag.

Kyle threw open the heavy lock and hoisted the garage door up with one arm. "Morgan? What are you doing here?"

She walked right by him and sat cross-legged in the center of the workshop. "I thought you might be hungry, so I brought you some food," she answered, as she started taking wrapped items out of the large bag. "I got you a couple of cheeseburgers, but I didn't get any drinks."

He stood there, holding the door for a moment. Then he snorted a laugh and let it rattle down to the ground. "We're having dinner?"

She smiled at him. "Think of it like a picnic. Are you hungry?"

His mouth slowly moved into a smirk. "Yeah, I could eat. I'll get us some water." He grabbed some paper towels and took the worst of the grease off his hands as he walked to a small bar-fridge in the corner.

"Great!" she called after him as he walked away. "I like that best with dinner anyway."

Kyle came back with a couple of water bottles that were misted with condensation. He handed one to Morgan and sat down beside her.

"Cold water!" she said with a laugh, and handed him a couple of burgers. He thanked her and dug in to the food.

"That's really good," he mumbled. "Thanks for this."

"No problem," she said with a mouth full of hamburger.

After he swallowed his first bite, he gave her a sideways look. "So, what gives?"

"What?"

He shrugged. "Why are you doing this?"

She finished chewing and swallowing and gave him a smile. "We're always at school, or rehearsing. We never spend any time together just being ourselves. Besides, you're constantly on the go and I figure you could use a commercial break, you know?"

He considered that. "It's a nice idea. Thank you, Morgan." He turned his blue eyes to her brown and she found herself staring at him.

She smiled and looked away, suddenly bashful. She took another bite and so did he. Nothing was said for a couple of minutes.

"Kyle," she finally said, "I know about your dad. I'm so sorry."

His face clouded over as he chewed. "Your dad told you?"

"No!" she said quickly. "I stumbled across a news clipping."

He nodded, and his face softened. "A google search?"

"Something like that."

"I'm glad it wasn't your father. He promised me he wouldn't say anything."

"He didn't," Morgan reassured him.

"I believe you. The guy has integrity." He chuckled. "More than my old man, anyway."

They both sat in silence, enjoying their food. Morgan looked at his arms, taking a finger and tracing the scar on his right forearm. "That was a knife, wasn't it?" she asked.

"Yup," he answered, not looking at her.

The silence hung in the air. She finally laughed and looked at him. "We come from very different worlds, you and I."

"We do," he agreed. "I like your world better."

"What do you mean?"

He looked at her. "Your world has a great family that takes care of each other. Friends who help and work together. It's pretty cool."

"Yeah, I guess I'm lucky," Morgan said, nodding.

"Me too," he said, taking his last bite and washing it down with some water.

Morgan scowled. "You think you're lucky?"

"Yeah, I moved here," he said, and he gave her a smile.

She found herself returning it and felt suddenly flustered. "Well, I'd better get home. My parents are expecting me, and I'm sure you still have work to finish."

"I do," he answered, as they both stood up.

She led the way as they walked to the big garage door, and she stopped and waited for him to open it. He easily hefted it high with one arm. "Hey, Morgan ... thanks for that. It was nice."

She looked up at him with a sly smirk. "Have you forgiven me yet?"

He smiled too. "I'll let you know."

"Okay, Kyle. See you tomorrow."

"See you tomorrow."

She took a couple of steps and heard the big door slowly clatter down. Her strides were long and her head was held high. She'd been excited and nervous to spring this surprise, and was amazed that it was so easy to be around him. He was quiet, but he was always present. Whenever she was with Kyle, he was very much with her.

Morgan fired up the convertible and drove home without turning on any music. She didn't need it.

CHAPTER 63

Morgan flew through the air, barely managing to put down her left hand and end up landing on all fours on the mat. "Damn!" she swore.

"No, that was close," Kyle encouraged her. "You positioned your body, got a hand down. Now it's a matter of kicking over your legs."

"Again," she grunted, as she rose to her feet. She ran her hands over her forehead to wipe away the sweat and smooth out her long ponytail. She was wearing black leggings and an old grey t-shirt that had seen better days. She was barefoot, as was required on the MMA club mats.

Kyle nodded and got back into position. He was wearing his white martial arts pants and a tight, black compression shirt. "Remember, gather the legs under you after you twist and I think you'll nail it."

She nodded and her eyes grew hard. She reached out her right hand and Kyle seized it. He turned his back to her as he threw his hip into her and took her off the ground, folding at the waist to send her high in the air.

Morgan concentrated on the turn of her body and planting her left hand. She saw the mat with her eyes, and one thought screamed in her mind. *Gather your legs!*

She tightened her core and lifted her knees toward her chest, straightening them at the last moment. Her feet hit the mat and she straightened fast … too fast. Her eyes were wide as she looked at Kyle and continued backwards, falling hard on her rump.

"Are you okay?" Kyle asked, standing over her.

She had both hands covering her face, and her body was shuddering with laughter. "That will look fantastic to the judges," she giggled as she reached for Kyle's hand.

He helped her up and put a big hand on her shoulder. "Morgan, you did it! That was it. You just straightened out a little too fast and it put you over."

She stretched her arms over her head and twisted from side to side. "I have to extend, or stand a little slower?"

"Not too much slower. If you're not fast enough, you fall on your hands and knees."

She grinned. "And if I stretch out too fast, I'm on my butt?"

He smiled too and nodded. "You're looking for 'just right' on this trick. Nothing else will do."

She cocked her head to one side and raised her eyebrows. "So what are we waiting for?"

He sighed and lowered his base to get in position.

Morgan reached out her arm and the whole process started again. This time, she flew over his back and she landed square on her feet with an audible thump.

"YES!" she cheered and raised her arms high, throwing her head back. "That felt amazing!"

"You nailed it," Kyle confirmed.

She ran to him and wrapped her arms around his neck. He hugged her back and then released her. Morgan continued to hold on as she whispered a muffled, "Thank you, Kyle."

He patted her back awkwardly. "Now let's do it again, because you did a great job."

She pushed away from him with a grin and immediately returned to position. "So, let's go already."

"Okay then." He stepped into her again, and she got more height, legs arcing up high in the air. She not only stuck the landing but immediately moved into a fierce stance.

He nodded. "That was a sweet landing. I can't see what you're doing in the air, but you're sticking the end. Sure you don't want to quit dancing and dedicate your life to Judo?"

She laughed. "I think I'm more of a striker," she said, and threw a playful kick at her partner.

He quickly backed away from her and got into a stance himself. "This is what the dance is supposed to be, right?"

Morgan lowered her fists and stood tall. "That's exactly right. It's a fight that ends with a little romance."

Kyle, too, stood normally and nodded. "I thought the throw was the last part."

"It's the biggest part of what we do, but I need you to collect me, and then we'll embrace at the end."

"I don't get it."

"Here," she said, reaching out her left hand. "Take my hand with yours and give me a tug towards you."

He did as she asked, and when he gave her a pull, she kept his hand and wrapped herself in his arm as she twirled gracefully into him. She reached up with her right hand and put it behind his neck, pulling his face closer.

She blinked and told him what was next. "Okay, good. Now you keep your left hand out for balance as you dip me backwards, and then hold me close."

He did as he asked. "Close enough?"

She swallowed and gave her head a quick shake. "No, it has to look like we're about to kiss."

He blinked and nodded his understanding, pulling her closer as she spread the fingers of her right hand on the back of his head. Her dark brown eyes were inches from his face as they stared at each other.

"Is this it?" he asked mildly.

She swallowed again. "Y-yes …"

"Okay, then," he smiled, as he stood tall and released her.

Morgan took a step back and flushed as she caught her breath. "Good, that was good. Can you rehearse after school tomorrow?"

He nodded. "Yeah, Jake and I are all caught up at the shop. I'm on top of my schoolwork. We're good."

"I'm going to ask Olivia to record us as well. I want us both to see what the judges are going to see."

"Makes sense," he agreed.

She put her hands on her hips, took in a deep breath and let it out. "Okay, I'm going to take off now. See you at practice tomorrow, okay?"

He laughed. "I said I would."

She smiled sheepishly. "Yeah, okay. Tomorrow."

He waved to her. "Good night, Morgan."

She thought about saying more, but changed her mind. "Good night," she said, as she turned and hustled across the mats.

"Hey, Laflamme!" he called after her.

"Yes?"

"You killed it tonight."

She pointed at him and gave him a wink. "You too! Don't you stand me up tomorrow, Kyle Branch."

He laughed and waved his goodbye again as she grabbed her bag and fetched her shoes from the entrance. "Yes!" she whispered to herself as she walked out of the gym. Everything was coming together, and she was coming to love rehearsal again. Bernie had been great, but Kyle was much more easygoing, and somehow more focused at the same time.

She took out her cell phone and saw she had a text. The one she was hoping for.

"Perfect!" she cheered and fired up the car. Their dance costumes were ready. She had another stop to make.

CHAPTER 64

M s. Blake and Olivia were sitting in the utility room after school, chatting about the hip-hop team and what they had accomplished, when Kyle and Morgan walked in.

"Hey guys," Olivia said. "I can't wait to see your routine!"

Morgan walked over to her and handed over her phone. "I need you to record this so I can watch it later. Do you mind?"

"Happy to do it."

Morgan walked over to her partner and moved into a fighting stance, like she had seen from so many of the athletes at the martial arts club. "Let's show them what we've got, Kyle. Get ready to record, babe."

"Ready!" Olivia called, aiming Morgan's phone.

Kyle and Morgan hit their first lift perfectly, and every lift after as well. They could hear their audience holding their breath during some of the more complicated maneuvers. Olivia watched through the screen of the phone, an eager smile on her face. Ms. Blake didn't blink as she took it all in.

When they came to the end, Kyle looked at her with an eyebrow raised. It was as if he was saying, *are you sure you want to do this?*

In answer, she stepped into him, and he did as he was required. He seized her arm, turned his back to her, and dug in his hip. When he dropped his shoulder and she went airborne, they heard gasps from the two observers.

Morgan turned her body, planted her bare hand on the tiles, and gathered her legs. Her heels hit the floor hard and she stepped back into a graceful pose. It was half grace and half fierce as her hands balled into fists and she transitioned into a fighting stance. Her eyes glared throughout.

Kyle seized her left hand with his right and gave her a firm pull. She responded by twirling into him, winding his arm around her. He threw back his left arm for balance as he lowered her parallel with the ground.

Morgan put her right hand behind his neck and spread her fingers, pulling him to her. His left hand came under her waist to hold her, and they froze, inches from a kiss.

He straightened himself, and her with him. They took a step apart and grinned at each other, breathless. "You can stop recording now, Olivia," Morgan said with a chuckle.

The wide-eyed blonde tapped the screen of the phone and exploded, "Oh my *God*, guys! That was ... that was so good!"

"What on earth was that thing you did at the end?" Ms. Blake said, applauding soundlessly.

"It's a Judo trick," Kyle answered. "She nailed it."

"I've never seen anything like that," Ms. Blake said, shaking her head. "Never! Not in any performance at any level."

Morgan gave a deep curtsy. "It'll be better when we apply the music."

"I'm kind of surprised you haven't done that yet," Olivia mentioned.

Morgan looked at her. "I know what you mean. The thing is, we needed to rehearse and understand every lift before we start putting it all together with the music." She looked at Kyle and smiled. "And ... we're there."

"What music were you thinking of using?" Olivia asked.

Morgan exhaled and smiled at her. "I've been listening to a lot of music, but I think Adele's 'Set Fire to The Rain' will work best."

"Oooh, that's perfect," her friend agreed.

"Yes, and I found a slightly longer version with a Rumba beat. That's going to make the transitions a lot easier."

Morgan looked at Ms. Blake. "What do you think ... about all of it?"

Ms. Blake knitted her hands together and walked closer to them. "Well, I've yet to see it set to the music, but I have some thoughts I can share."

"Please," Morgan encouraged.

"Well," she said, looking them up and down. "Your presentation is unique. Physically, you're going to tower over the other competitors."

Morgan and Kyle looked at each other and couldn't help but laugh.

"That's good, though!" Ms. Blake said, laughing herself. "You have to stand out to win a medal."

"And the routine?" Morgan pressed.

Ms. Blake brought a hand to her chin as she thought. "I found it electrifying! I mean, it was fierce, and the ending was just … just unforgettable! But I'm not a judge."

"Meaning?" Kyle asked.

"It is *way* outside of what they're used to seeing. You're going to get big points for the choreography, but there's a chance you're going to lose at least one point because Morgan is stealing the lead."

"I don't understand," Kyle said with a shake of his head.

Morgan turned to him. "Communication between partners is also judged. The male partner is not supposed to be led by the female. It's supposed to be a little of both."

Kyle folded his powerful arms over his chest. "I don't see how we can avoid that. I'm too new to this."

"You can't avoid it, just minimize it. You might escape detection," Ms. Blake explained. "But you can score big points with your pageantry, creativity, and transitions."

"You think we have a chance?" Morgan asked, her eyes wide.

Ms. Blake let out a big sigh. "I'd have to see it to music. But you definitely have a chance."

"It was a pretty amazing routine," Olivia offered.

"You have to remember," Ms. Blake continued, "this is a new category for your age group and every single competitor is going to be in unfamiliar territory. Some people are going to play it safe and stick to a more traditional approach. You're going a different way. Nobody's going to know what the judges were looking for until it's all over."

Kyle turned to Morgan. "I think you're asking the wrong question."

She frowned at him. "Okay, what's the right question?"

He looked her in the eyes. "Do you like this routine, and are you proud to show it to the judges and the audience?"

The young woman set her jaw as she looked up into her partner's face. There was no hesitation when she answered. "I am *very* proud of this routine, and I'm looking forward to showing everyone something they have *never* seen before."

Her partner smiled. "Then there's nothing more to discuss."

"But plenty to do?" Morgan asked.

"That's right."

"Okay, then." She turned to her friend. "Olivia, can I see my phone so we can watch the recording?" She looked back at Kyle. "Time to fill in the gaps."

CHAPTER 65

Contrary to popular belief, you can't save time. It can't be put away for a rainy day, or accumulated for profit. You can reduce the amount you use on a task, but it keeps on moving at the same pace.

Nonetheless, time was moving at an unbelievable clip for Morgan Laflamme and her dance partner. Between school, the hip-hop rehearsals, and Cabaret preparation, she barely had time to blink.

After reviewing the video that Olivia had shot, she was able to see a few things Kyle could do to make his movement smoother, but she was surprised to see that she was the one who needed the most work. Her footwork was impeccable, but her hands were all wrong for the story she was telling.

She started taking private lessons with Paul Stewart to improve her fighting stance. He was a great teacher, and she studied the proper movements whenever she would pose or strike. While Kyle was working with the youngsters in their uniforms, she was in the ring, wearing her leggings and t-shirt, getting coached by the ever-patient owner of the gym. She learned fast, and her hands soon showed the art that came with discipline.

The Cabaret rehearsals moved from the utility room to the gym. They needed the larger space to prepare for nationals. The utility room was available, but it was a quarter of the size of the area they would be using to gain the favor of the judges. One of the criteria was the way a couple used the space, and Morgan wanted to be sure they used it to great effect.

It turned out that Morgan was right when she selected a Rumba version of Adele's beautiful song. Kyle quickly used the box step and some of the easy turns to help transition to their flashy lifts. In a matter of hours, she had linked all their moves into one cohesive performance that built in drama and display until its breathtaking conclusion.

There was nothing left to do except practice the routine so often it became second nature. When she had prepared in the past, she always had to bully or cajole Bernie into the ferocious repetition needed to prevail. Not so with Kyle. He was always ready to rehearse, he completely believed in the idea of rehearsing in his costume, and he believed in her.

Tonisha had turned up the heat too, pushing the crew to be tighter and better in every way. Lucas was back and better than ever. Hector seemed to dig a little deeper, and Olivia had a brief but enchanting solo. She could pull off the athletic moves and still look cute doing it.

They were only discussing their attire at this point. There were many opinions, and Tonisha was sure to listen to them all and pick the freshest look. Morgan didn't care, and she had faith that her friend would get it right. It was one of her talents.

A couple of days before nationals, Ms. Blake called the entire dance crew to the utility room to discuss a few things. She explained that they would be taking a school bus in, and that they would probably be there for a couple of days.

"We qualified for Nationals based on last year's placement. You see, we only have a hip-hop crew and our Cabaret performers," she pointed out. "It's not like the other dance competitions, where they can have many teams on the floor at once."

"We have to qualify for the top-tier competition, right?" Tonisha asked.

"That's right," Ms. Blake confirmed. "Both of our teams are going to have to make a big impression in the opening rounds to move on." There was solemn silence as that reality sunk in. "We have the hip-hop trials on Friday morning, and the Cabaret goes on Saturday." She looked at Kyle. "Anyone not competing on Friday is still welcome to attend. You're a team, and the principal has given permission for you to be there to cheer on your teammates."

Kyle smiled at her. Lucas grinned at Kyle and winked at Morgan, but she pretended not to notice.

"There's more!" she said to get their attention, as the dancers began starting many private conversations. "Cabaret is the last event, and they're holding a completely informal dance after. There will be refreshments, food, and all kinds of music. It's a chance for all the dancers competing to socialize and enjoy some time with each other. We have permission to keep the bus there and give everyone a ride back to the school when it's over."

A few of the dancers cheered, and their conversations started up again. This was an exciting time, and they had prepared for months. The nervous energy was almost palpable.

Morgan stole a glance at Kyle. There was no emotion on his face, and he didn't seem surprised by any of it. She was fascinated by the fact that he never showed what was going on in that head. Frustrated, too, because lately she was very interested in what he was thinking.

CHAPTER 66

They boarded the old yellow school bus at sunrise on the day of nationals. Everyone had their expensive backpacks and shoe bags. Some had makeup on, but most wore their faces bare, because they would have to put on a healthy dose of stage makeup later.

Morgan sat by Olivia near the front of the bus, and her friend was babbling away, beyond excited. "Oh my God. Nationals!" she squealed.

Hector and Lucas were sitting behind them, also excited, but much quieter. Lucas was fighting off a yawn when he noticed that Morgan was stealing glances to the parking lot.

He smiled. "Don't worry, dancing queen. He'll be here."

Hector pointed out the window. "And there he is, chica."

True enough, the patchy grey Volvo pulled into the lot and planted itself in the first space it came to. The door opened and Kyle stepped out. He carried the same old backpack and a plastic bag that no doubt held his lunch.

The other dancers on the bus saw his approach and called out to him. A few of the younger sophomores cheered, while a couple of others cheekily offered to let him sit by them.

Kyle sauntered up to the bus, up the stairs, and plopped into the empty seat behind the driver. He waved to the dancers who were calling to him, and when he caught Morgan's eye, he gave her a slow smile and a gentle nod.

A smile crept on her face, and she found herself disappointed when he looked away from her. Instead, he was looking at Ms. Blake, who was making small talk.

"That's our Kyle," Lucas said with a chuckle. "Even on the day of nationals, he is one cool customer."

"You think it's because he doesn't compete until tomorrow?" Hector asked.

"No," Morgan said, looking back at them. "He was the same when he took out those football players. As calm and cool as you please."

Lucas nodded and looked out the window. "I can't imagine him taking out Two-Ton Tony like he did."

"I asked Tony about that," Olivia said to all of them. "He said that Kyle stood there and said, 'So do you want to do this? Because I want to go home.'"

"For real?" Hector asked.

Olivia nodded. "Yeah, Tony said he was mad at the time, but now he's kind of grateful that Kyle gave him an out." She shook her head. "I wish he'd taken it."

Morgan raised an eyebrow at her friend. "Am I missing something? Are you and Tony getting closer?"

Olivia grinned. "You could totally say that."

"Boyfriend material?" Morgan asked with a giggle.

"Could be!" the blonde laughed. "Pretty sure he's going to ask me to prom."

"Already got my date," Lucas deadpanned from behind them.

They all smiled at his news, and their conversation was interrupted by Ms. Blake standing to get their attention. "Okay, team. Remember you are a team and you stick together. This is going to be an ocean of people and activity. Seniors, please look after the sophomores, and anyone who is new to this competition should stick close to someone who has been here before. We MUST register together, and then you're free to roam. It is YOUR responsibility to find out what order we perform and the scheduled time. When it's our turn, they will NOT wait for anyone who is missing. Whoever is there must go on. We need to get registered and find our room. Then we throw it down!"

The dancers cheered, Ms. Blake sat down, and the bus lurched forward. They made their way out of the school parking lot and eventually to the

San Diego Freeway. The energy was high, and every dancer was chattering away with someone close by. But not Kyle Branch.

He was looking out the window instead, his blue eyes scanning the roads and the sky. Morgan was listening to Olivia, but she would steal glances at Kyle. *He is so out of his world*, the dancer thought to herself. Part of her wanted to sit beside him and see what was on his mind. Part of her worried how that would look to everyone else. *Why should I care what anyone else thinks?*

The decision was made for her when Ms. Blake moved to sit with Kyle. She was doubtlessly telling him more about what to expect. Whatever she was saying, he couldn't help but smile.

The big yellow machine took an exit, and they found themselves moving toward a tall hotel on Von Karman Avenue, which dominated the horizon.

They pulled into the driveway of the Irvine Marriott and into the drop-off area, framed by towering palm trees. The old school bus had to wait for a large coach to finish unloading another team of dancers, but it didn't take long for them to grab their bags and suitcases and make their way through the sliding glass doors. Then Southwood's team rolled in.

"Don't leave anything on the bus, and stay with me!" Ms. Blake instructed the students. She turned, thanked the driver, and went down the steps. Kyle was right behind her, and the rest of the students scrambled to grab their bags, double-check the seats, and hustle off the bus.

The sliding doors stayed open as the steady stream of dancers filed into the opulent lobby. It was a sea of humanity. People were lined up at the check-in desk to get their rooms, and a concierge was surrounded, dealing with any request that came her way. Dancers sat in the chairs and on the floor, leaning back against the walls for support.

Ms. Blake took them to an intake table with a banner that clearly read, "Registration." It was clear that the people at the desk knew the teacher from her years of volunteering. She was pointing to Kyle, and he was handed a tag that he put over his neck. The dancers behind them came to the table, found their names on a list, and were handed a schedule.

Ms. Blake walked with Kyle, and they took a moment to talk with small groups of dancers as they lined up. As they got close to Morgan's circle of friends, she noticed the word "Instructor" in bold on Kyle's nametag.

She pointed at it and grinned. "Really?"

He laughed. "It lets me follow the team, and I get in for free."

Ms. Blake patted his arm. "He's important."

"It's cool. The hip-hop captain likes him, anyway," Tonisha said with a grin.

"What's the deal today?" Olivia asked.

Ms. Blake motioned for them to come closer. "We have to perform in the Santa Barbara room. If we make the cut, we compete in the Catalina Ballroom for a medal."

"Then we better find *both* rooms, because we're here to win!" Tonisha said.

"That's what I like to hear," Ms. Blake agreed. She continued down the line and explained things to the other dancers on the team.

Morgan looked at Kyle. "We'd better find the Santa Barbara room, then … if that's okay with you, mister instructor."

He shrugged. "Well, there's a big sign saying it's down that hallway."

Lucas grinned. "See! You're already instructing us. Don't let it go to your head."

"Let's go!" Olivia said, and started marching toward their destination.

CHAPTER 67

The Santa Barbara room was a good size, but nothing fancy. A faded blue carpet covered most of the floor, except for the parquet wood flooring where a stage was set up. It was for the judges to observe and determine the scores.

Dancers were everywhere, warming up, stretching, talking, and stealing glances at the competition. The Southwood team were no different. They were all dressed in matching denim jackets, the females wore dark leggings, and the males wore black jeans. They all sported black sneakers with white laces and soles. It was a playful uniform that allowed them to move easily.

Standing in the center of all the activity was a smiling Ms. Blake and the unflappable Kyle Branch. Ms. Blake's hands were folded and her eyes were soft as she took in all the young dancers. Some she'd known for years. Kyle stood with his hands in his pockets.

Hector and Lucas flanked Kyle and explained how it all worked. The idea was that this first performance wasn't for a medal, but to qualify for the medal round. It wasn't lost on him, and when they finished, he nodded and said, "Then you'd better win this round."

"Damn right, Gigantor," Tonisha said with a grin.

They watched a few performances from local schools, and a couple from Utah and Arizona. They were good, but the timing wasn't always where it needed to be and there were a few miscues. The nerves that come with a national competition can take a team down a peg. Suddenly, Tonisha's relentless and demanding rehearsals made sense to all of them. They were ready. They were prepared.

Eventually, their time came, and they took the stage quickly and found their positions. The music started and the team started to move. Tonisha was fierce, and every move was strong and full of vitality. Olivia was perky, and she smiled through her solo, every move energetic and on time.

Kyle was entranced as he watched. He'd always arrived at the end of the rehearsal, and had never seen the entire dance. He smiled as he saw Hector and Lucas moving in sync. He'd never noticed how close they were in size, and though they were different people, they were able to move in perfect unison.

He also noticed Morgan, gracefully bouncing and selling every single move in the back row. She made it look easy and she never missed her mark. Her ponytail was like a whip that moved with the music, almost opposite to how she moved her body.

The number came to an end, and the dancers froze at exactly the right moment. Kyle and Ms. Blake clapped loudly, and so did the few spectators that had come to see the qualifiers. The judges smiled and were jotting notes down on their score cards. The dancers held up their hands, high-fived each other, and trotted off the stage.

They ran right to Kyle and Ms. Blake. A few of the sophomores hugged the guidance counselor. "I am SO proud of you!" she crowed. "What a performance!"

Lucas and Hector ran to Kyle, and he gave them a calm fist-bump as they all grinned. Olivia was having none of that. She ran to him in her excitement and wrapped her arms around him. "We did it!"

"Not yet," Morgan said, as she came close to them. She wanted to hug someone, but she had to wait for Olivia to let go of her partner. The two dancers and best friends embraced.

"We HAVE to make it to the next round," Olivia said. "We nailed that!"

Ms. Blake nodded her head in agreement. "You really put on a show. We have to wait and see."

Morgan sidled up to her partner and stood beside him. "What did you think?"

Kyle gave her a sideways glance. "Great. Very … clean."

She couldn't help but laugh. "Oh, that word again!"

"I see what you mean, though, about the 'tall girl,'" Kyle said.

"What?"

He looked up at the next group of performers as he explained. "You're one of the best dancers up there. Everything you do looks great, and you make it smooth. The only reason you're not front and center is that you're the tallest."

Morgan too turned to look at the next performers. They were getting into a new formation. It was clumsy. She crossed her arms over her chest and smiled, leaning her head against her partner's shoulder. "Thanks, Kyle. Thanks for being here."

"No problem," he replied. "Now, we wait."

Group after group strutted their stuff on the stage. They were all good, and they had all practiced. Everyone watched and judged each other. It was natural, as only two groups could go on to the Catalina room and fight for a medal.

It was hard to stay patient as the groups performed, but when the last group had finally completed their routine, the waiting was unbearable. Some of the dancers stretched, others nervously fidgeted, and the rest talked about nothing. Ms. Blake and Kyle could keep it together, but the rest were nervous wrecks.

Eventually, a small woman with glasses and her blonde hair in a bob stood up in the middle of the stage. She was flanked by the judges, who were sitting in their seats and smiling as the chairperson prepared to read the results.

"Well, that was a marvelous display of teamwork and dance," she gushed into the microphone. "You're all winners in our eyes!"

"Ugh! Corny," Olivia muttered with a roll of her eyes.

"Be nice," Ms. Blake said, still smiling at the speaker.

"Sadly, only two groups can go on. The runner-up in this preliminary competition is Brighton High from Utah!"

The dancers from Brighton High exploded, jumping up and down and hugging each other. All the other teams sagged and nervously looked at each other. They knew their chances of moving on had gone way down. A couple of Southwood sophomores groaned, and the tension in the room mounted.

When the cheering from the Brighton dancers had subsided, the head judge took to the microphone again. "Congratulations to our friends from Utah."

Everyone applauded half-heartedly.

The blonde woman couldn't help but look at Ms. Blake. "Southwood High is the winner of this round!"

The dancers around Kyle leapt into the air, cheering and raising their arms. They were hugging each other, dancing on the spot. Only Kyle and Ms. Blake were cool, and they gave each other a look.

Tonisha noticed and gave them a sideways glance. "Did you know?" she asked.

They both couldn't help but laugh. "We saw every performance," Kyle explained with a shrug. "You were the best. No doubt."

"Now we have to find the Catalina room," Olivia said with a grin.

"I found it on the map after I saw you dance," Kyle answered. "Figured we'd need to know where you were performing next."

"Can you show us?" Lucas asked.

"Follow me, and I'll take you to the Catalina room," Kyle said, and started walking.

The dancers all grabbed their things and scrambled to follow Kyle as he strode towards the door.

Morgan and Olivia gave each other a glance. "Medal time?" Olivia asked with an eyebrow raised.

"Medal time!"

CHAPTER 68

If the Santa Barbara room was underwhelming, the Catalina room was the opposite: a massive room with many folding seats for spectators and a huge parquet dance floor. The stage for the judges was larger, and covered with navy cloth.

The dancers' eyes widened and their hearts beat faster as they took it all in. It was exactly where they wanted to be, and they all were anxious about the task at hand. They had moved on to the medal round, but they hadn't won anything yet.

It was announced that there were only six groups in the finals. There would be five minutes between performances, and then there would be a fifteen-minute wait for the results. The order was announced, and everyone started to warm up and stretch; the room was buzzing with conversation. The groups came from all over the United States and were diverse in their approach. Some were glamorous and others looked like juvenile delinquents.

The word came down that they would be third to perform. After a few gasps and gut-checks, the dancers started warming up again. They all had their game faces on, and Tonisha had fierce eyes that constantly watched her team, or the stage. She was itching to get up there and show them. She wanted to show them all.

Kyle looked around and noticed a lot more spectators for the final event. He recognized a few of the dancers from the Santa Barbara room. Their journey had ended, and they wanted to see how the groups that defeated them fared. It wasn't hard to understand why. If the group that beat you won the whole thing, that was some consolation.

Morgan looked up at Kyle. "Any last-minute advice from our 'instructor?'"

He raised his eyebrows and smirked. "Knock 'em dead."

"Sounds good," Olivia laughed, as she bounced on the spot to warm up.

After two strong performances, it was time for Southwood to show the judges why they were there. The dancers were tense as they lined up beside the dance floor, but all jitters and fidgeting ended when they heard the call. Tonisha led them on to the floor and they sprinted to their positions.

From the first beat to the last, Southwood brought their best. There was a fire to their performance, and every member gave it their all. Kyle and Ms. Blake barely breathed as they watched. The sophomores showed a little more energy. The audience cheered after each soloist, and Olivia received the loudest ovation when she finished her cheeky moves.

The last beat dropped and the last pose was struck. It was over. The audience showed their appreciation with extremely loud claps and whoops. The judges smiled and nodded, quietly reflecting the same enthusiasm that came from the crowd.

Ms. Blake was jumping up and down, cheering and clapping. Kyle was clapping loudly and wore a satisfied smile. "They nailed it," he said to the teacher standing beside him.

The dancers bowed, waved at the audience to show their gratitude, and hugged each other as they came off the stage. Tonisha waited for every dancer, just off the floor. She embraced each one before they ran back to their teacher and Kyle.

Together, they watched the next three performances, secretly hoping they would not compare. They quickly realized that these were the strongest teams from the preliminaries, and there wasn't a weak crew in the bunch.

Morgan bit her lip nervously, while Olivia had grown quiet. "What do you think?" she asked her dance partner.

Kyle narrowed his eyes. "It's close. Very close."

The fifteen-minute delay was excruciating. Olivia alternated between pacing and sitting. Morgan sat cross-legged on the floor and played with her hair. Tonisha was talking with Ms. Blake about anything that popped into her mind, while Ms. Blake patiently listened, knowing that was what she needed.

Morgan looked up at her partner. He was standing like a statue with his hands in his pockets. She knew there was a lot going on in that head, but she could never figure out what it was he might be thinking. But she liked the calm way he carried himself, and she was happy he was there.

Suddenly, the crowd stopped buzzing, and silence filled the room as the older blonde woman with glasses stepped up to the microphone. It was time to find out.

"Well, the judges have discussed this at length. You didn't make it easy," she added with a nervous laugh. "We have narrowed it down to the three medalists." She held up a piece of paper and started reading. "In third place, Brighton High from Utah!"

The crowd applauded, and Southwood clapped their hands for the team that had come with them from the Santa Barbara room. They also knew they had scored higher, and were wondering if that meant silver or gold.

The silver medal was to be announced next. "In second place," the woman announced, "from Illinois, Columbia High!"

The crowd cheered again, and the happy silver medalists piled on to the stage, laughing and hugging as they took their places.

The Southwood dancers all huddled together, not knowing their fate. At this point, it was gold or nothing.

"Time for our gold medalists!" the woman called to be heard over the noise of the crowd. She took a last look at her paper. "Southwood High! Come and get your first-place medals!"

The audience went crazy, while the dancers screamed and gathered in a big huddle that bounced up and down. Kyle and Ms. Blake found themselves pulled into the middle of it. The older woman laughed with abandon, while Kyle looked a little overwhelmed but still managed to laugh at the madness around him.

The dancers eventually calmed down enough to make their way to the stage and wait for the medal presentation. The announcer and a couple of the judges worked together to distribute all the medals. They called on the audience to congratulate them one more time, and it was done.

Ms. Blake and Kyle waited for them to come back to their bags, where they were sitting, and Morgan went right up to Kyle.

"It's you and me now."

"Tomorrow," he said with a nod.

Morgan smiled. "Tomorrow."

CHAPTER 69

Kyle was standing by the large window of the drive shed, wearing nothing but shorts and watching the sun rise, when he heard a groan and some movement on the bed behind him. Roscoe had jumped up and was settling in for some more sleeping.

He smiled and looked back at the sun. "Got some things to do today. Big stuff, Roscoe. Two huge things. I hope it all goes right."

Roscoe started snoring. Kyle smiled and kept his eyes on the sun. "You're right. There's nothing to worry about."

"Why aren't you taking your car?" Taylor asked, sitting on the sofa and watching her sister.

Morgan shrugged. "Kyle says he fits better in his old car than my little speedster. He does, actually."

"And you don't mind him driving?"

"No! I am *so* nervous," she answered. "I'm happy he's driving."

"You weren't this nervous last year."

Morgan thought about that. "Yeah, that's true. But I didn't have a brand-new partner competing for the first time."

Taylor shook her head. "He's competed in martial arts tournaments before. He's used to that sort of thing."

"Well, they're two different things, but ... I guess if he's competed in front of people before, that will help him today."

260

Mrs. Laflamme walked into the room. "I think you're worrying too much, dear. You and Kyle have worked so hard. You're ready." She walked up to her daughter and hugged her from behind.

Morgan smiled and leaned back into her shorter mother, comforted. She saw the patchy grey Volvo pull into the driveway. She turned, hugged her mother, and waved at her sister as she left. "See you guys later!"

"Break a leg!" Taylor called after her with a grin.

Morgan ran to the car and threw her bag on the backseat. She jumped in the passenger side and smiled at her partner. "You ready?"

Kyle gripped the wheel with both hands and didn't look at her. "Yeah, I'm ready."

Not another word was said until they made it to the Marriott. After Kyle had found a parking spot and shut down the car, they climbed out and started walking. They weaved through the parked cars until they saw the entrance to the lobby by the valet parking. Ms. Blake was standing there waiting for them, and she wasn't alone.

The entire dance crew was there, smiling at them and laughing as they saw the two dancers' expressions. Olivia ran to her best friend and gave her a hug. Tonisha, Hector, and Lucas were right behind them. There were hugs for Morgan and fist bumps for Kyle. Ms. Blake watched with a warm smile and her hands clasped in front of her.

"Let's get you registered and changed," she said to the two dancers.

"Yeah, this is *war*," Kyle said with a sly grin.

The dance crew and their teacher waited at the end of the corridor for their teammates to finish changing and come out to register. A couple of smaller rooms were designated to be dressing rooms, and their friends were putting themselves together to perform. Kyle was finished first, and he turned the corner, making long strides toward his classmates. A couple of smaller male dancers were behind him. They looked like children compared to Kyle.

He looked fierce in his faux-leather vest, arms exposed. The scars on his forearm and shoulder were quite visible. Black pants and shoes completed the look. He carried a plastic bag with his street clothes in one hand.

"Wow … muscles," Olivia said with a chuckle.

Kyle walked up to his friends, and they were all looking him up and down. He smiled, held his arms out, and turned around slowly for them to inspect the outfit. "How do I look?"

"I gotta admit," Tonisha said with an appreciative nod, "you look pretty tough."

He looked at her and smiled. "Wait until you see the girl."

The words had just left his lips when Morgan strode into the corridor. She held her head high, and her perfect ponytail accented her dramatic red lipstick and dark eyeshadow. Her top had a high neck, leaving her shoulders bare. Panels in her faux-leather skirt would break with each long stride to reveal a pale and toned leg. Her heels were strapped high up the ankle. Her left arm was wrapped in the same material as her skirt and top. Like Kyle, she held a backpack with her street clothes in her left arm, while she moved her bare right arm with every step. She looked like a gladiatrix from another time. There was a fierce purpose to her march.

The dancers all looked at each other when they saw her, then right back at Morgan. They were mesmerized as she approached them. She finally came to a stop right beside her partner, looking up and giving him a smile. Morgan turned her eyes back to her team. "Well, what do you think?"

"I think my mother can sew," Lucas answered with a grin.

"Truth!" Hector agreed.

"Here, let us take your bags for you," Ms. Blake said, gesturing for the dancers to help. Olivia grabbed Morgan's things, and Lucas quickly took Kyle's plastic bag.

Morgan looked up at Kyle. "Well, let's go get registered," she said, and let out a big breath.

"Good idea," he said, and offered her an elbow.

She smiled, putting her hand on his arm, and they turned and walked toward the registration table. As they walked ahead of the dancers, the students behind them were still discussing their striking appearance.

"They look like Gods," Lucas whispered to his friends.

"Or like rulers of some savage jungle," Olivia offered.

"There *is* something regal about them," said Ms. Blake.

Hector laughed. "They aren't going to have any trouble standing out."

The entire dance crew watched as every person who walked by their friends turned their heads to steal another look at the couple. Dancers, judges, children, and every spectator who saw them pass took great interest in them.

They marched to the registration desk and lined up. As they did, Morgan was fidgeting, and her eyes moistened. She reached up to wipe away a tear, careful to keep her makeup from being ruined.

Kyle noticed and spoke up. "You okay?"

She laughed, self-conscious, and looked up at her partner. "Sorry! I just … I've been looking forward to this day. There were so many times I didn't think I was going to be here."

Kyle turned his eyes forward. "Well, here you are."

"Thank you for this, Kyle. Thank you so much," she whispered.

He laughed. "I'd say 'you're welcome,' but then I remember how it all happened."

She smiled too and leaned her head on his shoulder. "Have you forgiven me yet?"

He grinned and kept his eyes forward. "I'll let you know."

She laughed and lifted her head. It was their turn to step up to the table and register. They filled in their paperwork, signed their forms, and couple number eleven were ready to compete.

CHAPTER 70

"This place has been good to us so far," Ms. Blake said as they walked into the Catalina convention room. "Since this is a new category, it's a small group. Only twenty couples have signed up."

"I'm so glad you suggested it," Morgan said, looking at the large parquet dance floor. She was watching the judges file in and take their seats. Some were talking to each other, while others filled their glasses with water. There was a stack of scoresheets at every table: the scores that would make or break them.

Morgan turned to Kyle. "Okay, we're couple number eleven, but that doesn't mean we go in that order. They usually do a draw to see who goes when."

"Why not go in the order they registered?" he asked.

"Tradition," Ms. Blake explained.

"When DO we perform?"

"You're the eighteenth position."

"Good!" Morgan exclaimed. "We want to be fresh in their minds when they're deciding a winner." She turned to Kyle. "Oh, there's another thing you have to know."

"What's that?"

"When they announce us, they'll say your name first."

Kyle frowned and looked at the ground. "Well, that's stupid."

Morgan raised an eyebrow and chuckled. "Why do you say that?"

He shrugged and started pointing at the other couples. "If you look at each competitor, you'll see the females are the fanciest when it comes to their dress. Also, from what I've seen, the women are the ones who add the pageantry and grace to the routine. They're the stars of the show. Should be them that get named first."

"Tradition," Ms. Blake repeated, and patted him on the arm. "But I like the way you think."

The dance crew were chatting behind them. They all had their phones out and were sending texts. It didn't take long to realize what they were doing. Students from Southwood started showing up and taking seats in the gallery. Before long, the gallery was completely full, and there were school jackets everywhere. A surprising number of football players showed up. Two-ton Tony took the time to wave at the couple.

"Wow, a lot of students here for this," Morgan said as she returned the football captain's wave. "On a Saturday too."

"I'm not surprised," Ms. Blake said with a smile. "The culture at Southwood has done a complete about-face, and you're a big part of it. Everyone is a little kinder, and a little more relaxed, since you showed them the way."

"I think what happened to Lucas opened a lot of eyes," Morgan answered. "It made the football team rethink a lot of things."

"That's true," Ms. Blake agreed. "But it was that dance you organized that had the biggest impact."

"You think?"

"Absolutely," the guidance counselor added with a solemn nod. "The whole student body was hurting after that. They knew it was wrong and terrible, but they didn't know what to do about it. They didn't have an answer until you held that dance."

Morgan thought about that, and she looked at her partner with a grin. "See that! We did good."

"Hey, that was all you and the dance crew," Kyle answered, holding up his hands in protest. "I just provided the place."

Ms. Blake chuckled. "You'll never understand this, young man, but you did more to help our school than you can possibly imagine."

The lights lowered and the competition was beginning. After a brief announcement by the older blonde woman with glasses, the first couple was called up and their music started.

All the dancers watched them perform in silence, and clapped dutifully when the couple had finished their routine. After about five routines had finished, Morgan turned to Kyle. "What do you think?"

He considered his answer. "They're good. But they're kind of struggling with the timing and the plot."

Morgan turned back to watch the couple dancing on the stage. "What do you mean by that?"

"If you watch carefully, you'll see the guys sometimes have trouble getting their partner elevated in the lifts. They wobble, or take a back-step to make it work. Their timing is off."

Morgan brought a hand to her chin and watched as the couple on the dance floor performed a lift. "I see what you mean, but what did you mean about the plot?"

"You made this great story going in our dance. The action and lifts get more and more dramatic until the big finish. Most of these couples busted out a good lift right at the start to make an impression, but it never gets any better."

"There are a lot more lifts in our routine," she observed.

"Your choreography is … better in every way," Kyle said with a glance her way.

She hugged his arm and leaned into him. "Thanks, big guy. Maybe it's because I know my partner can handle anything I dream up."

Ms. Blake walked to stand in front of them. "Okay, you lovely couple. The sixteenth couple is dancing. Time for you to go to the warm-up area and loosen up." She tilted her head forward and regarded them over her glasses. "Show them all, kids!"

They looked at each other, stole a quick drink of water, and looked at their teammates. "Thanks so much for coming," Morgan said to them. "Nice of you to invite the entire school too."

The dancers laughed and gave them some encouragement as they started walking toward the front of the room.

"Where are we going?" the big fighter asked, as they made some distance from their friends.

Morgan reached back and took his hand. "Here, follow me to stage-right."

He didn't try to recover his hand as they walked. In fact, their hands naturally linked fingers, and they walked over to a small area with mats and a hard floor. Other dancers were there, moving around.

Morgan's heart sang as she held her partner's hand and guided him to a spot in the warm-up area that would accommodate them. After everything she'd done, everything they'd been through, he was willing to hold her hand and be there for her. She was still nervous, but it was more excitement than fear. Months of work were about to come to fruition, and she couldn't *WAIT* to show the judges and the audience what they could do.

CHAPTER 71

"**D**ancing in the eighteenth position, couple number eleven … Kyle Branch and last year's ballroom champion, Morgan Laflamme!" the announcer called.

Morgan took her partner's arm, and they strode confidently to the floor. They heard the cheers of the Southwood students, and a few of the dance crew called them by name. They also heard the murmurs as the crowd discussed this unusual and exotic-looking couple.

When they were almost at the middle of the dance area, Kyle stopped walking, and Morgan continued a little further until she was standing in front of him. There was a pause, and then the strains of Adele's "Set Fire to the Rain" started up.

Morgan moved to her right, and Kyle stepped with her. He put his hands on her hips and hoisted her high in the air. She spread her arms gracefully and leaned her head back. He backed up and placed her on the ground, and Morgan went with the momentum and spun away from him as he followed. She froze in a martial arts stance, and he set his feet too.

They came together in a box step, and then struck a smooth grapevine to traverse the floor. When they stopped, Morgan stepped toward him and lifted her right leg high. Kyle set his left hand under the leg, and she leaned into the arm he placed under her armpit. He bent his knees and effortlessly shoulder-pressed her up until his arms were straight. After four quick rotations, he lowered her to his chest, and she continued to lay flat until they came to a stop. He suddenly let her go, but he grabbed her wrist and she unraveled to hover above the floor. The crowd applauded at the grace and control of the move.

Kyle continued to hold her leg and her wrist, swinging her around until she gracefully slid to the ground and struck a pose. He helped her up, but she abruptly pushed him away, as if she was trying to escape.

Morgan came to a stop in the dead center of the floor, and Kyle came up behind her. He reached for her arms, but she quickly pulled them away and retreated. Kyle's reaction was to turn his back and take a couple of steps away from his partner.

There wasn't a sound in the ballroom. The audience was riveted to their performance. A few phones came out, and people started to record what they were seeing. They knew it was special, and there was a lot of anticipation.

She moved quickly toward her partner and threw the leg closest to him up like an attack. He easily turned with her movement, placing one hand on her ankle and the other on the small of her back. He easily pressed her up with one hand and she laid back; the leg held by the ankle was straight, and the other was gracefully bent. She moved her arms like she was flying. The crowd cheered, seeing her so high in the air and flowing across the dance floor as Kyle walked.

When they made it to the far end of the floor, he lowered her slowly until her bent leg found his hip, and she stood tall. He bent his leg on the same side for balance, and Morgan stretched out her arm, as did he. It created a pose where she was high in the air and their opposite arms were extended, framing the pose. The audience cheered, appreciating the difficulty in what they were doing.

Kyle lowered her, and they returned to a Rumba box step, perfectly in time with the music. The crowd watched, feeling that the couple were setting up their next move. They didn't have long to wait. Morgan turned away from her partner and leaned back. Kyle lowered himself to catch the small of her back with his shoulder, and reached for her ankle with one arm. He straightened his legs, and she was balanced on his shoulder as they started to spin. Kyle raised his free hand as they spun faster and faster. He let go of her ankle, and Morgan responded by slowly sliding down in front of him. She never touched the floor; Kyle put both hands under her armpits and started walking back across the floor. He held her still as she held her arms out and pointed her legs to look like she was flying. Again, the cheers of the crowd surged. Kyle eventually lowered her and fell to one knee as Morgan planted her feet and quickly moved away from him.

Kyle remained on his knee, and the two dancers looked at each other across the dance floor. Morgan struck a fighting stance and looked fierce. She ran around him, and as she did, he switched to sit flat and put a hand out behind him as he reclined. Morgan closed the distance, and Kyle put a hand on her hip. She put her arm on the same side on his shoulder for balance, and Kyle slowly and carefully stood to his feet, keeping his partner elevated with great control. The crowd erupted at the show of strength, how effortless it looked.

To finish the move, Kyle lowered her into his embrace, not allowing her feet to touch the ground as they rotated slowly. He had his hands around her waist and up her back to control her, while her arms rested on his shoulders. She pushed him away again, and he took a few steps away as she retreated.

She came to the center of the floor and curled in a ball, as if she was crying. Pure pageantry. Kyle took long, graceful strides and moved his hips, as Morgan had taught him to do. The crowd was silent; every eye was on them to see what would happen next.

He slowly reached down and touched her back. She stood quickly but gracefully and turned into him as they box-stepped again. Kyle took a deep breath and let it out, preparing for the next lift.

On cue, she lifted her inside knee up, and Kyle grabbed her shin while the other hand went to her tailbone and muscled her up in the air. He kept hold of her ankle for balance, and the hand on her rump straightened to elevate her for height.

The crowd clapped wildly, seeing her so high in the air, and Morgan moved her arms gracefully as she surrendered herself to the move. The crowd cheered louder as he released her ankle, and he kept her high in the air with only one hand. They were cheering for the power and balance of the move, but Morgan was the star. Her legs were perfect, and her arms flowed with the rotation Kyle was providing.

When the music dictated, he lowered her, and she planted her heels and made some space between them. It was time for the finale.

Morgan struck a fighting stance again. Her hands were like blades and her dramatic eyes flashed fierce as she looked at her partner.

Kyle brought a leg back and struck a pose of his own. He looked like a big warrior waiting for battle, and his blue eyes blazed into hers. He gave her a small smile and a nod to show her it was time to bring the house down.

She took a quick breath, let it out, and charged at her partner. He held his ground, just off the center of the floor. She almost ran past him as they came together, but he caught her arm and turned his back and hip into her. Morgan relaxed and prepared herself for what would come next.

He bent forward, lifting her feet off the ground, and contracted his core, snapping her high over his head as the crowd gasped. Morgan moved her body around and brought her legs underneath her, planting square on her heels and taking one step back as Kyle held on to her arm.

The crowd exploded with cheers, and it wasn't only Southwood High students. Teams from all over the country were on their feet as Kyle gave Morgan's arm a tug and she spun into his embrace.

He bent forward, and she allowed him to lower her backward toward the floor. They looked in each other's eyes as she raised a hand to his face, and her mouth opened as if they were going to kiss. They held the pose, and the song ended at the right moment.

Cheers and applause came from all over the room. Spectators, dancers, coaches, and a couple of the judges were applauding.

Kyle's blue eyes peered into Morgan's, and he smiled at her. "We can't do it any better than that!"

She laughed as he straightened up and righted her. They turned to the crowd and bowed, then repeated it for the judges. Kyle offered his arm, and they walked boldly from the dance floor to the waiting area stage left. A few of the other competitors were clapping as they walked in.

A petite blonde woman ran up to Morgan and touched her arm. "Oh my God! That was amazing! What on earth was that at the end?"

"It's called 'the Laflamme," Kyle answered with a grin. "She invented it."

Morgan did a double take and brought a hand up to her mouth as she started to laugh.

"Well, I love it!" the blonde responded. A few other dancers echoed her feelings.

They stole a glance over at their friends in the gallery. The dance crew was jumping up and down. Ms. Blake blew them a big kiss. The football players around the room were pumping their fists and cheering wildly. The crowd continued to show their appreciation for a full minute, even after they finished and left the floor.

"Now what?" Kyle whispered into his partner's ear.

She let out a sigh. "Two more performances, and then we find out where we placed."

Kyle smiled and nodded. "I can tell you this much, I feel sorry for anyone who has to follow *THAT.*"

CHAPTER 72

"It's kind of crazy, when you think about it," Kyle said, watching the last competitors performing.

"What?" Morgan asked.

"You work for months putting together a routine. You try so many things, have so many difficulties, and then in about three minutes, it's all over. You're done and there's nothing left to do."

"It's true," she answered. "You put it all on the line for a performance or two." She turned to face her partner. "You were so great out there, Kyle."

"Hey, thanks. But I think you were the one who made that work. Your choreography, and you were the one who took on that stunt at the end. Pretty gutsy! Imagine what it would have looked like if you landed on your butt and slid across the floor?"

They both laughed at that.

The last performance wrapped up, and the applause faded as the last couple went over to the holding area. A few coaches made their way over to talk to their charges as the judges discussed the results. It would be another fifteen minutes before anyone knew the outcome.

Ms. Blake made her way to the side of the stage and jogged up to them with her arms out. She grabbed them both in a big hug and jumped up and down with excitement. "You did it! You were fantastic out there!" She stepped back and clasped her hands together. "I am SO proud of you two kids."

She looked at Morgan. "You, young lady, have an amazing talent for choreography. I've never seen anything like that, and I've seen a LOT of performances."

Morgan smiled. "Thank you!"

Ms. Blake turned to Kyle. "And you, you big beautiful boy!"

Morgan and Kyle burst out laughing as he blushed.

"You were the perfect partner, and you made every lift look so easy."

"My partner made it pretty easy," Kyle explained.

Ms. Blake shook her head and pointed at him. "Modest to the end."

He shrugged. "Just honest."

They all turned when they heard a commotion in the judges' area. There was a full-blown argument going on. Three or four of the judges were shouting at an older gentleman, who was wearing a sour look on his face. He shouted something back and stormed out of the Catalina Ballroom.

"Wow," Morgan said, eyes wide. "What was THAT all about?"

Ms. Blake shook her head. "I've never seen the like. Apparently one of the judges doesn't see things the way the others do."

Kyle frowned. "You think that's about us?"

Morgan's face fell. "It could be."

The blonde woman with glasses marched up to the microphone and called everyone to attention. "Please return to your seats, and we would ask the dancers to line up in order and hear the results." She seemed flustered as she made the announcement. Ms. Blake turned and walked back to her seat to see the outcome.

"We're the eighteenth couple, right?" Kyle asked.

"No, we're couple number eleven, so that's where we should be in line," Morgan explained.

They counted down the line until they found their spot and filed in. Kyle held out his arm, and Morgan placed a hand on his forearm. Her emotions were running high as they waited to be called out. "I can't believe it's over and we're not going to work together anymore," she said, eyes teary.

"It does seem strange."

"Maybe … maybe we could spend some time together when we're not dancing." She looked up at him. "How about another picnic at the auto shop?"

He smiled at her. "Sounds nice, are you buying?"

She laughed. "Sure."

"You're on."

They didn't have any more time to talk, as the line started moving and they found themselves walking onto the dance floor again and standing in a long line facing the audience.

The blonde lady held a wireless microphone and stood in front of the dancers. "This is the first time we've opened Cabaret for this age group, and I think they showed us that it was worth doing. Please put your hands together to thank all our dancers for their hard work and their performances!"

The crowd dutifully clapped, but stopped almost immediately. They wanted the results. Everyone did.

She held up the card in her hand. "In third place, Peter Gravely and Susan Wright from Hughes Center High in Cincinnati!"

A small couple jumped up and down, hugged each other, and stepped forward to receive their medals. Susan was a petite redhead in a white dress, and her partner was a slender boy with dark hair. They were elated. The crowd applauded for the happy couple.

The announcer clapped too after placing the medals around their necks. She made her way to the microphone and looked again at her paper. Her hands were shaking, and she let out a sigh as she steadied herself. "In second place, with an amazing performance … Kyle Branch and Morgan Laflamme from Southwood High, right here in Irvine!"

Morgan's eyes went wide in shock. Kyle turned and hugged her, but she stared into space. The crowd responded with a mix of applause and angry shouts. People were shaking their heads and protesting the decision. In their minds, couple number eleven had won, and nobody else was close.

The competitors themselves clapped, but they too looked at each other in surprise. This was not the outcome that they'd expected. The announcer came to Morgan and Kyle with a couple of medals. Her eyes were sad as she put a medal around the shocked young woman in front of her. "You were fantastic," she said quietly, as Kyle bent low to help her out.

"Thank you so much," Kyle said, and shook her hand. Morgan stood there, staring straight ahead.

Boos and angry shouts were still being heard as the announcer made her way back to the center of the floor. "Quiet, please," she asked the crowd. She looked at her card again and spoke up. "In first place, your champions … Pavel Toski and Tatiana Laslow from Brighton High, in Salt Lake City!"

The audience clapped as a startled couple looked at each other and started celebrating. They didn't look convinced as the medals were hung around their necks.

The audience made no secret of their outrage. Some threw a couple of paper cups onto the dance floor. It was looking ugly.

Kyle took Morgan by the hand and walked to the third-place finishers. He smiled and shook their hands. "Congratulations! Let's go congratulate the winners," he said, steering them toward the other couple. "We thought YOU totally won," the redhead volunteered as they walked over.

The winning couple was standing there, miserable, as the crowd continued to grumble. Kyle dragged the stunned Morgan behind him as he walked up to them and held out his hand. They were shocked as they shook the towering young man's hand, and he congratulated them on their victory. The third-place finishers did the same.

The audience stopped grumbling and clapped for the show of sportsmanship from the couple who should have won first place. People were still shaking their heads and muttering, but the tone had softened quite a bit.

The announcer clapped too and spoke into the microphone again. "That's what we like to see. Now it's time for our dance to close out the competition. There are no awards for what happens next. Stick around and have some fun!"

The crowd cheered, and people came streaming onto the dance floor as the competition ended. Coaches and spectators ran up to teammates and relatives to hug them and offer some kind words.

Morgan was still standing still, staring silently into the distance. Kyle reached down and took her hand gently. "Are you okay?"

She never had a chance to answer him, as Olivia charged up to them and hugged them. "You two were amazing out there!" she gushed.

"Hermano! You rocked that!" Hector offered, as he and Kyle bumped fists.

Lucas laughed. "You two looked like a god and goddess compared to the others. Top notch!"

Tonisha was not as happy. "That is CRAP! You two clearly won that!"

Kyle shrugged. "The judges saw it differently. That's how it goes."

"ONE judge," Ms. Blake said, as she moved closer. "Unfortunately, that was enough to keep you from winning."

"But ... but ... we were the best ones," Morgan stammered.

Ms. Blake leaned closer to her and whispered. "Oh, honey. You were. You knew you were taking a chance with such a radical performance. That old boy was a traditionalist, and he didn't understand what you were trying to do."

"Lucas and I recorded your performance on our phones," Hector told them. "We uploaded it and it's getting hits like crazy! Everyone wants to see that move at the end."

Lucas nodded. "Yeah, this is probably the biggest thing to happen at nationals. I've never heard of anything bigger."

"That's right," Tonisha agreed. "You two busted out a NEW move that nobody's ever seen."

Random people were coming up and patting Kyle on the arm, saying things like, "You guys won that!" or "You were robbed!"

Through it all, Morgan just stared. She didn't move and barely blinked. Kyle looked at her with a frown. "Morgan?" He stole a worried look at Ms. Blake and grabbed his partner's hand as a slow song came over the speakers. "Excuse us," he said, as he pulled her onto the floor.

"What are you doing?" she protested, as she pulled back.

"Taking the lead!" he laughed, and pulled her into his embrace. She allowed him to take her hand and move her slowly to the music.

"What happened out there?" she said, tearing up.

"Glad you asked," he said with a smile as he turned her away from the dance crew. "You won that competition in EVERY way. Let the couple from Utah keep their trinket. You've won a lot more than that."

"What do you mean?" she asked, as she put her head on his shoulder.

His hand moved from her hip to pat her on the back. "Look, people win and lose these things all the time. How many of those dancers didn't win? More than that, you showed that audience something special. They'll be talking about that performance, and that decision by the judges, for years. Nobody is going to remember who won or lost this competition, but EVERYONE is going to remember that stunt we pulled to end the number."

He pushed her back so that he could see her face. "Morgan, what you did today will always be remembered, and I'll bet the whole world is going to watch that video the guys uploaded. You're probably going to be famous!"

Her face softened as she considered his words. She wiped away a tear and nodded her head. "Thank you, Kyle. I just ... I just wanted to win."

"I get it. I really do. But you did more than win," he said with a laugh.

He turned his attention from her as someone tapped his shoulder, right on the scar. They both were surprised to see the older announcer standing in front of them.

"I'm sorry to interrupt," she said with a nervous laugh. "I was wondering ... could you show me that move you did at the end of your performance?"

"No," Kyle said with a shake of his head.

Both Morgan and the announcer looked at him with wide eyes. "You won't show me?" she asked, incredulous.

"We won't?" Morgan echoed, looking at her partner.

"No. We're not going to show you *one move*," Kyle said, as a grin spread on his face. "It's a waste of time. But we'll show you the whole dance again, if you want."

The announcer smiled at him, understanding. "YES! Why not? I think everyone would like to see that again. I'll go get your music ready," she said, and hustled away.

"What are you doing?" Morgan asked him.

"Adding to the legend of Morgan Laflamme," he said, still grinning. "A command performance, no less. One more time?"

She nodded and grinned back. "One more time!"

CHAPTER 73

The music died, and the announcer spoke into the microphone. She was flanked by most of the judges, smiling in their direction. "Ladies and gentlemen, I'm sorry to interrupt. If you were here for our Cabaret competition, couple number eleven did something we've never seen before, and we very much want to see it again!"

The crowd erupted in cheers, and many eyes turned their way. "Oh my God. Is this happening?" Morgan said, as she squeezed Kyle's arm.

"Sure is," he answered, not looking at her.

The announcer tapped on the microphone. "They have graciously agreed to repeat their performance for our entertainment. Please clear the dance floor. Couple number eleven, Kyle and Morgan … *you're up!*"

The crowd moved to the edges of the dance floor and clapped wildly. A few people whistled, and the football players could be heard cheering loudly. Phones were taken out, and people prepared to record this unprecedented event.

Morgan and Kyle walked to the center, all smiles. They took their position and waited for the music. This time, they didn't hold back. They smiled at each other, enjoying every move and every lift. The crowd cheered for every one of the fancy moves until the song was nearly done. Cameras flashed, and it was almost hard to hear the music over the crowd.

When there was only one move left, Kyle held up a hand to stop his partner. Timing the move with the music didn't matter anymore. He looked at the crowd and started raising his arms up and down to encourage their cheers. The audience responded and clapped with anticipation.

He looked at a grinning Morgan and nodded to let her know he was ready. She came in a lot harder than she had dared during the performance, and when Kyle grabbed her, it was strong. He turned his hip into her, elevated her feet off the floor, and sent her flying over his back. Morgan crossed her legs gracefully as they arced through the air. She gathered them underneath her and landed her heels loudly on the dance floor, sticking the landing perfectly.

The crowd went insane, and flashes abounded as Kyle held her arm and wound her in. They ended up in an embrace, Kyle lowering her backwards as she brought her hand to his face as if they were going to kiss. She looked in his eyes, made her decision, and moved in to kiss him. But he moved back.

"Today is the day I let you know," he said, above the roar of the crowd.

"What?" she asked, blinking.

"You asked me to tell you when I was able to forgive you." He leaned closer to her, and the crowd started cheering again, for what they knew was coming next.

"I forgive you, Morgan," Kyle said, as he squeezed her tight and kissed her.

He knew what he was doing, and Morgan was lost in the moment as the crowd laughed and clapped. That was not the first time Morgan Laflamme had been kissed, but it was definitely the best.

EPILOGUE

"Graduates of Southwood High, I give you your valedictorian, Morgan Laflamme!" Mr. Hayes called into the microphone attached to the lectern.

The students, wearing their blue robes and flat-topped caps, cheered and clapped. Morgan stood up in the front row and made her way up the stairs and across the stage. Her long hair draped down her back to her waist. She wore sensible black shoes and a modest cream blouse under the blue robe. After shaking hands with the principal, she placed some paper on the lectern.

She cleared her throat and looked at the crowd. "So here we are," she said with a chuckle. "It has been a *crazy* year!"

She heard murmurs of assent from students and parents alike.

"I'd love to tell you that it was all great, but that wouldn't be true. Some terrible things took place this year. Things that should not have happened."

The crowd was solemn as they considered her words. They all knew what she was talking about. In the graduate's area, Morgan saw Olivia wrap an arm around Lucas, and a couple of other people behind him gave him a pat on the back.

"It could have broken us, but it didn't. We looked at what was done, and we refused to accept it. We thought about what happened and worked together to try and help. We looked at the future and decided that we were *done* with that kind of nonsense."

Applause was loud as she finished that thought. Morgan smiled. "I'm sorry I won't be attending school next year, because I see the leaders of our community and I know that they're going to continue what we started. Everyone at Southwood is welcome, and everyone is safe." She looked around the crowd until she found Two-Ton Tony. She smiled at him as she spoke. "We have a new captain for the football team."

Cheers started as soon as she said the words, and she pointed at him. "Two-Ton Tony is a great leader and a great guy. I actually think his heart might weigh a ton."

The crowd laughed and Tony looked at the ground, shaking his head with embarrassment.

"He's committed to helping out students who need it, and making sure his team knows right from wrong. I can think of no greater leader."

She moved the papers around on the lectern. "I learned a lot this year. I really did. It took my entire high school career for me to figure out what Ms. Blake and the other teachers were showing me all along."

There was some applause for the popular guidance counselor, and Morgan found her on the stage and waved.

"Most of you have heard that she's retiring this year."

The crowd muttered, and there were a few boos, followed by good-natured laughter.

"I know, right?" Morgan laughed. "Well, she's given me permission to let you know that she is *not* retiring, and she'll be here to help students next year!"

Parents, teachers, and students all clapped, and a few stood up to show their gratitude. Morgan smiled at her teacher. "She said something about 'being bored with all that peace and quiet.'"

The crowd laughed at that, as did Ms. Blake.

Morgan held up a finger. "Now, valedictorians are supposed to talk about how we're about to face a 'new beginning' in our lives. Or how we should go out into the world and 'strive to achieve our goals.'"

A few of the audience members smiled and others laughed. It had the virtue of being the truth.

"No, not me!" Morgan said, holding up a hand. "No clichés in this speech. In fact, I don't have too much more to say."

Hector started applauding wildly, and the people around him laughed.

"Thanks, Hector," Morgan deadpanned. "I'm going to encourage you to do something *different*." She looked down at the ground and put her hands on both sides of the lectern to steady herself. "I would love to tell you that

I didn't make any mistakes this year, but I did. Big ones. I wronged a good man for my own selfish purposes. I wanted something so badly, a goal that I set for myself, that I didn't think about right or wrong. All that mattered was the goal. Along the way, I figured out my mistake and worked hard to make it right. I don't know if I did, but I definitely learned something."

She looked at the audience and held up her arms. "See? That's the great thing about mistakes. They help shape us into who we are, but they do *not* define us. We define ourselves, and we are what we do."

The audience started clapping, and the graduates nodded their heads as they considered her words.

"I'm not going to tell you to go chase your goals. I figure you'll do that anyway. I'm going to encourage you to look at the people around you and see their goals. I want you to see what you have in common, and be kind."

She stopped talking and shook her head as she looked at her peers. "Isn't the world always trying to divide us? Right? We are divided by gender, sexual orientation, politics, religion, education, and wealth. You might have more in common with someone who looks different from you than someone who shares the same skin color. We're divided into tribes, and we're constantly pitted against each other. Nobody wins when you think like that. It's crazy!"

There was more applause from the crowd.

Morgan laughed and threw up her arms. "The dumbest thing about the situation is that *none* of us chose our circumstances. Nobody chooses the color of their skin or decides to be born into poverty. But we shouldn't resent each other, because the girl who was born into wealth didn't have any more choice in the matter than the boy who was born into nothing."

She smiled at Ms. Blake and turned back. "I'm not encouraging you to do something that I'm not willing to do. I'm already making plans to do it myself. I won the birth lottery. I was born into a family with two great parents who could afford to send me to dance lessons. Not everyone is that lucky, and I don't take that for granted anymore."

Morgan took a deep breath and looked at her guidance counselor with a smile. "I'm taking a gap year, and Ms. Blake is allowing me to come back to help the dance team. I'm also going to start a dance club for *any* students that want to dance. It won't cost a thing, and we'll entertain all styles."

The audience clapped, and her dance crew called out their encouragement. "Good for you, girl!" Lucas hollered.

"You rock, Glamazon!" Tonisha called with a laugh. The people who heard her laughed too.

Morgan brought her hand to her face to contain her own laughter. She looked back at the crowd. "I'm going to have to find a job—a real job. It won't be a great one, but that's okay. I'm going to start paying my own way."

She took a breath and let it out. "I'm also going to see if I can volunteer downtown. There are a few organizations who work with kids who don't have much. They could never afford the dance lessons I got growing up. Well, I'm going to make sure they have the same chance that I did."

The crowd applauded, and her parents smiled at each other. Taylor was silent, smiling as she watched her sister address the crowd.

"And this is what I'm telling you. You often hear people say that they want to make the world a better place. But how do you do that? How will you know when it *is* a better place? I don't know!" she said with a laugh and a shrug.

"I'm going to tell you something simple and true. What I'm telling you, what I want you to take into your heart and truly believe, is that when you reach out and help somebody, I guarantee that the world *will* be a better place. You will make it better for them, *and for you!*"

She looked back at the staff on the stage, smiled at the audience, and picked up her paper. "Thank you so much for this honor," she said, and started walking back to her seat.

The audience exploded, and the graduates all leapt to their feet. For the second time that month, Morgan Laflamme received a standing ovation.

Morgan turned off her car and started walking to the drive shed. She had ditched her formal clothes from the graduation ceremony and now wore flip-flops, shorts, and a tank top. She heard the gentle strumming of a guitar and a strong baritone voice singing.

In a world filled with numbers,
Opinions, news, and facts.
I need something more to complete me
Something to help me relax.
Show me the right moves.
Show me the steps I must take.
Show me the rhythm, but please, please show me the way.

"Kyle?" she called as she ran up the creaky old wooden stairs. There she found Roscoe, curled up on the sofa.

"Hi there, boy!" Morgan cooed with a grin, and sat beside the big dog, scratching behind his ears. Roscoe plopped his head on her lap and closed his eyes.

"Oh, hi," Kyle answered. He was barefoot, wearing jeans and a white t-shirt, sitting on his bed with the guitar. "How did the speech go?"

"It went great," she answered with a smile. "Did I hear you playing and singing a song?"

He nodded. "Yeah. Keeping myself busy. Roscoe doesn't seem to mind."

"I didn't recognize it."

Kyle looked at her and smiled. "I wrote it. I'm not good enough to play anybody else's stuff yet."

She returned his smile. "I liked it." She looked at the ground and then back at him. "Why didn't you go to graduation today?"

Kyle looked at the ground as he walked the guitar over to the corner and then sat in the chair near the bed. He let out a sigh. "It's different when you don't have a family to share it with."

She nodded her understanding. "Do you know what you're doing now? I mean, are you going to school?"

"Not this year. If I save for another year, I'll have enough to start and finish a degree. I'm going to look at local universities and colleges. I want to keep living here for as long as I can."

"I'm actually taking a gap year too."

"Can't make up your mind about what you want to do?"

Morgan smiled. "Yeah, but not in the way you think. That video Hector posted has well over a million hits."

"Is that right?"

"It sure is," she verified. "I'm getting offers from many different dance schools to work, teach, or study. I have to consider my options before I make a decision." She pointed at him. "Like you, I like where I live, and I'd like to stay a little longer."

He nodded and his blue eyes held hers. "What are you doing today?"

She looked at Roscoe as she petted him. "I'm glad you asked. Olivia is hosting an afterparty when the dance tonight is over. A lot of people were asking me to get you there."

"Really?"

"Yeah, it should be fun. Will you come?"

"Are you going?" he asked, narrowing his eyes.

"I am," she said firmly. "Will you come with me?"

"Okay. It'll be a new thing for me."

"I'll look after you, keep you safe," she said with a grin.

"Thanks so much," he replied. "We can go in your car if you like."

She shrugged. "I like your car, actually. It's grown on me."

"What time do you want me to pick you up?" he asked as he stood up.

Morgan stood up too and put her hands on her hips. "Are you kicking me out?"

He laughed. "No! I'm trying to figure out what's going on later. Settle down."

She walked until she was standing close to him. "That's good to hear."

"It is?"

Morgan grinned with a gleam in her eye. "Yeah, I actually came over here hoping I could convince you to kiss me again."

A slow smile spread over his lips. "Well, I have a different idea." He walked over to the bookshelf and found an odd-looking, yellow plastic block. "I found this at a yard sale," he explained. "It's an eight-track record of some classic Rumba music." He looked at his guest. "I thought maybe we could dance a little ... if you wanted. Maybe you could show me something else?" He placed the eight-track into the player, and Rumba music started playing from the ancient machine.

Morgan walked to the player, turned it up a little, and went to Kyle. He held out his hands to dance, and she took them and put them both on her hips. She threw her arms around his neck and smiled at him.

"Stealing the lead again, Morgan?" he asked.

"You bet," she answered, as she leaned in for a kiss.

CPSIA information can be obtained
at www.ICGtesting.com
Printed in the USA
BVHW051720151022
649212BV00001BA/46